BY INTENT

The less-than-pleased expression on his face could have given her frostbite. Not to mention the slow rise of his left eyebrow. She fought the blush that rose to her cheeks.

"Alyssa Knight," he said.

She winced inwardly as he pronounced her name with the dreaded tone one would reserve for the tax solicitor.

"I'd heard you were back in town. Guess it didn't take you long to get into trouble. What are you doing down at the courthouse? Speeding ticket, lawsuit, or car accident?"

"It's wonderful seeing you again as well, Nathan. Or should I say Judge Hughes?" She cocked her head to the side and fixed a smile to her lips although his comment slid across her skin, slicing like a paper cut.

"So what brings you here?" he repeated, then stepped out of line to let the longhaired man behind him order.

"Besides an imaginary court case?" She moved to let another customer pass between them. "I was having breakfast with a friend."

He raised a thick eyebrow. "At 6:40 in the morning?"

She shrugged. "Is that a problem?"

His mouth twitched as he took a step forward to the counter. "No, just a surprise."

"I live to be a surprise."

Angela Weaver

By Intent

BET Publications, LLC
http://www.bet.com
http://www.arabesquebooks.com

ARABESQUE BOOKS are published by

BET Publications, LLC
c/o BET BOOKS
One BET Plaza
1900 W Place NE
Washington, DC 20018-1211

All Kensington Titles, Imprints, and Distributed Lines are available at special quantity discounts for bulk purchases for sales promotions, premiums, fund-raising, and educational or institutional use. Special book excerts or customized printings can also be created to fit specific needs. For details, write or phone the office of the Kensington special sales manager: Kensington Publishing Corp., 850 Third Avenue, New York, NY 10022, attn: Special Sales Department, Phone: 1-800-221-2647.

First Printing: September 2004
10 9 8 7 6 5 4 3 2 1

Printed in the United States of America

For my grandmother, Ollie Williams.
Thank you for the best chocolate pound cake in the world
and for loving my incorrigible self.

And a youth said, Speak to us of Friendship,
And he answered, saying: Your friend is your
needs answered. He is your field which you
sow with love and reap with thanksgiving.

—Kahlil Gibran

Winter

"Tear up your resignation letter and I will give you two months' vacation and double your current salary."

She didn't turn at the familiar sound of the highbrow British voice coming from the doorway, but her slender fingers paused midway between the bookcase and the shipping carton sitting atop her office chair. An antique clock chimed three times. At that time of night, the silence on the executive floor had drawn her attention to the sound of the temperature control switching on only minutes before.

Alyssa Knight lowered her gaze to the top of the mahogany William IV desk. Nestled amongst the satin folds of a black velvet box sat a diamond engagement ring Harrison had given her after the team closed on the Matsumoto Shipping subsidiary spin-off. She was almost tempted to touch it. She already knew how the platinum warmed to her skin, how the heavy circlet would slip onto her finger, and how the marquise diamond sparkled like a living thing.

Ignoring her silence, he continued. "I personally spoke to the head surgeon at the hospital. Your father will make a full recovery, sweetheart. There is no need for you to go back to Chicago."

She stifled a sigh at another one of Harrison's overtures to get her to stay. Brushing a strand of her shoulder-length hair behind her ear, she lifted her eyes toward the window. Alyssa took a deep breath and filled her lungs with the lemon scent of a polish the cleaning lady had used on the furniture during her nightly duties.

Instead of gazing upon the empty streets of London's financial district, she let her mind's eye drift back to a time when as a little girl she flew down the sidewalk on a brand-new pink bicycle. She could still feel the hard white rubber handlebar grips, the December wind on her cheeks, the pounding of her heart. Moreover, she heard her family's shouts of encouragement. That winter morning Alyssa had felt as though she could fly.

"Maybe I need him," she murmured, her voice raspy with fatigue. She'd slept a total of fifteen hours in the past four days. In London, businesses might pause for tea, but would not stop for her leaving. There had been documents to review, e-mails to send, phone calls to make, and good-byes to give. Not to mention the unfinished business of packing up her one-bedroom garden-floor flat in Kensington. She would not permanently leave London until the next month, but it was time to bid her first of many farewells.

Only the whisper of fabric warned her of his approach. "He has your mother, and after this business deal I will take care of you. Look at me, Alyssa . . . darling."

She didn't need to look at Harrison with her eyes, because she knew him all too well. Yet, Alyssa turned and raised her face. The sight of him played havoc on her nerves, upsetting the nibbles of a tuna sandwich she'd had for dinner. With his alabaster skin, ash-gray eyes, wavy silver-flecked hair, and an athletic physique, no one could deny that Harrison Brandell II was a distinguished and handsome man.

Taking care to brush her palms against her midnight-blue suit, she noted that he wore the silver necktie she'd purchased for him at a small shop in Milan.

"I've already made my decision, Harrison."

He stood straight with his hands in his pockets, the confident grin he perpetually wore flattened. "I need you, darling. We have to close the Caspian Energy deal and you've already got that new French construction CEO eating out of the palm of your hand. Come on, this is worth at least fifteen million pounds to the bottom line."

Her fingers tensed and for a brief moment disappointment flared in her honey-brown eyes. She stood still when he moved to embrace her.

"All you have to do is help the team through the placement process and then we can start working on our wedding," he whispered seductively in her ear. His fingers toyed with the single pearl she wore on a gold chain around her neck. "Mother can handle most of the details and then you and I can fly to the States and visit your family. Maybe take a vacation and spend some time at the villa in Tuscany."

Alyssa's lip curled into a bitter smile. Classic Harrison: always about the end of the game, the result, the closing of the deal. He wanted to focus on a wedding even before she had accepted his marriage proposal. Only recently had she realized that he had been grooming her for a new position and title. She would be promoted to his wife.

"No," Alyssa said slowly. He could not seem to understand that in the realm of business she could negotiate a deal, compromise to accomplish a target, but she would never settle in her personal life. It was not the thing for her to take second best in a relationship.

She disentangled herself from his arms and moved to stand on the other side of her desk. Curling her fingers into the leather backing of her executive chair, Alyssa met his guarded stare.

"No, what?"

She heard the tinge of impatience in Harrison's voice. She'd told him exactly four weeks ago that she couldn't accept his ring. He'd pressured her to reconsider, but the time they'd spent apart had only solidified her feelings. They had met at a global financial conference. He'd been a guest speaker and she'd played a part in organizing the event, as her boutique investment firm had been a main sponsor.

His unshakable confidence and charisma, coupled with a

relentless pursuit, had made it next to impossible for her to say no. They had only been seeing each other for three weeks before she'd walked into her office building on a Monday morning to discover that Harrison had bought the company she worked for. Within a year of the takeover, he'd managed to turn their small London financial firm into a European powerhouse.

She had already been a rising star in the investment banking division, but having the owner as her boyfriend had guaranteed that Alyssa would be in the spotlight. Regardless of their new relationship, she'd moved up because of her talent and willingness to sacrifice her personal life for her work. In less than two months, she'd been moved to the executive floor to enjoy a corner office with a fantastic view of the city. Her new manager had been eager to tell her that Harrison had made sure that the office planners had chosen the best paintings, the best furniture, and the best location just for her.

Yet, she'd spent so much of her time at conferences, on planes, in meetings, at client events, or at dinner parties that she had little time to appreciate it.

"No, I have not changed my mind. No, I'm not staying. No, we are not planning a wedding, because I'm not going to marry you, and yes, we've discussed this, Harrison. We've discussed us and my answer is still the same," she stated flatly, inwardly amazed at the evenness of her tone.

"Bloody hell." He balled up his fists. "I just told you your father is going to be fine. If this is because of the other week, I already apologized for my inexcusable behavior. The upcoming board meeting had me on edge, that's all. I was out of line and I overreacted but I made sure that he received the best of care and was compensated well for the injury."

Alyssa raised a well-arched eyebrow while holding back a snort of disbelief at the gross understatement. Harrison had sent her dance instructor to the hospital with a fractured rib and a black eye. She shivered slightly. The rage she'd seen in Harrison's face haunted her still.

"This isn't about any of that. This is about me. I'm not happy here and I've been thinking about going home long before Pop's illness." The full truth was that not only did she miss her parents, but she also believed that she had finally put Lily's death behind her.

She watched as he placed his hands behind his back. "I'm prepared to offer you a bonus of seventy-five thousand pounds paid on signature of a year's contract."

Alyssa had to blink twice as she saw a fleeting trace of apprehension cross Harrison's eternally confident features. It had always seemed to her that the man who bought and sold millions in a day, directed the course of a business enterprise that spanned the globe, and played host to London's elite on a monthly basis knew no fear.

She remained silent for a moment and then moved to place her favorite Oxford University finance textbook in the box. "My mind is already made up."

"This office and my bed won't be empty for long," he warned.

But his heart would be, she mentally added, as the fact that he'd never really cared for her the same way she'd cared for him had never been more apparent. He would commit to nothing unless it added money to the bottom line or earned praise from his father.

Harrison would forever put business, social standing, power, and his father's approval in front of all else. It had been after a weekend at his parents' estate in Surrey that he'd proposed. Despite her nationality, middle-class upbringing, and her color, for she was darker than Harrison, Sir Brandell had approved of her. She had supposed it was because of his penchant for baseball and American jazz.

Having filled the two shipping boxes with the few contents that she'd accumulated during her tenure at the firm, Alyssa bent to pick up her long jacket, briefcase, and purse. Grasping the straps with a strong grip, she walked toward the door and passed close enough to Harrison to inhale the wood-smoke scent of his expensive cologne.

Once she reached the doorway, Alyssa stopped and turned around, sparing one last sweeping glance at what represented the career she'd spent most of her waking time pursuing. The plush beige carpet, recessed bookshelves lined with rare books, art pieces borrowed from the firm's private gallery, and a Queen-Anne-styled table with plush leather-backed chairs that served as her conference table made up the room's decor.

Her perusal stopped on Harrison's straight back. He stood by her desk, right in front of where she had left the engagement ring. Alyssa swallowed hard against a powerful emotion that welled up in her throat. It took her a moment to recognize that it was not the affection she'd usually felt. No, it was pity.

She turned around and faced the empty office corridor. During their entire courtship, he'd treated her like a princess and taught her more about the finance industry than she'd dreamed possible. He'd adored her American brashness and made her laugh with his dry British wit. Alyssa couldn't lie to herself; she would forever be fond of him.

"I wish you well, Harrison." With that she walked away.

Chapter 1

"Child, you and your brother just go out and get some fresh air."

Alyssa smiled, remembering the phrase from her childhood along with the comforting sound of her grandmother's dulcet tones. It brought back images of summers spent exploring the nooks and crannies of the South Carolina farm with her older brother, Alan.

She took a deep breath, then let her head fall back to stare through the clear overhead glass of the Jeep Wrangler Sahara. The bright glow of the spring sun warmed her face as the crisp air filled her lungs. Although the automobile wasn't Barbie pink with streamers on the handlebars or equipped with a worn leather saddle that Grandpa would put on Ole Betsy to give her a ride in the pasture, the convertible Jeep was perfect for her.

"I'll take it," she stated.

"Well, little lady. Why don't we go into my office and discuss this some more?"

With a half smile on her face, she took off her seat belt and sat back in the seat, enjoying the slight breeze that filtered into the space and mingled with the lingering scent that accompanied new cars. As soon as she nailed down this deal, she would be finished with over half of the to-do list she'd written during the over-eight-hour flight from London's Heathrow Airport to Chicago's O'Hare.

It had taken her six weeks. A little over a month after her plane touched down she had a new job, moved into her aunt's old condo, secured a new doctor and lawyer, reconnected with old friends, and renewed her driver's license. Now all she needed was a car.

A good investment strategy, disciplined savings, and a nest egg of handsome performance bonuses would nicely supplement her lower salary and secure a very comfortable lifestyle. The job as program manager at the youth center would allow her to give back to the community. Bringing the skills that had served her well in the international finance arena, she would organize and reinvigorate the youth center's program for teens.

The world called Chicago "the Windy City," but she called it home. Alyssa grew up hearing wintertime blues and summertime jazz, playing double Dutch under tall trees on clean sidewalks, watching the performances of the Chicago Ballet. Gospel music and Mahalia Jackson's powerful voice would flow through the three-story brick row house her parents had scrimped and saved every penny to buy.

London's centuries-old buildings and historical wonders made it a grand city. Suspended between the most pleasing aspects of its numerous pasts and rapidly changing present, the British capital had been a wonderful place to live. However, Chicago, proudly displaying the hope for the future along with vestiges of its heritage, would always possess the key to her heart.

"Dan." She touched him on the cheek and aimed the smile that had charmed the heads of corporate enterprise and foreign diplomats toward the slightly balding, gray-haired man. Alyssa knew what she wanted; the only trick was to get it in the shortest time possible. Having spent half the morning gathering information on the car of her dreams, she'd walked into the showroom of Chicago's number-one Jeep dealership exactly one hour after lunch.

"Uh . . . huh . . ."

A fiery blush spread over the car salesman's fair complexion. Less than twenty minutes after shaking hands with him, she knew Dan Stowers was from Alabama, married to his high school sweetheart for twenty years, had three kids, and liked to watch football. Taking a moment to retrieve the envelope she'd tucked into her purse before leaving home, Alyssa pulled out the computer printout, scanned the contents, reinserted it into the envelope, and neatly dropped it into his lap.

"I want the all-weather-guard equipment, mudguards, the keyless entry, the 3000 security system, the rugged package, the hard top/soft top option in black, power windows, locks, air-conditioning, four-wheel drive, antilock brakes, body side steps, fog lamps, and a spare tire cover."

Dan's brow creased into waves. "Uh-huh . . . got that . . . okay . . . that's going to be a custom package."

Alyssa proceeded to point at the various accessories inside the Jeep. "On the inside, I want the seven-speaker sound system and the six-disc changer, and the nice floor mats. In the back I want cargo mats and a cargo net to hold things in place when I'm driving off the road. Oh, did I say this has to be a five-speed automatic transmission? Because it needs to be," she added in a clipped accent.

"Is that everything? That's a pretty loaded vehicle."

"No." She tapped her finger against the gearshift. "I want it in yellow and I'm only willing to pay three thousand over the invoice. How soon do you think you might have exactly what I want?"

"Well, I think we've got a shipment coming in tomorrow. I'd have to get it customized though."

"I really want what I want and I'm willing to wait." Alyssa aimed another smile his way before reaching over to adjust her seat. It only took her a moment to locate the control and recline the seat back to a more comfortable position. "But to be completely forthright I don't like waiting and I'd rather not wait too long."

"You're asking a lot. I have to talk to my manager and we usually need a deposit for this kind of order." He unbuckled his seat belt.

"Talk to your manager or whoever you have to." Reopening

her purse, Alyssa reached into her leather billfold, pulled out her platinum card, and waved it in front of the man's ever-widening eyes. "Bring me back a purchase order that's to my liking and we can close the deal this afternoon."

"You really mean business, don't you?" His surprised gaze moved back and forth between her face and the unlimited credit card in her fingertips.

Putting the card back into her wallet, Alyssa closed her eyes. "Yes, now you run in and talk to your manager while I take a nap."

She cracked open an eye. "I'll wait here . . . and, Dan?"

"Yes, Ms. Knight?"

"Never call me little lady."

Two hours later after a short drive out of the city and into the suburbs of Chicago, Alyssa parked her mother's BMW sedan in the parking lot next to a parish hall and rectory. Her older brother, Alan, had given the German automobile to her mother on her birthday. Alan's high-profile sports career as a professional baseball player afforded him the chance to spoil their parents. A soft smile graced her lips as she thought of surprise gifts that decorated the family home.

Since the fateful day of her mother's early-morning phone call, Alyssa had thought of nothing but the past and all of the dreams she used to cherish. What a shame that her father's faint brush with death had been the impetus she'd needed to change the course of her life.

Picking up the bouquet of wildflowers lying in the passenger seat, she turned, pulled the door handle, and exited the car. Using her left hand to shade her eyes, she looked toward the top of the small gentle hill at the sight of St. James Church. Surrounded by trees and set back from the road, the Catholic church and cemetery had a quiet and timeless atmosphere.

One of the oldest church buildings in the Chicago area, it was a calm and tranquil sight that afternoon. She locked the car doors and crossed the small driveway to enter the grassy cemetery.

As she walked past old and new gravestones, Alyssa took a deep breath and swallowed back the idea that the once vivid young woman who had been more of a sister than a best friend was laid to rest there. It took her a while to arrive at Lily's final resting place but the headstone was not hard to find amidst the colorful assortment of roses, lilies, orchids, and other flowers left by family and friends. Her eyes paused on the inscription written in Spanish.

> *Yo siento amor para vivir*
> *I feel love in order to live*

Alyssa kneeled down on the soft green grass. Fifteen years ago they had met while wearing pink tutus and pristine ballet shoes. They danced their first recital together, held sleepovers at one another's houses, gotten braces the same week, and double-dated to the junior prom. They had always had one another and their love of dance.

"You would be so angry with me, Lily. I've haven't set foot in a studio for over two months."

She placed the flowers alongside the others and closed her eyes, seeing not the grave of one who died too young, but the smiling face of the best friend and best dancer she'd ever known. The night of Lily Santiago's death had been their final performance at the cultural festival. They had practiced every waking moment for their annual performance.

She could still hear the strumming of the guitar, complete with the clapping and stomping of the dance group. None of them could have imagined that Lily's solo of the Spanish bolero would be her last. Clenching and unclenching her fingers, Alyssa wished more than anything else that she could go back to that night, but moreover she longed to remember something other than nameless fear and waking up in a hospital bed.

Head bowed, she whispered a gentle prayer and asked for

forgiveness. In lieu of holding tight to the happy memories of her friend, she'd turned away from the painful reality of her death. Lily would have turned twenty-eight today. Alyssa reached out and ran her fingers over the smooth headstone as tears threatened to squeeze out from the corners of her eyes.

"Take care and know that you are missed and you are loved."

Wiping away the wetness from her lashes, she stood and silently bade a sad farewell. Robbed of her illusions of youthful immortality, she'd run from Chicago with broken dreams, disillusionment, and a profound sense of loss. Now she was home, and this time Alyssa vowed things would be different. The sun began to sink lower in the sky while she returned to the parking lot.

As she walked down the hill, she noticed that another vehicle had parked close to hers. A tall red-haired man assisted an older gentleman in a wheelchair. For a second, she made eye contact with the man in the wheelchair before turning her face away.

The eye contact lasted for only a brief moment but her steps faltered over the grass as the world spun slightly, a startling feeling of recognition sweeping over her. She quickly discounted the notion, as she would have remembered such a person not only because of his distinctive features but also his use of a wheelchair.

Shaking her head, Alyssa made her way to the car, unlocked the door, and slipped inside. Without conscious thought, she glanced into the rearview mirror and watched as the two men continued their slow journey. Resolutely, she stuck her key into the ignition and pulled away.

The Honorable Nathan Beale Hughes was never late and always on time or early. At the age of thirty-four, he had become one of the youngest men ever elected to the state bench in northern Illinois. After graduating first in his class from Harvard Law, he could have joined many of his fellow graduates in taking policy or political positions in Washington, D.C., but he'd bypassed the infighting and high life for the judicial system.

Only having recently celebrated his thirty-fifth birthday, he was a proud home owner and an up-and-coming state court judge in the Cook County, Illinois, judicial system. A steadfast dedication to justice, appropriate professional experience, and legal intellect along with an excellent reputation for fairness had earned him an interim appointment to the bench and a landslide victory in the subsequent election.

Taking care to lock the door of his renovated town house, Nathan readjusted his tie before starting toward the sidewalk. It had taken him months of research and a week of intense negotiation to close on the three-story single-family residence, but the results more than pleased him. With its location in one of Chicago's older colorful neighborhoods, he had access to parks, running paths, public transportation, museums, and theaters. He also had access to the most sought-after commodity: a residential parking permit and a parking space.

With a grin on his lips, Nathan keyed his remote control and unlocked the silver Mercedes CL Class Coupe. Just as he cupped his hand under the door latch, the mobile phone in his trouser pocket emitted a short ring.

Pulling the phone out, Nathan flipped open the small device and hit the talk key, forgoing the opportunity to check the display for the identification of the caller. Few people had his home phone number, even fewer his mobile phone.

"Hughes," he barked.

"We still on for tomorrow?" The baritone voice of Matthew Powell came through the airwaves clearly. Nathan's good friend and fraternity brother since his days as an undergraduate could have gone into the music industry had his passion for psychiatry not taken him on a different path.

A grin broke out on Nathan's face. "How could I pass up

the opportunity to eat the Sunday dinner of one of the best cooks this world has ever seen?"

"Better be careful that your Mama doesn't overhear you."

Nathan settled his six-foot-three-inch frame into the luxury automobile and shut the door. "No chance of that happening. I'm not the one still living at home."

"It's not like I want to live at home. Come on, Nate. I can't break her heart; can you imagine the chaos that would descend upon the greater Chicago area if I were to leave my mother by herself?"

Nathan placed the handset into a cradle located inside the center armrest. Once connected, the mobile phone seamlessly integrated with the car's audio system and transferred the phone call to the car speakers and onboard microphone. He sat back and rested his head against the leather headrest. "I can see the headlines now. Widowed mother meets retired and widowed fast food franchise millionaire, then rushes to Las Vegas for a drive-through wedding."

"Hey, Hughes, that wasn't funny. This is my mother we're talking about."

"That's exactly the point. You're the psychiatrist, Matt. You should know that your mother would be just fine without you. You, on the other hand, would have serious problems if you were to live alone without someone to take care of you."

He drove the point home with a tap on the steering wheel.

"Getting back to the reason for the phone call, I also wanted to tell you that I got Lauren's wedding invitation in the mail today. It's hard to believe that little bit is getting married. It seems like just yesterday I was helping you load all her stuff into the back of a truck to take her to college."

The smile on Nathan's face dimmed at the mention of Lauren's impending nuptials. In his single-minded pursuit of law, family had taken a backseat to ambition. One of his greatest regrets was that the close bond he'd once had with his little sister had unraveled as time and distance grew between them.

"Do you know if Sabrina's going to be in the wedding party?" Matthew questioned.

"Why?" His jaw tensed slightly as it always did at the mention of his stepsister's name.

"Just need to know if I should put in my order for a ringside seat to the boxing match."

Nathan's loud laughter was muted in the expanse of the car. "No. There'll be no fights at the wedding. According to the rules of a double wedding, there can only be a limited number in the bridal group. Not only did both my mother and Mrs. Knight cross Sabrina off the list, but my stepsister herself politely declined before they could tell her."

"What? You have to be putting me on."

"Nope, it looks like she's going to be busy with impending motherhood."

"Motherhood?" Matthew's snort of disbelief carried over the airwaves. "More like vanity. She didn't want to be caught in a wedding photo in less than perfect shape. And here I was looking forward to the fight of the century."

"Guess you'll have to settle for something a little more tame. Speaking of weddings, my mother and Ralph are headed to New York soon to help Lauren with the planning."

"Oh, now I get it. No Hughes Sunday dinner tomorrow so it's okay to come to my place."

"Not at all. I am allowed to skip the family dinner every once in a while and I'm already looking forward to seeing your mother and having a nice quiet meal."

"No problem with that," Matthew replied.

Nathan glanced over at the center console and made note of the time displayed on the digital readout. He had approximately forty minutes to get to the other side of Chicago and be prompt for his dinner appointment.

"Sorry to cut this short, but I've got a meeting to get to. We'll catch up tomorrow, okay?"

"Serious? You've got a meeting on Saturday?"

He put the key into the ignition and turned the switch. "The justice system doesn't stop for weekends."

"Good luck."

"Thanks." Nathan touched the end button on the center control and ended the call. Taking a moment to input the address of the steak house into the navigational system, he put the car in gear and headed east.

Thirty minutes later, after cruising through light traffic on North Shore Drive, he pulled off the expressway and turned onto the local street. Following the directions of the onboard navigation system, he pulled over to the curb beside the valet parking sign, put the car in park, and waited for a red-jacketed young man to open his car door.

Smoothly pocketing the car voucher from the valet, he exited the car into the warm spring air and looking neither right nor left, walked up the granite stairs, pausing only to open the heavy oak doors of Franklin, an upscale steak house.

It took his eyes a moment to adjust to the lowly lit entrance area. "Good evening, Judge Hughes. Senator Thorpe is waiting for you."

Nathan nodded and proceeded to follow the black-suit-clad host through the small waiting foyer that opened into the dining area. Overhead he could still see the dying embers of sunset through the glass-domed ceiling. Low-hanging chandeliers highlighted rich oak paneling, high-backed chairs, Persian rugs, and wood floors decorated the room.

As was the normal way with politicians, John had one hand holding a mobile phone and the other resting comfortably around a fountain pen poised over a leather-bound writing tablet. With a tall build, straight black hair that grayed at the temples, and a nondescript face, John Thorpe resembled a high school science teacher. In reality, he was one of the most powerful elected officials in the country.

Nathan took a seat at the square walnut-colored table,

wondering once again why it was that the onetime dean of the University of Chicago's law school and current United States senator had requested the dinner meeting. He picked up the menu; it took him little time to settle on the grilled lamb.

"Sorry about that, Nathan." John placed the phone on the table.

"How are things?"

John took a sip of his beverage. "Busy," he replied, somewhat distracted. "More budget demands and less money. How about we go ahead and order?"

The senator only had to lift his menu from the table before a hovering waiter appeared by their table.

"Care for wine or spirits?" asked the waiter.

"No, thank you," Nathan responded before handing over his menu.

After sitting back and crossing his legs, he politely inquired about the man's family. "How are Winfred and the boys?"

"Just fine." He smiled. "She's in Florida visiting her sister. The boys are doing well in school. So how are things down at the courthouse?"

"Pretty good. The warmer weather seems to decrease my caseload."

"Well, that's great timing since I hear that congratulations are in order."

Nathan's brow furrowed. "How so?"

"I recently learned of the great success of your sister, Lauren. She's getting married to the son of an incoming member of the Senate, I believe?"

Nathan's reply was firm and polite. "Yes; however, Lauren was a highly successful interior designer before her engagement to Nicholas Randolph and I expect that she'll continue her career after she's married."

"Of course, of course."

Nathan's expression remained impassive as the other man's face reddened slightly. The arrival of the dinner entrées could not have come at a better time.

They ate in a strained silence for a while. Finishing his meal, Nathan put down his fork and knife. He wiped his mouth with the white table napkin. "So, John, what exactly is it that I can do for you? Your telephone message was rather vague."

"Actually, it's more along the lines of what I can do for you. As you probably know, Judge Henson will turn seventy-five in eight months."

Nathan nodded. As a senior judge within the federal justice system, Henson's opinions had influenced the district court for over three decades. Federal court judges were appointed to their positions for life and it was not uncommon for a justice to serve on the bench until death. Judge Henson, however, had let it be known publicly that he would retire upon reaching the age of seventy-five.

"Harmon Gillespie is in line for the chief judge position and the move leaves an office open. Someone needs to replace him and we have to get the ball rolling to lobby the Senate Judiciary Committee to set a schedule for confirmation hearings."

"Naturally." He nodded. "But what exactly does this have to do with me?"

"Well, Nathan." John placed his napkin on the table. "I've been asked by the president of the United States to approach you with the offer."

Nathan's fingers clenched on the frost-covered water glass while his mind calculated the average age of the northern Illinois district judges he knew. The approximate number was twenty years more than his thirty-five. "Not that I'm not flattered by the offer, but I'm a little young to be taking his seat."

"Not necessarily. Nathan, you must realize that your reputation isn't limited to Cook County. You have an excellent academic and professional record. Your written opinions have earned praise from your fellow judicial colleagues. The attorneys that come into your courtroom see you as highly competent and fair-minded. The work you do in the community along with the support you've given the party over the years is impressive. But what really matters is that you have received an excellent evaluation from the American Bar Association Standing Committee, which for all intents and purposes guarantees the president's nomination."

Taking a sip of water, Nathan sat forward and placed his hands on the table. "And the party is heavily courting the minority vote this year," he added. "Now that you've given me the merits, drill down to the closing, John. Nothing comes for free or easy."

"True." John moved his notepad and opened a file underneath. "People in Washington have scrutinized your every decision and opinion, checked your background from preschool to graduate school, talked with former professors, colleagues, the American Bar Association, judges, and attorneys."

"And?"

Nathan watched as the senator steeped his fingers. "As you may well know, it's a new political environment compared to the time I was your age. However, the constituency still likes to vote for people who uphold the traditional family values: the white picket fence, apple pie, and going to the circus with the children. It's something that everyone can relate to. It's the same with government officials. Because appointment to the federal bench is for life, stability is highly valued. It's your bachelor status."

Neither spoke while the waiter came and took away the dishes.

"Would you like coffee or dessert? We have raspberry truffles as our special dessert of the evening," the man said.

"No, just add a twenty percent tip on the bill."

"Certainly, Senator." The young man barely cracked a smile. Instead he bowed slightly and slipped away.

Once the waiter was out of listening distance, John asked, "So what can I tell the president?"

"That I'm honored by his recommendation but I can't give you an immediate answer." Nathan pushed his chair back.

The other man stood and picked his mobile phone and portfolio up off the table. "This is all confidential of course."

Nathan nodded, got to his feet, and shook the outstretched hand. "Understood."

"I'll be waiting for your decision."

Nathan was a judge who made important civil and legal verdicts on an everyday basis. Turning, he strode toward the restaurant entrance. He had yet another decision to make, and this time it was personal.

Chapter 2

Sophie Johnson took a sip of creamy foam on top of the caramel cappuccino she knew she shouldn't have been drinking. The fact that they didn't publish the calorie and fat content of the beverage was a sign.

No. She shook an unpolished fingernail in the air. It was a warning that if she knew how much her waistline was going to hate her after she finished drinking, she wouldn't have shelled out almost four dollars for a cup of sugar- and cream-laced coffee.

She let out a small huff and then inhaled the thick smell of coffee beans, vanilla, and honey. Over the din of voices and the whir of the espresso machine, it was barely possible to hear the smooth jazz coming from the ceiling speakers.

Sophie put her mug down, turned around in her seat by the window, and looked toward the center of the room. The marble-textured floor of the popular café and eatery was filled with the polished black patent leather shoes of what seemed like half of Chicago's legal profession. Her eyes searched the crowd, picking out some of the police officers that frequented the courthouse.

It took her a moment but she finally located the person she sought. Standing by a round wooden serving table with her toe tapping a slow rhythm stood Alyssa Knight. Noticing the appreciative stares that her friend received from a number of the men in the room, Sophie let the "ifs" flow.

If she hadn't met and married the love of her life.

If she hadn't gained thirty pounds during her pregnancy.

If her husband hadn't died in a boating accident.

If she went to the gym instead of staying late at the court-house.

Then maybe she'd look half as good as Alyssa did.

Even after having met with Alyssa a week after her return to Chicago, Sophie was still amazed. The girl had been pretty even when they were kids. But now . . . she smiled wryly. In one word, Alyssa Knight was stunning. A perfect oval face height-ened by arched crescent eyebrows with deep eyelids and long deerlike eyelashes; long almond eyes with honey-brown irises; what older women would call a smoker's cheeks, stretched over a smooth complexion that she could liken in color to a young oak tree warmed by the summer sun.

Alyssa's rich dark brown hair accented with reddish high-lights looked fantastic. Sophie touched her own mane of fine-textured auburn hair and then thought about putting some color in it. Her son would like it. Her family, on the other hand, would think she was going through some kind of emotional cri-sis. And Bernard? Her dead husband's cousin wouldn't notice if she dyed her hair blond and dressed up in a skintight catsuit like the teenage girls in cable television music videos.

Sophie would love it if she could hate Alyssa, but they went too far back for that. They had grown up together on the same block, gone to the same church, skipped rope, and talked about boys and dreams. Besides, she thought as she aimed a pitying glance at a nice-looking cop that was trying to catch Alyssa's eye as she weaved her way toward their table, she didn't have a vain bone in her body.

"Sorry I took so long." Alyssa took a seat.

Sophie leaned back in the wooden chair, and then pointed to the tray in Alyssa's hand. "I was just enjoying the atmosphere. What's this?"

"I thought that I'd grab us some kind of treat, seeing as how I got you out of bed so early to meet me."

Sophie looked down at one of the two oversized blackberry

scones and inwardly groaned. Outwardly, however, her right hand reached over to pick up a plastic fork. At this point in her life a little extra indulgence wouldn't tip the scales one way or the other. "Girl, I would have been here anyway. Only I'd have been sitting at my desk, munching on a doughnut, sipping a cup of instant coffee, and looking at a computer screen."

"You work too hard."

"Have you been talking to my mother or my son?"

"Neither," Alyssa retorted quickly. "I've been getting lectured by my mother, who had a nice long talk with your mother after Women's Day at the church last week."

She let out a laugh at not only Alyssa's words but also the way her words were now sprinkled with a light British accent. "They're at it already?"

"Do they ever stop is more like it." Her friend smiled and waved her hand. "It makes no difference that Mama is helping Alan with wedding plans, while making sure Pop follows the doctor's orders. She's afraid that I'll bury myself at the community center."

Sophie took a sip of coffee and gave Alyssa a close look. She'd sensed from the first time they'd had dinner together after her move back to Chicago that there was more to her coming home than her father's illness. The other woman had practically run from Chicago after their college graduation. Not that she could blame her; Lily's death had hit them all hard. "Will you?"

Alyssa's fork stopped halfway between her mouth and the plate. "Will I what?"

"Bury yourself with the youth center. They've got more work than the law should allow, and knowing you like I do, you won't quit until it's done."

"I'm not Superwoman. I just like to get things done."

Sophie pointed her plastic fork at Alyssa. "Well, if you didn't act like it, you wouldn't have half the church singing your praises and Bernard saying that you're the second coming."

"Isn't the pot calling the kettle black?"

"Well . . ." Sophie polished off half of the scone and paused before starting on the remaining half.

"Well what?" Alyssa raised a perfectly arched eyebrow. "It took me over a week to get on your schedule and it's at such an incredibly early hour."

"I'm sorry about that." She sighed and shook her head. "Sometimes I think I'm turning into a female version of Hughes."

"Hughes?"

Sophie watched as Alyssa leaned in closer and cocked her head to the side.

"You didn't tell me you had a new man in your life."

Sophie stifled a giggle and waved her right hand. "New man, my foot. You need to get your mind out of the gutter. I'm talking about Judge Nathan Hughes."

"Nathan Hughes." Alyssa's voice rose. "As in Nathan Beale Hughes, Lauren's older brother, the high school all-star football running back, sang in the church choir, president of the debate team, and graduated valedictorian from high school and college?"

"That would be the one."

Alyssa took a bite of her blackberry scone. That Nathan had been elected to the bench hadn't been a surprise. Her mother had barely waited until she'd unpacked her carry-on luggage before filling her in on all the news regarding all the families and kids she'd grown up with. What she hadn't known was that Sophie worked with Nathan. "Why am I not surprised Nathan grew up to be a workaholic?" she asked rhetorically.

Her friend's eyes widened. "That's right. You two practically grew up together. How long has it been since you've seen him?"

"Years." Alyssa fought the urge to wince, remembering the last time she'd run in to Nathan. She was sure she'd given him a less-than-flattering impression of her grown-up self.

"Well, don't worry. He hasn't changed a bit." Sophie shook her head slowly. "The man's like clockwork: always on time, always dependable, always right. They call him 'old reliable' down at the courthouse."

"Kind of like you?" This time Alyssa pointed her fork at Sophie. The attractive widow spent all of her time either at work, church, her son's school activities, or at home. Alyssa had become reacquainted with Curtis, Sophie's son, three weeks ago, and the little charmer had already gotten her to accept an invitation to go to a swimming party.

"Watch it now. . . ." Sophie leaned back in the chair and patted her mouth with a paper napkin.

"Well, you said it yourself," Alyssa replied smugly.

"I know. I'm just not trying to kill anybody," Sophie said solemnly.

"What?" Alyssa frowned in confusion.

"If I up and changed, my boss would have a heart attack."

"So, they've got great surgeons over at University of Chicago Hospital." She shrugged. "That's just an excuse and you know it. Why don't you take a half day off and come to the spa with Mama and me?"

Alyssa smiled as her friend gave her an arch look.

"Look who's turned into Ms. High Maintenance."

"I bought a pamper package for the both of us because she wouldn't go unless I came along."

"How much would it cost?" Sophie asked bluntly.

"Eighty dollars," Alyssa lied with a straight face. The actual price of the pampering session was about three times the cost she quoted.

"Eighty dollars," Sophie repeated with a suspicious twinkle in her eyes.

"I know the owner and she's giving me a special discount for an old favor."

"Let me think about it."

"Don't think. Just do. Thinking will keep you chained to a desk working your life away. Just change your routine and do something for yourself."

"Speaking of routine, it must be 6:30 A.M."

"Why?" Alyssa asked after taking a sip of her tea.

"Because there's Judge Hughes."

Alyssa straightened, then followed the direction of Sophie's gaze. Amidst the group of caffeine-seeking clientele of the coffee shop, the tall man checking his watch and carrying a leather attaché case exuded authority and confidence from the buckles of his gleaming polished shoes to the top of his close-cropped jet-black hair. She took a deep breath and let it out, easing the spattering of butterflies in her stomach. It wouldn't do to deceive herself and think the sight of him hadn't made her heart perform a quick stop-and-go.

Nathan . . .

There had been a time when she'd had a secret crush on Lauren's older brother. She'd always been attracted to men with high IQs and a healthy dose of drive to succeed. Yet, once during her junior year of college, a brief flirtation with self-destruction had Alyssa trading men with book sense for boys with sports smarts.

Her eyes wandered over his profile. Sophie had been wrong. Nathan Hughes had changed quite a bit since the last time she'd seen him. The boy who'd sat in the same pew for over ten years had disappeared and in his place stood a male specimen that caught a woman's eye and held it tight.

Nathan stood at over six feet tall with a deep brown-sugar complexion. His muscular physique showed through the tailored dark gray suit. He didn't just wear the suit; he made it look good. So good the image he portrayed could have landed him on the cover of a fashion magazine instead of a law journal.

". . . getting changes made to this year's event-funding proposal should be a piece of cake."

"What?" Coming back to her senses, Alyssa returned her attention to Sophie.

"Nathan's sole administrator of the foundation that provides a substantial amount of the budget for the activities you'll be organizing."

Alyssa blinked twice and put her fork down. "But I was led to believe that the funding application would go through a committee approval process."

"Normally that's the way it works, but this is a special case. The Hughes fund was one of the first major contributors to the youth center. I thought you knew. Didn't Bernard tell you?"

"No, he didn't." The smile fell off her face and Alyssa opened her mouth to ask another question. However, the ring of the other woman's text pager cut her off.

"Darn it, gotta cut breakfast short. One of the clerks is sick and I need to make sure the case notes are prepared for Judge Knowland's morning docket."

Alyssa nodded and stood up just as Sophie was putting on her jacket. "The life of a woman in demand."

"Sorry about this."

"That's okay. I think I'll just say hello to Nathan."

"I'm glad you're back, girl." Sophie leaned over and gave her a hug.

Alyssa gave a quick squeeze, then pulled away and looked Sophie in the eyes. "Me too. So do you want us to pick you up on Monday? We need to be at the spa by one o'clock in the afternoon."

She watched Sophie roll her eyes before picking up her briefcase. "I'll call you tonight."

Alyssa sat back down and tapped her fingers on the table. Of all emotions, she hated guilt the most. Especially the kind of guilt that crept up at the sight of the person you'd wronged. Oh, Lord, she wanted to stand up and stomp her foot at the irony of the situation. The one man that she'd been friends with since childhood, only to have kissed him in jealous anger and gotten him beat up by a former boyfriend, happened to be the same person whose support she would need to fund her teen program.

She reached into her purse, pulled out a small-mirrored lipstick case, and reapplied the bronze shade. Surely Nathan hadn't become one of those people who held a grudge to the grave. Alyssa put her purse on her shoulder, then placed the remains of breakfast in the waste bin. Taking a deep breath, she plastered a smile on her face and walked to the front of the coffee shop to approach Nathan from the side as he waited in line.

"Can I buy you a chocolate-covered doughnut to go with your coffee or will I be arrested for bribery?"

As soon as the words came out, she wanted to stuff them back in and run full speed for the door. It had taken less than one minute for her to backslide fifteen years. Back to the days when Lauren and Nathan would sit in the kitchen at her house and drink sweet tea with lemon while doing homework.

In the brief silence after she'd spoken, he neither moved to give her a hug nor held out a welcome hand. Any small flair of hope that she'd held briefly that he might have forgotten, much less forgiven her, died at the blank look on his face. She swallowed and resisted the temptation to avoid his gaze. Instead she studied his face.

Nathan's deep brown-sugar complexion was smooth and almost completely unblemished, with skin pulled tight over a strong jaw. The sight of a lone chickenpox scar gave her a silent bit of glee. It was only fair, seeing that Nathan had given the childhood illness to her older brother and she had thus been infected as well. Wide heavy eyebrows framed piercing brown eyes and tightened lips.

The less-than-pleased expression on his face could have given her frostbite. Not to mention the slow rise of his left eyebrow. She fought the blush that rose to her cheeks. The multicolored gypsy skirt, red chiffon peasant blouse, and leather Greek sandals completed a less than professional look, but one of the things she loved about her new job at the center was the lack of formality that had on occasion chafed her at the investment firm.

"Alyssa Knight," he said.

She winced inwardly as he pronounced her name with the dreaded tone one would reserve for the tax solicitor.

"I'd heard you were back in town. Guess it didn't take

you long to get into trouble. What are you doing down at the courthouse? Speeding ticket, lawsuit, or car accident?"

"It's wonderful seeing you again as well, Nathan. Or should I say, Judge Hughes?" She cocked her head to the side and fixed a smile to her lips although his comment slid across her skin, slicing like a paper cut.

"So what brings you here?" he repeated, then stepped out of line to let the longhaired man behind him order.

"Besides an imaginary court case?" She moved to let another customer pass between them. "I was having breakfast with a friend."

He raised a thick eyebrow. "At 6:40 in the morning?"

She shrugged. "Is that a problem?"

His mouth twitched as he took a step forward to the counter. "No, just a surprise."

"I live to be a surprise." She moved to stand in front of the glass case containing a number of breakfast pastries and bread though, unnoticed, she shot him a look of annoyance. His presumption of her being in trouble grated on her already sensitive nerves.

"What are you drinking this morning?"

"Chai latte," she answered without thinking. Before she could say anything else, Nathan ordered a coffee and a tea and paid the cashier.

Alyssa opened her mouth to protest but he moved faster. In less than two minutes, he'd put the paper cup filled with spiced tea and milk in her fingers and he'd positioned both of them to the side of the coffee bar.

"You're welcome."

"I was supposed to buy you a doughnut, Nathan," she reminded him as she cradled the steaming cup.

"I don't eat them."

Involuntarily her eyes traveled down the length of his torso and did a quick check of his stomach. He had been on the skinny side when they were young and although he'd filled out with muscles, his stomach was as flat as ever. She'd bet that if she reached out and poked the starched white cotton shirt underneath the striped tie, it would be like pushing against a brick wall.

She looked pointedly down at the cup in her hand. "And I don't make it a habit of offering to buy someone breakfast only to have it politely refused."

Tipping his coffee cup in an imaginary toast, Nathan took a step forward, a hard smile curving his handsome mouth. "No, you only make it a habit of kissing your friends to make your date jealous."

Her light eyes narrowed as she struggled to keep Nathan from seeing how much his comment upset her. Alyssa placed her cup gently down on the bar. Yes, she had walked right into that one. Yes, she deserved it, but what she didn't deserve was the cold look in his eyes and the scorn in his voice.

Running her fingers through her hair, Alyssa unlocked her tight jaw. "Been waiting a long time to say that, have you?"

They were related by marriage but not by blood. Their families had friendships that had grown and flourished over four decades. Yet none of the shared birthday parties, picnics, trips to the zoo, ice cream, and Popsicles mattered. Nathan Hughes was not a very forgiving boy and she just discovered he had grown up to be an unforgiving man.

"Yes." He grinned at her, a full grin. A real grin that creased his eyes and revealed a set of perfectly white teeth. For a second, Alyssa had the crazy idea to tell him to stop. Just stop and stay that way. Her gaze trailed upward from his full lips, pausing on the hidden dimple, to meet his eyes. Try as she might, she couldn't help but let loose a smile of her own.

"Anything else you feel the need to say? Maybe hello, welcome back, nice to see you?" She aimed for the questions to come out teasing; instead she missed the mark and hit worried.

He shook himself as though he'd done something wrong and the smile faded. "My mother was wondering when you'll stop by the house for supper."

She regarded him curiously. "Still living at home?"

"No, I have my own place near the North Side. I do, however, regularly have dinner at home after church on Sundays. And yourself?"

Alyssa ran her fingers through her hair and then shook her head. "I've been living off and on back at the house since I returned from London, but last week I moved into a condo Aunt Hilary was renting out."

"That's good," he commented offhandedly.

"Nathan . . ." A million excuses and apologies ran through her head, but didn't manage to get past the wall of pride in her heart. She'd be damned if she'd prostrate herself in front of him, especially in such a public place.

"Excuse me." Nathan fought the urge to let down his guard. Fate was capricious, the future a mystery, but the past was resolute, something that could be learned from but not altered. The large honey-brown eyes of the young woman standing opposite him were not those of the girl he'd once known.

He lifted his left hand and pointedly looked down at his watch. Alyssa recognized the brand and model. The gold Swiss-made Rolex President timepiece would cost over fifteen thousand dollars out of the jewelry case. She'd stood alongside Harrison as he bought its eighteen-karat gold cousin after a meeting in Berlin. She'd seen it a second time as her mother prepared to return the expensive watch Harrison had sent to her father as a get-well gift.

"Sorry to cut the reunion short but I've got to get ready for court."

"Great seeing you, too," Alyssa murmured to his retreating back. A small pain started in the back of her head and spread to her overfull bladder. Dumping the half-full cup of tea, she headed in the opposite direction that Nathan had taken. First she'd find a bathroom, and then she'd dig into her purse for an aspirin. It looked as though her new life wouldn't be as carefree as she thought it would be.

* * *

Nathan walked out of the coffee shop and headed toward the glass doors of the building that housed the Cook County Courthouse. His long strides took him across the Civic Center Plaza and underneath the shadow of Picasso's steel sculpture, past the early morning visitors and regulars: cleaners, clerks, security, trial lawyers, couriers, and deliverymen. The tall handsome judge was too distracted to see the admiring glances of the court reporters and female attorneys flowing his way or even the beautiful sunrise over the Chicago skyline.

"Morning, Judge Hughes."

Nathan raised his head in acknowledgment of regular security detail in the building, and then he checked his watch. One hour until his court opened for morning session. Normally he'd be mentally running the cases on his docket, but his mind refused to concentrate on business.

Alyssa Knight had come home.

He'd thought that time would take it away but she still affected him just the same. *Hell*. He rubbed a hand over his newly cut hair. He'd bet that all the boys in high school had had a crush on her at one point in time, but with the threat of her older brother, Alan, no one had dared to ask her out.

In that desire to be closer to her, he'd had one thing in common with his classmates. Something in him had wanted to protect her, to hold her, to be the recipient of her smile. She'd never been an ugly caterpillar but she'd grown into an attractive woman, and like any man he knew beauty, and Alyssa had it all. A dancer's body with a woman's curves. Long legs, kissable lips, and expressive eyes.

Along with a high degree of irresponsibility, fickleness, and selfishness. Nathan cut off the direction of his thoughts as his body responded to the images.

He shook his head in bemusement. During the last family Sunday dinner, his mother had taken great pains to tell him that Alyssa had returned to Chicago. However, seeing was believing and he'd noticed everything about her. He took a sip of his coffee while he waited for the elevator.

As he watched the numbers on the side of the elevator bank count down, his mind drifted back to the graduation night. It was then that he'd seen the grown-up Alyssa. She'd come to the university party on the arm of the captain of the basketball team and NBA draft pick.

That night Alyssa had woven a spell around the men. One that even he hadn't been able to escape as he'd taken a step forward, an unfamiliar tightening of his stomach making his jaw clench as he watched her smile into the face of her escort. The silver evening gown shimmered over Alyssa's svelte body and her midnight hair lay perfectly coiffed over her shoulders.

He'd stood by watching as her date proceeded to refill her drink with the spiked punch. Then after she'd danced with the entire basketball team, Nathan had pulled her aside. "I think it's time for you to go home, Alyssa."

"I'm not ready yet. I want to dance." She'd smiled at him as she leaned against the wall. He hadn't touched a drop of alcohol, but he experienced the effects just by looking at Alyssa's lips. Red lipstick, not hooker red, but burgundy, still heated his blood.

"You're drunk."

"How would you know?" she shot back. "Did you read about the condition in a textbook?"

"Yes, I did. As a matter of fact I remember seeing a picture of you directly above the caption."

"Very funny, Nathan. But Reggie can take me home."

Nathan looked over at the team's leading three-point shooter as he danced closely with another girl. "Not only is he in no condition to drive, it looks as though he's found other company."

He'd watched Alyssa's eyes widen and the next thing he knew she'd wrapped her arms around his neck and forced her lips to his. The surprise of having her body pressed up against his and her mouth upon his had robbed him of thought. The loud shout behind him had cleared his senses. Only it was too late to keep the hand from clamping on his shoulder, past time to dodge the fist on track for his face. Nathan found himself on the carpeted floor with a hurting jaw as the basketball team took both their captain and Alyssa away.

More than his pride had been injured that night. The childhood affection and respect he'd had for Alyssa had significantly diminished. Yet the attraction that had been born the moment her lips touched his had not. He could imagine the set of gorgeous legs that lay hidden under the gypsy skirt. Eyes like a Mona Lisa, a smile that could warm an Eskimo, and an energy that seemed to radiate from her skin.

Nathan came back to himself when the elevators opened and he stepped inside and rode up to the ninth floor. Getting off, he made his way to the side of the floor that held the judges' chambers and let himself into his own office.

"Good morning, Judge Hughes. This just arrived hand-delivered for you."

Nathan turned to see Liz Banderra, the administrative assistant he shared with another judge, enter his chambers. He took the heavy vellum envelope from her hand and recognized the elegant cursive writing on the front. A frown marred his features. They had dined together last weekend and she'd made no mention of sending a letter. No matter, he could ask Gillian Mathis about it tonight, as he would be in attendance at her monthly dinner party.

Picking up a letter opener, he sliced through the envelope and scanned the contents before placing it on his desk. It was an invitation to an auction benefiting one of Gillian's pet charities. The well-off divorcee had both the time and talent to devote her energies to chairing local and national fund-raising campaigns. Her prominent family and well-connected ex-husband allowed her entry into the offices and wallets of Chicago's financial and political elite.

"On the docket for this morning is a breach-of-contract suit followed up with a malpractice. Your first case starts in about forty minutes and your schedule is full for the week, so no surprises, okay?"

Nathan looked over at Liz as she tapped her pen against her notepad. The petite Latina woman had come to work in the office last year. She'd made herself indispensable with her combination of efficiency, organization skills, and legal knowledge.

"When was the last time I surprised you, Liz?"

"The time you came down with the flu. Your little bout with that bug set your calendar back three weeks. I had attorneys calling me so much I thought for a minute I had turned into the police switchboard."

A small smile curved Nathan's lips as he walked over to the closet. "Understood."

After Liz closed the door, he pulled his black judicial robe off the hanger and then walked over to the stained wall mirror. Nathan shook his head as he put on the robe. It never failed to make him think about the enormity of the responsibility he'd been entrusted with. His convictions and faith in the legal system allowed him to do his work and sleep at night. But that morning he didn't feel the same. Too many things were happening in his life. Nathan zipped up, went over to his desk, and sat down.

Holding the cup of coffee in his hand, he thought about the prospect of being nominated to the federal bench. All it would take was running the gauntlet of a Senate confirmation hearing and he would be sworn into a lifetime position.

His eyes sharpened on the statuette of a woman holding a set of scales that sat to the left of his desk. Unlike most of the images of Justice, this one was of Themis. That particular representation of the Goddess of Justice and Law did not wear a blindfold, nor did she hold a sword.

Fair and equal administration of the law, without corruption, greed, prejudice, or favor

Nathan rubbed his chin and sat back. As a judge, his duty was to equally uphold all of the tenets of the American justice system. As an African-American, he felt it was his personal mission to meet the needs of his people. The federal bench would be a better position to help but it would also be a step toward an even bigger goal, that of the associate chief justice of the United States Supreme Court. He would be a part of living history with his decisions affecting the course of American politics, law, and social discourse.

He looked over at the antique bronze timepiece perfectly situated on his credenza. Nathan had approximately thirty-five minutes before he was due in court. If there had been one other thing that stood out in his mind as an effect of his talk with his former law professor, it was the idea of marriage.

He took a sip of rapidly cooling coffee and leaned back. One day he imagined starting a family. He could picture himself sitting next to the Christmas tree laying down model railroad tracks. Playing with a small wooden train just as his father had done with him and his little sister, talking to his children about his own father, the man who was his hero.

Yet the thought of settling down led him to the inevitable issue of choosing a wife. Nathan looked over at the auction invitation on his desk. Gillian Mathis would make the perfect judge's wife. An elegant, highly educated, self-sufficient, and cultured lady. There would be no surprises, her manners were impeccable as well as her breeding, and she would complement his lifestyle.

Making a mental note to call John and accept the president's nomination, he picked up his leather portfolio, got up out of his chair, and exited his chambers. Amidst all his thoughts of the future and the present, a stray image snuck in as he strode into the courtroom. Unaware, his features softened as the image of a brown-skinned gypsylike waif with a twinkle of gold in her eyes and a curve to her lips danced in the back of his mind.

Chapter 3

"Really, Mama, you can't leave until after I get the apartment together. I wanted to have you and Pop over for dinner. I thought we'd celebrate."

Marva McCollum Knight snorted before sticking her head out of the closet and looking toward the bed. Hazel eyes narrowed at the sight of her youngest child lying sprawled across the lovely patchwork quilt that had been in her family for three generations. She wanted to shake her head. After getting home from the nine o'clock service, she and her husband had changed out of their church clothes into something more comfortable. Alyssa had not.

The time was already past two o'clock in the afternoon and the girl was back in her pajamas. It seemed to Marva that almost overnight Alyssa had changed from a high-powered career woman to the little girl who would sit for hours between her legs to get her hair braided.

To be entirely truthful, part of her wanted to put aside her own wants, walk over to the bed, hug her daughter tight, and never let go. Having her baby girl home even for a brief time had reminded her again of how much she missed having company in the house. This trip to New York to help Alan with his wedding was just the thing to bring her and her husband together, but more than that she resolved it was time to ask Walter about visiting her family's home in South Carolina.

She'd been born on a farm, raised to live on the land, grow her own food, and can her own preserves. The call to return home had snuck up on her like a thief in the night. Only the thought of leaving her daughter caused her to have second thoughts. "Alyssa, you'll be fine."

"But isn't the bride's family supposed to plan the wedding? Why aren't Cassandra's parents working on this?"

"Make no mistake, her parents want to help but your brother is determined to give her the perfect wedding and pay for it." She smiled before reaching into the closet again.

Alan acted just like his father. Her Walter had driven three hours on dark back country roads to ask her father for her hand in marriage. She still didn't know how but he'd also paid for most of the wedding. Marva would never forget the day she'd walked down the aisle of the family's Baptist church wearing her mother's cream-colored hand-stitched wedding dress.

Grabbing a hold of her favorite pantsuit, she left her closet and hung it inside the garment bag. "Not to mention I think that it's very important for us to spend some time away."

"Why?" Alyssa pressed, sitting up on the queen-sized four-poster bed.

"Your father needs a vacation and I need some grandkids."

"Could you repeat that last part for me please?"

Marva walked over to stand in front of the antique dresser and crossed her arms. "The sooner your brother puts a wedding band on Cassandra's finger, the sooner I might get the chance to have kids around the house for the summer since it looks like you'll never get to settling down any time soon," she reprimanded her child.

Although she enjoyed being a teacher, Marva felt more than a little guilty. She'd grown up wanting to be a singer, but the lack of a truly good voice and fear of failure had kept her from her own dreams and so she'd channeled a lot of her energy into raising a daughter whose birthright was to be center stage in anything she desired.

It had been her idea to enroll Alyssa in dance class at the age of eight. The night of the hit-and-run accident and her daughter's subsequent rejection of dance had killed her dreams twice. Her only consolation was that Rachel, her youngest, had found her calling. Her baby girl left home for a second time to spend a year at a retreat in California in the hopes of writing a Pulitzer Prize–winning novel.

"Mama, why are you packing now? You don't leave for another week or two."

Searching for her chemise, she shook her head. "Because I've got a busy schedule with the church and at the high school. You of all people should know how I am about getting things done."

"Mama." Alyssa sighed.

Marva closed her eyes and exhaled through slightly parted pearly white caps. She sometimes wondered what it would be like to have her first name back. Not *Mrs. Knight, Sister Knight, Mama, Mother, Sweetheart, Hilary's sister.* How would it feel to be just Marva again? To be the woman who turned brown dirt into a garden that could feed a family and fill the basement pantry with tomatoes, squash, and corn, and blackberry, peach, and strawberry preserves? She reckoned that it would be the same as trying on an old apron and having it stretch at the seams.

Turning her mind back to the present, she looked up from her underwear drawer and shot a look of exasperation at Alyssa.

"I've never been one to brag or raise my kids to be proud, but I tell it like it is. You are a beautiful, successful, and intelligent daughter of mine. Now why a man hasn't managed to keep your interest longer than four months is beyond me."

"Harrison and I were seeing each other for almost a year."

"He doesn't count. I didn't think you should have dated him, anyway."

"You have to be the only mother in the world to think he's not three feet away from perfect."

Ignoring her daughter's sarcastic comment, she continued. "While we're gone you just take care and stay out of trouble. Hilary's supposed to be back in town the week after next, but you never know with that sister of mine."

"What's Aunt Hilary up to?" Alyssa asked, focusing on something other than her mother's words of caution. She'd always liked her mother's younger sister. The woman's flair for languages, love of travel, and gift for telling stories had earned her journalism awards for her travel guides. Too bad her husband, Reese, didn't like to venture far from the comforts of civilization or the borders of the U.S.A.

"Lost her mind again but this time she left your uncle."

Alyssa started to laugh and then caught sight of her mother's disapproving stare. "Did she leave him in the house alone?"

"Not this time, she had the sense to get him settled at some golf resort in Arizona before she jumped on the plane. Got a postcard from her last week and she's in some Latin American country that I can't pronounce. Said she was going to live in a tree for a little while."

"Aunt Hill's in a tree?" Alyssa started chuckling all over again.

Her mother nodded. "And she's set to interview some lost native tribe that still thinks Elvis is alive and Stalin's going to rule the world. I swear Hilary's craziness is going to give me an ulcer. Sometimes I wonder if I should have introduced her to a more firm-handed man. Mama told me she'd run all over Reese but I never believed her."

"No one else seems to be having problems about her trips."

"Don't think for a minute that's the case. I'm not the only one who's worried that she's going to fool around and get lost or, worse, killed. You should have been at last month's family dinner; Edward gave Reese a pair of handcuffs and told him to cuff her to the bed. Hilary almost knocked him upside the head with the fruit bowl."

"Well, I think that her trip sounds exciting."

Marva snorted. "You would. Sounds like suicide to me. You know they're cutting down the rain forest. I donate my spare change to some environmental rights group every time I go to the grocery. But with Hilary's luck, you can bet that she'll pick the wrong tree to sleep in."

Marva took a deep breath and then snapped her fingers. "Speaking of donations, let me tell you before I forget that I've got tickets to a charity auction coming up."

Alyssa shook her head. "I don't like social events."

"Since when? Five minutes ago? Don't lie to your mama. Somebody from this house needs to be there, and since you're the only one in town this weekend, it had better be you."

"Why don't you give them to Sydney?" Alyssa was sure her younger cousin would enjoy herself amongst Chicago's elite.

"She's not going anywhere any time soon."

"What's wrong with her?"

"Still getting over a broken leg. Don't know what it is about this new generation. Bungee jumping? She gets that mess from her mother. I don't know what possessed her to try something like that. It's too much like lynching to me. If one of your friends jumps off a bridge are you going to do it too?" Her mother shook her head and then zipped up the garment bag. "I know I raised you smarter than that."

Alyssa lowered her head to hide a grin. She'd come as close to jumping off a cliff as humanly possible. Rappelling off the cliffs of Crete had been a thrilling and memorable event in her life that she'd both cherished and vowed never to repeat. Getting back to the subject at hand, she tried another excuse to get out of going to the auction. "I don't have anyone to go with."

Her mother put her right hand on her hip and held her left hand up. "Well, you can call Joseph, Peter, William, Marcus, Tony, or whoever else has been coming around to talk with you after church. You've got some of the most eligible men in Chicago trying to take you out and you haven't got the time."

Alyssa brushed over the part about her settling down and fought the urge to roll her eyes upward at her mother's little drama. Mama placed a hand over her chest. She looked like she was getting ready to swear an oath to go into battle instead of praying for peace.

"Now, if you're done with your excuses why don't you run downstairs and check on my pot roast?"

"Yes, ma'am." Alyssa saluted before slipping on her house shoes and stomping downstairs to check on her mother's dish. After turning down the oven, she stopped following her nose and instead allowed the sonorous sound of the trombone to lead her to her father.

She paused on the last step of the entrance into the basement den of the house. She and her older brother had spent some of their happiest moments playing down in Pop's little hideaway. She still had a small scar on the top of her right ankle from the time she stumbled and fell down the stairs.

The morning sunlight came shining in through the upper windows and warmed the normally cool room. The brick fireplace, in-wall shelves filled with records, and slightly worn furniture that her father had refused to part with after they had renovated the living room made the basement her favorite room in the house.

"What finally brought you downstairs, pumpkin?"

"Mama's fussing about Aunt Hilary and Sydney again." She smiled with an honest happiness she hadn't felt in a long time. It was being home, being there. It was hearing her father's voice.

Before taking a seat in her favorite recliner, she leaned over and planted a big sloppy kiss on the semibald salt-and-pepper temples of the one man whom she would always love: Pop.

"The answer is no." He took off his glasses and rubbed the bridge of his nose.

"You haven't heard the question."

Alyssa watched as Pop took a moment to get up out of the leather recliner chair Alan had given him as a Christmas present. "Don't need to hear the question. I can read your mind."

"Really?" Her lips curled upward. "So you're not going to New York? You might want to tell your wife because she's got an empty suitcase sitting on the armoire."

"Told her I'd get my stuff together some time this week."

"Pop, you really are going to fly to New York?"

"The good Lord willing." He continued his perusal of his record collection.

"So how did she convince you to get on a plane? You've told me over a hundred times that if God meant for people to fly, He would have given us wings."

"That woman threatened to divorce me and take away my records."

"She threatened to take your music?" Alyssa's eyes widened and her bottom lip dropped.

"Uh-huh. Said she'd take every last one. Down to the Coltrane records I got at the street fair back in 1963."

"That's not like her."

"Don't I know it?" He shook his head and slapped his knee. "This wedding is important to your mama but I keep getting the feeling that something else is on her mind. Has she said anything to you?"

Alyssa pulled her legs up to her chest, wrapped her arms around them, and laid her head on top of her knees. "Besides stay out of trouble? No, she hasn't said anything."

"Well, I guess I'll have to wait. It's always the way of women to keep us men waiting."

Alyssa's lips curled into a mock frown as her father walked toward the antique walnut two-speaker music cabinet and took the needle off the record player.

"Not true. When have I ever kept you waiting, Pop?"

"Before you were born. Marva promised that she'd deliver you as a birthday present. Not only were you three weeks late, but it took you over seven hours to get your tiny behind into this world."

"Now it's my turn to wait for the two of you to get back so I can have a housewarming party."

"You can always stay here at the house while we're gone."

"Pop." She elongated his name. "You know I never liked being here in this big place by myself. I'd always make Alan stay home with me. Besides, I need to be at the apartment in case I get more crates from London."

"By the way, Harrison called to check on me and see if you were settling in."

She sighed. "Oh."

"You didn't come back home because of my little scare, did you, pumpkin?"

"No." Alyssa didn't lower her gaze but she had to keep from crossing her fingers.

"You wouldn't lie to your father, would you?" He brushed his hand across her hair before returning to his chair.

"I was thinking about doing something new. Your operation did play a part in getting the ball rolling, but I already had the idea."

"There is a world of difference between a man's actions and his words. You remember that, don't you?"

"How could I forget?" she said wryly, remembering her father's lengthy sermons on the subject of dating.

"Now, did Harrison's actions or lack of them play a part in this decision of yours to return home?"

Alyssa shook her head, both proud and chagrined at Pop's perceptiveness. "Maybe I wanted him to choose at first. Choose between falling in love with me, putting me first, and needing to please his father. I wanted him to fight for me. Just like you and Mama."

"Good."

"To be completely honest, I don't think he would have ever placed me first and I won't compromise and be second or third. Harrison would have supported me financially and in a small way mentally, but then it comes down to emotional commitment . . ." She shook her head. "He couldn't give me the kind of security I needed."

"Well, all I know is the minute you told your mama that you weren't marrying him and were coming home, she and I both slept a little easier."

"Glad someone got some sleep."

As a song faded away to begin another, her father pointed to a slip of paper on the coffee table.

"You got a message on the answering machine this morning. Dan at the car dealership called and said your Jeep's ready." Pop's brow creased. "I didn't know you'd bought it. You said that you planned on looking."

"I did look." She smiled.

His light eyes narrowed. "Why didn't you let me know you actually planned on buying a car the same day? Those slicksters will take a woman for her last nickel. I would have come with you and helped out."

More like taken over. Alyssa struggled to keep from rolling her eyes up into the back of her head. She could negotiate million-dollar deals, move across the Atlantic, and live on her own, but she couldn't buy a car without being taken advantage of?

"Thank you, Pop, but I did okay."

He rubbed his head. "What's wrong with your generation? What happened when you moved out the house? You make needing us menfolk to give you a hand sound like a horrible thing."

"You've been busy with therapy and I didn't want to bother you."

"Don't try to dress it up."

"Well, all right. I've sinned." She threw her hands up and laughed. "I'm independent and I like it."

"Your mother and I taught you how to look out for yourself and I guess that means that you're independent, but that don't mean that letting a man help out makes you dependent."

"Yes." She stood up, moved to take a seat on her father's lap, and gave him a hug. "Men like to feel loved and needed, especially fathers. They need hugs and love from their baby girls."

The loud doorbell buzzer interrupted their moment.

"Yeah, that right." He squeezed her back. "Now get upstairs and tell those Girl Scouts at the door that they picked a houseful of diabetics and selling cookies here would be like putting all of us in the grave."

His brow furrowed. "And don't forget to make sure the chain's on."

"Yes, Pop," she called out over her shoulder as she bounded up the stairs.

First, Alyssa looked through the peephole, then opened the door with the chain in place. She spotted a plain manilla envelope sitting in the center of the welcome mat. After taking off the chain and reopening the door, she picked up the envelope. Alyssa turned it over and let out a small breath to see her name in black typed letters. Noting that it was unsealed, she reached inside to pull out its contents.

"Who is it, baby?"

Careful to place the newspaper clipping behind her, Alyssa stood at the bottom of the stairs and smiled up at her mother.

"It was just a newspaper salesman," she conjured from her imagination. "I told them that we weren't interested."

"Jesus," her mother swore, then looked up to the ceiling. "Forgive me, Lord, but they just never give up. Just last week I had them call on the phone. Right after dinner. I told the man, and he sounded like a nice boy. I told him that I had a long-distance call on the other line and then hung up. I hate to be rude, but they should have enough courtesy not to call so late in the evening and it does get on my nerves."

Alyssa plastered a smile to her face and nodded. "I'm sure they won't be bothering you for a while."

"I'm sure they wouldn't if they knew I canceled my subscription because they kept pestering me. You have to have some level of politeness. Now, did you check on my roast?"

"It's doing just fine."

"Good. Well, why don't you get some real clothes on and after eating you can help me in the garden?"

"And deprive Pop of the honor? No, thank you. Besides, I have to meet someone."

"Since when?"

Since five minutes ago, Alyssa thought. "I'm going to go by Sophie's, Mama."

"You're going to put a friend before your own mama? Knowing full well that I asked you about this last week?"

"Mama . . ."

She pointed her petite finger as if it were a loaded gun. "Call Sophie and tell her you're going to be late and then get your behind in some clothes."

Chagrined at having forgotten her promise, Alyssa bowed her head in defeat. "I'll be up in a minute."

As soon as her mother's back was turned, she returned to the object in her hand as though it were a live snake. As far as she knew, only her family and the superintendent of her building were aware that she would have been staying overnight with her parents as her apartment was fumigated.

Reaching into the envelope, Alyssa slowly pulled out and unfolded a yellowed document: YOUNG DANCER KILLED IN HIT-AND-RUN ACCIDENT.

The blood drained from her face and she swayed, leaning against the wall for support. Her eyes locked on the picture of the accident scene, and any measure of peace she'd gained over time vanished as the mixture of terror and fear curled in her stomach.

Only later, after she'd bid good-bye to her parents and driven toward Sophie's, did she wonder about why the article had been dropped on her parents' doorstep. Waiting for a traffic signal to change, Alyssa turned her head and looked down at the page that lay in the front passenger seat of her mother's car. A cloud passed over the sun; the light turned green, and even in the warmth of the BMW, the chill of a winter wind crept over her skin.

"No man in his right mind would let a woman like that go. Douglas Mathis might have the Midas touch with the health insurance industry and making money, but in divorcing Gillian his judgment could seriously be called into question."

Nathan leaned against the foyer wall, allowing the flow of conversation to continue around him. Before her guests sat down to a five-course Caribbean dinner, Gillian's large entrance hall had been a reception area with a tuxedo-clad bartender serving cocktails and whiskey. Nathan knew that if he had stepped into the kitchen, he would have seen a uniformed chef and his staff folding the crabmeat crepes and drizzling hot red pepper sauce over the coconut shrimp.

For the past two hours he'd spoken with movers and shakers within all the various public and private sectors of Chicago. Playing politics was not something that he preferred to do often and certainly not for extended periods of time. With the coming challenge of Senate confirmation hearings, he would have to be fully engaged in bipartisan politics that held ultimate approval of his bench appointment.

One gained, not by luck, but by preparation. Since making the decision that he wanted the job of U.S. Federal Court Justice, he'd formulated an agenda that would guarantee him the seat.

He surveyed the room, taking another swallow of the club soda before setting the glass down on an empty tray. Tonight he would change his bachelor image to that of family man and soon thereafter, a father. While Chicago's African-American elite prepared to depart the opulently decorated suburban home, he focused on the hostess as she bade good night to her guests.

As usual, Gillian's elegance, as well as her wit, never failed to please him. The black cocktail dress she wore displayed her figure. His dark gaze lowered. She would settle easily into his life, into his family, and be an asset to his career. He would wait until later and speak with her alone.

It was after one o'clock in the morning when the caterer and the wait staff as well as the cleaning crew had vacated the house. Now the entrance space stood empty except for the crystal chandelier, French paintings, and banister stairs leading to the second floor. The luxury dwelling once again became a beautiful showplace. He watched as Gillian slipped off her silver-heeled shoes and lowered herself into the plush chintz sofa.

"Nathan, come sit down and share a glass of wine with me."

She gestured to the pair of wineglasses and the open bottle of burgundy wine that sat on a silver serving tray on the coffee table.

Taking off his jacket, he laid it over one of the overstuffed chairs and took a seat alongside her on the sofa.

"Shall we toast?" he asked after pouring two glasses.

"Please."

"To you, Gillian, for your latest social triumph."

"Now that makes me feel better." She smiled, lightly touching her glass to his. "I've spent all evening waiting for disaster to fall."

Nathan took a sip and then put the glass down in order to direct his full attention toward her round face. "Why is that?"

"The caterer almost canceled on me. Not to mention you've been watching me the entire time. If I didn't know you better I would be suspicious."

"You should be, Gillian." Nathan met her dark eyes.

"What's wrong?" She moved closer to him and placed her hand on his knee. "Did Davis upset you?"

"No, on the contrary, he offered me a partnership heading the corporate law division at his firm."

She sighed with irritation. "I told him that you wouldn't be interested, but the man never listens."

Nathan raised an eyebrow. "He asked you first?"

"Actually he called to find out if you would be coming tonight. I was tempted to say no."

"Why is that?"

"Because of the utter lack of politeness. He would not have graced us with his presence had I answered less than truthfully. Not to mention, Bishop Sinclair needed to ask him about representing the church in a civil suit."

"Anything I should be concerned about?"

"No." She took a sip of wine. "Now why don't you tell me what's bothering you?"

"I have a proposal for you."

"Nathan, how can you talk about business right now?" She

placed her head on his shoulder and stroked his leg with her clear-polished fingertips. A tendril of her hair tickled his neck as her feminine scent warmed his blood. Not for the first time did he notice the lush curve of her breasts.

"I'm to be nominated to take over an open federal judgeship once Judge Henson retires."

She lifted her head while her lips curved into a wide smile. "That's excellent! You will obviously use this as a stepping stone for greater things."

"That's one possibility."

"How can I help you?"

He turned and took her hands and cradled them within his own. "You could marry me."

Nathan's sharp glance caught the look of fear that crossed Gillian's face before it was replaced with a forced laughter that quickly stilled. "You can't be serious." She scooted away and met his stare. "Wait, you are serious."

"It's time I found a wife and started a family. We have been friends for years, Gillian. It's not that much of a stretch to see the possibility of marriage."

"Not to mention that it's a very good public relations move," Gillian guessed shrewdly.

"I won't lie to you. It's been put to me that being married should ease the confirmation process."

He let go of her hands and leaned back. "Are you surprised?"

"No." She pursed her lips. "It's quite Machiavellian, but I feel that I know you well enough to see that in your eyes this makes complete sense."

"Do I take that as a yes?"

"I'm flattered, but I can't marry you or any man. Even the promise of having you in my bed every night isn't enough to tempt me to remarry."

He watched as Gillian reached out to pick up the wineglass and drink deeply, then place it on the silver tray.

"Would this be because of love? I believe we have the potential to grow to love each other."

She gave him a long measured look before stroking his cheek. "You are a kind, honest, upstanding, wonderful man, and I know you would be a good husband, Nathan—"

"But." He allowed a slight grin to curl his lips.

"After my divorce, I vowed that I would never wear another man's ring on my finger."

"What did he do to you, Gillian?" he asked, surprised and somewhat annoyed, yet not enough to disregard her emotions in favor of his own.

She shook her head and lowered her eyes. "It is more of what we did to one another. I married for many reasons and none of them were the right ones."

"I won't miss out on this opportunity because of a mere technicality in regards to marital status."

Gillian nodded in agreement. "The city needs more minorities in positions of power." She flicked a diamond-and-emerald-clad wrist to indicate the empty living room. "That is the main reason behind my having these soirées."

Nathan stood and drew her up with him. Pulling her into his arms, he held her close and sighed. "You are one helluva woman, Gillian. Will you not reconsider my proposal? We would make a great team."

He felt her head come to rest on his shoulder. "I would give it all away," she whispered softly.

Nathan pulled back but kept her hands within his own. "What do you mean?"

"The money, the jewelry, this house, everything, if I could be the woman you think I am," she said with poignant understatement.

Nathan stared fascinated by the sheen of tears in her lovely eyes. The haunted look that lent her an image he had never seen her display before: vulnerability. "Gillian."

She shook her head and pulled away. "I wish you luck in your endeavors."

"That sounds suspiciously like a good-bye."

She reached down and picked up her wineglass. "It is in a way."

"It doesn't have to be."

"You've made your decision, Nathan, and I've made mine. You need a wife and I need a discreet lover. There is no middle ground between the two."

He nodded at the wisdom of her words. "Still friends?"

She raised her glass with a trembling hand. "Always."

Chapter 4

Alyssa turned up the stereo and tapped her finger to the steady beat and relaxed bass of the radio. Looking into the mirror, she finger-combed her hair and adjusted the position of her sunglasses on her nose.

Even though she had already planned to see her old friend, the conversation with her father regarding Harrison and the mysterious delivery of the newspaper article had unsettled her. It wasn't until the next evening after work that she acted upon her growing restlessness and gave in to the urge to dance. Looking up as a group of young women streamed out of the double-doors of the seven-story brick building, Alyssa wondered if she'd made the right decision. Maybe it was too soon.

She'd known that Lily's older brother had started his own dance studio in the middle of south Chicago. The popular Latin and ballet dance school had a reputation for taking in only the most talented dancers. After pulling up to the converted warehouse, she sat in the car for ten minutes before gathering the courage to get out.

Taking a deep breath, Alyssa took a moment to pull her hair back into a ponytail and then exited the Jeep into the humid air. Shaking off the thought of miserable days of endless summer heat, she grabbed her gym bag.

The wide freight elevator deposited her on the second floor and she stepped out into a deserted hallway. Following the strumming of the guitar to what she hoped was the entrance to the dance studio, she turned to the left and walked slowly toward the back of the building. Alyssa examined the cavernous room with its unadorned brick and mirrored walls. An open ceiling hung with air vents and shiny fat pipes. The windows flushed with burnished golden rays of sunset splashed through what seemed to be a million diamond-shaped panes. She took a deep breath, the mixture of roses and perspiration lingering in the air.

"I was wondering how long you planned on avoiding me."

Alyssa looked in the direction of the deep voice and her eyes locked with Andrés Luis Santiago's deerlike eyes. His were just like those of her best friend. Just like Lily's.

He stood leaning against the balance beam wearing black leotards and a white shirt. She hadn't seen him in years. Yet seeing him now didn't hurt as she thought it would. Lily's older brother had been her dance partner and a good friend. He'd been the only member of the group who'd supported her decision to apply to Oxford University. Lithe with a dancer's body, he would have taken the dance world by storm had Lily not been killed. With dark brown wavy hair, a Roman nose, and a sunburnt complexion, Andrés was the image of his Spanish ancestors.

Alyssa dropped her gym bag on the side bench, slipped off her black Armani sandals, and smiled at her old friend. "I wasn't avoiding you, I was moving into an apartment, running errands for my mother, starting a new job, and—"

"Laying wildflowers on Lily's grave." He finished her sentence for her.

Alyssa nodded and turned her face to the left to survey the dance studio. She'd hoped to stem the hot pressure of tears in her eyes, but the sight of the mirrored wall and the pine-colored waxed floors brought back a fresh wave of memories.

She opened her mouth, closed it, then took a few steps onto the floor. The wood felt cool under her stocking-clad feet. "This is a very nice place you've got here." It was best to let the past stay in the past.

"It's my heart and soul."

"Are you still teaching Spanish dance?"

"I have a class that meets on Thursday nights. Are you interested in joining?"

"No." She shook her head and turned back to face Andrés. Her stomach jerked at the mention of dancing in front of others. It wasn't until a year after Lily's death that she'd ventured into the university's dance studio with the intention of joining a class. Although the school offered a curriculum of diversified dance training, the thought of dancing with people other than her best friend had chilled her to the bone.

In London, it had been her well-kept pleasure to take private lessons. Whenever she had a free night or weekend when she was in the city, she would take the tube to the studio and for an hour or two lose herself in the music and the practice of the dance. The situation had suited her perfectly until the night Harrison had unexpectedly arrived.

"Why not?"

"I haven't been able to dance in front of people since Lily was killed."

The words rushed out of her mouth. Alyssa hadn't been able to say them for years. Lily Santiago had been run over and left for dead.

"Not even a small class?"

"No, Andrés. No one," she stated firmly.

"So you haven't kept up?" He walked around her, taking a measure of the body beneath the clothing. Alyssa looked into the mirror and lifted her chin.

"No," she responded to the hint of challenge in his voice. "I took private lessons."

"And you'd like to continue?"

She nodded her head. They may have grown up together. She may have eaten at his family's dinner table and he at hers, but in the realm of dance none of that mattered. If she couldn't keep up, he wouldn't waste his time.

"Let's see how good you are before we decide what to do with you. The changing room's to your left."

Alyssa picked up her duffel bag and went into the ladies' dressing room. When she came back twenty minutes later, dressed in black leotards and her hair pinned back in a bun, the room was empty. Taking her place at the ballet barre, she stared into the mirror while stretching. Tall for a woman, with curves that attested to her African-American heritage, she had remained in good shape by a haphazard regimen of dance classes and midnight visits to numerous hotel fitness centers and swimming pools.

Moving away from the barre, she waited patiently, standing in a position better suited to emphasize the grace and posture she'd spent years learning. She watched in the mirror as Andrés reentered the studio from the dressing room and walked over to the audio controls.

With one press of a button the entire room reverberated with music. It only took her mind a moment to realize that Andrés had chosen a modern interpretation of the flamenco. A genuine Southern Spanish art existed in three forms: *la cancíon, baile,* and *la guitarra:* the song, the dance, the guitar.

Standing in the center of the room with her back perfectly arched, she gracefully raised her arms toward the heavens. The art of Spanish classical dance was dependent upon the upper body, emphasizing beautiful carriage and arms. Aware of the eyes that were watching and assessing her every movement, Alyssa released her breath, focused her gaze inward while listening to the music, feeling the rhythm and flow. As she began to dance, her face softened and her lips curved upward into a dreamy smile. Of all the sensations coursing though her body, the strongest was one of joy.

Two hours later, after a much-needed shower and change of clothing, Alyssa knew that she would need a truckload of bath salts to soothe the muscle aches cause by the series of movements, jumps, twists, and dance sets. Although his choreographic style had its roots in the Spanish gypsy style, it seemed Andrés had tempered his new dance style with a balletlike slower pace that focused more on artistry than temperament.

"Lily would have been impressed by your performance today, Alyssa."

Putting her bag on a nearby wooden bench, she turned to Andrés. The mention of his sister's name emboldened her to ask the question that had been on her mind of late. "Did the police ever find the driver responsible for killing Lily?"

"No, they never did."

"Your parents must still be trying."

She watched as he averted his gaze.

"They moved back to Spain shortly after you left. Father was offered a new position and they felt it was best to get away."

"You chose to stay?"

"Chicago is my home."

So much has changed since I left, she thought. "Are you keeping in touch with the police about the accident?"

He broke eye contact again. "No, I stopped pushing long ago."

Alyssa meant to push the freight elevator's down button but the surprise of his statement had her stabbing it instead. "Why?"

"The past is the past. My sister is dead and no police investigation will change that."

She studied his face, and the rawness of the grief shook her.

"I know it won't bring her back," she said softly. "But what about justice?"

His lips tightened into a thin line. "I have had to live with the memory of her death every day. Some of us are not fortunate enough to have been able to run away."

Alyssa turned her face away and took a step back as she sucked in her breath. His words struck deep and hard as only the truth could.

"*¡Dios mío!*" he cursed, reaching toward her, but then caught himself and dropped his hand. "I didn't mean that."

"Yes, you did," she rebuked softly. "From your point of view I would seem to deserve it."

"No, Lily's death wasn't your fault."

"On that we agree," she replied, still unable to meet his eyes. "I wasn't behind the wheel but maybe I could have helped identify the person responsible." She clenched her fingers. "If only I could have remembered a color, model, license plate, anything."

"Alys, let the past go."

"I don't think that it will let me go," she responded after a brief pause. "The guilt, the sense of loss. I've even had nightmares about that night. I loathe the fact that the person that took her life is still out there, unpunished."

"How do you know that he hasn't suffered?"

Alyssa eyed him curiously as the elevator arrived. She back-stepped inside, careful to keep her hand out to hold the doors open. "I don't. One thing I do know is that they haven't paid their debt and time has only added interest. I will get my memories back one day and if there is justice in this world, one day there will be a reckoning."

Andrés Santiago watched Alyssa go and knew it wouldn't be the last conversation they would have regarding his sister's death. Returning to the studio, he picked up a sweeper and began to clean the floor of the place that had been before tonight a sanctuary. He'd designed everything from the placement of the light fixtures to the shape of the changing room stalls.

Having given up his dream of professional dance, he'd made a life for himself in Chicago. He paused from pushing the broom handle and stared at the spot where Alyssa had been standing only moments before. An old anger bordering on hate flared in his stomach. All too quickly it turned to self-loathing. A future probability had become reality. She was back and he would see her often, teach her how to dance, and relive the agony of that night.

Lily's best friend. He'd stood inches away from her as they danced, placed his hands upon her bare arms, and felt the softness of her skin and the strength of her muscles. He'd watched her eyes darken with passion as she gave herself over to the music.

There was no denying that in stillness Alyssa was striking, but in dance she was perfection. Long legs moved through intricate patterns; slender, bare fingers led strong arms. Yet it was the beauty of her unadorned countenance, the long slender neck, and the feminine sensuality she wore like a crown. Not for the first or the last time she made him wish he had made different choices.

Five weeks ago he'd gotten the late evening phone call informing him of Alyssa Knight's return, yet it was fear, not guilt, that sent him hurriedly dressing and seeking confession at the church.

Andrés finished sweeping and dumped the trash into the dustbin. After he put away the broom and picked up his duffel bag, his eyes narrowed on his shadowed reflection in the wall mirror. He would keep his promise of silence, he vowed, as an ominous feeling gripped him.

Since the night he'd cradled his sister's cold body in his arms he'd believed that he'd paid the ultimate price for his sins. Now it seemed God would not wait for his death to collect His due.

He would go to the church tonight and pray, but he already knew the answer to his daily plea. Freedom for him would only come in the grave. Taking out his keys, Andrés slid the heavy metal door closed and locked it.

At seven o'clock the next night, Alyssa put down the spiral-bound research paper, went into the kitchen, and prepared a light supper.

"Some of us are not fortunate enough to have been able to run away."

The sentence had echoed in her mind all day. It had driven her to return to the location of the hit-and-run after leaving Andrés's studio. His words had both haunted and compelled her to step out of her car and onto the corner adjacent to the performance hall. Everything looked the same, even the bright red fire hydrant where they'd created a makeshift memorial. It was only she who had changed.

When all the chopping, stirring, cooking was finished, she took her plate and a glass of wine to a small breakfast nook that overlooked the courtyard. There she ate mechanically, nibbling on the green salad, occasionally taking small bites of the crisp garlic bread and pasta while contemplating the enormity of the task she'd set for herself.

The only failure is not trying, she thought, putting her fork down beside the salad bowl. As she sat looking at the newspaper copy headlining Lily's death, she reveled in the silence. It would give her strength against the screams that had recently returned uninvited to her dreams and turned them into nightmares.

She would prove Andrés wrong. Six years she'd run from the night Lily died. No longer.

Chapter 5

Thursday afternoon, Alyssa stood next to the open window of her office and looked out. The view that her eyes encountered was that of a well-equipped playground and basketball court. The sounds of cars and children's laughter that greeted her ears were a far cry from the silence of her former office in the London business district. Priceless pictures rivaling the works of world-renowned artists lined her walls. Only these were not framed or hung and they had been created by talented fifteen- to seventeen-year-old Chicago youths.

She glanced down at her silver watch, smiling slightly. The youth center director had yet to arrive. Her meeting with Bernard should have started over a half hour ago. In London, every minute counted and appearances, although they could be as deceptive as a balance sheet, were crucial to nailing down a deal.

Turning, Alyssa paused as she caught a glimpse of her reflection in a decorative mirror. The long flowing skirt and light blouse she'd chosen to wear that morning would have raised many an eyebrow had she attempted to wear it to the London office. She'd woken up at five o'clock that morning, showered, and begun to zip up a pair of tailor made herringbone pants before realizing that she didn't have to wear a suit to the office and didn't need to leave the apartment for another two hours.

Alyssa leaned over her desk and picked up the phone only to lower it back to the cradle at the sound of heavy footsteps outside her door. She caught sight of Bernard Shaw as he walked down the hallway toward her office.

The tall, dark, heavily built black man looked more suited for the football field than the Chicago Mercantile Exchange. Before founding the youth center, he'd dominated trading on the futures exchange and earned a reputation as one of the best commodities brokers in the world. Now having traded his suit and tie for a pair of khakis and a polo shirt, he was well on his way of making the youth center a smashing success.

"My apologies, I couldn't get off a conference call." He took a seat in the chair opposite her desk. Alyssa walked around to the other side of her desk, sat, and leaned forward, resting her arms comfortably on a stack of papers.

"No worries. How are you doing?" she asked.

"Good." He grinned. "But not as good as you, I bet."

"Why do you say that?"

"Curtis told me that you and Sophie went to a spa."

"Yes, my mother as well." She smiled. The day of indulgence had provided a welcome respite from her thoughts of Lily's accident. "We had a nice day of pampering and relaxation."

"Good, I'm happy Sophie's getting out. It's been three years since Zach's death."

She'd only met Sophie's husband once at a Christmas party. The man's willingness to brave the snow to buy a pint of ice cream for a seven-months pregnant Sophie had made a good impression on her. "What happened when her husband died, Bernard? I'm hesitant to ask Sophie about it."

"Zach and I were supposed to take my boat out and catch some fish. I had a meeting come up and couldn't make it. My bullheaded cousin went out anyway. The weather forecaster's prediction of scattered showers turned into a thunderstorm. His body washed up onshore three days later."

"Goodness."

His mouth compressed. "I should have been there. If I hadn't decided that making money was more important than family, Sophie would have a husband, Curtis a father, and I'd have my favorite cousin."

"Zach made the choice to go out alone," she pointed out. "Surely Sophie doesn't blame you for what happened."

"She doesn't have to. I blame myself."

Alyssa gave him a close look. "Not just for the accident either."

"She is . . ." He paused to correct himself. "She was my cousin's wife. I was his best man at the wedding and I'm his son's godfather."

"Have you told her that you're in love with her?" She'd taken a stab in the dark, but Bernard's startled twitch confirmed her suspicions.

"No."

"Will you?"

"No." He looked up from his steepled fingers. "And neither will you. It was months after the funeral before she could as much as look at me without crying. Now she smiles, laughs, lets me spend time at the house, and helps out here. She's past grieving and so is Curtis. I won't ask for more."

"So you're willing to settle for less? Not very sensible or too smart." Alyssa shook her head. "I'm surprised to hear such complacency from a man who's spent his life challenging the financial industry and now the not-for-profit arena."

"How did we get on the subject of my personal life and when can we get off it?" His lips curved upward.

Alyssa continued on as though she hadn't heard him. Maybe she'd inherited her mother's hobby of meddling in the lives of others. "Just a little warning in case you're interested, Mama plans to set Sophie up with the new vice principal at one of her high schools."

"Who Sophie goes out with is none of my business."

If they had been having the conversation via the phone, Bernard could have gotten away with the lie, but since he was in her office and Alyssa had him in plain sight she could see that the sudden change in his body language belied his calmly spoken words.

"I came to tell you that I got word this afternoon about your funding proposal," he said.

"What's the scoop?"

"Good news or bad news first?" he questioned.

She cocked her head to the side, then sat back and crossed her arms. "How about the good news and we forget about the bad?" she suggested.

Bernard laughed before sitting back in the chair and crossing his legs. The slight movement brought her attention to the document in his lap. Alyssa would recognize the cover of the proposal anywhere, especially since she'd created it.

"Well, looks like the funding approval is close . . ." He hesitated as she leaned forward.

"But?" Alyssa prompted.

"Hughes nixed many of your new ideas. He especially disliked the camping trip."

Feeling as though she'd been kicked in the teeth, Alyssa gestured toward the proposal Bernard was holding. "Let me see."

He raised a thick eyebrow. "It's ugly."

"It can't be any uglier than my senior thesis on post-cold-war Eastern European economics."

Funding request denied; revise and resubmit. See notes.

Silence reigned supreme as she flipped through each page, noting the bold lines of red and the repeated use of the word *unacceptable*. In her mind she recounted all the questionnaires, opinions, research, phone calls, pricing negotiations, and just plain good ideas she'd come up with.

All for what? The curt dismissive sentence Nathan Hughes had written on the proposal jacket. The man hadn't even had the decency to write a letter. Alyssa turned each and every page. It didn't take long for her to recognize the pattern. If it wasn't a repeat of last year's events, it wasn't approved. There was no reason, just a two-letter word that she was beginning to hate: no.

She tossed the bound proposal on her desk and sat back in her chair. Not once in her entire professional career had she been denied anything. Alyssa was a winner, no matter what, but to see this. She'd done her homework, had been well prepared, and had gotten thoroughly rejected. While one part of her was still in shock, the other half was infuriated.

How dare he? She exhaled through her mouth and the breath came out in a low whistle. "It's going to be all right," she whispered to herself.

Taking another deep calming breath, Alyssa looked up and uttered one word. "Why?"

"I should have warned you, but Sophie told me that you might have a better chance than your predecessor at changing things."

Alyssa started to feel an ache in the back of her neck. "Tell me more, Bernard. I have to know all these things if I'm going to function effectively in this position."

"Sorry about that. Well, your predecessor scheduled the same series of workshops, museum trips, and career professional speakers every quarter."

"You mean she didn't make waves?"

"Exactly."

Releasing a loud pent-up breath, Alyssa stood up and went over to the window. Hours of budgeting, meetings, and preliminary reservations had gone into that proposal just to get turned down. If there was one thing in the world that she couldn't stand, it was failure or rejection.

Balling and unclenching her fists, she felt disappointment giving way to anger, then to determination. Perhaps Bernard was on point with his assessment of Nathan's motives. Alyssa, however, had her doubts. Like it or not she wasn't his favorite person and her name on the cover page couldn't have helped. She'd promised those kids that they would have a team-building outdoor camping and hiking trip that would rival those that they'd heard about given by the world-renowned Outward Bound program.

"What are your plans?" Bernard had come to stand beside her.

"Fight for it."

"Good," he responded, seemingly unsurprised. "Let me know the outcome soon, okay?"

"You bet."

"Oh, just wanted to let you know that the builder called yesterday about the cabin. Seems that they're ahead of schedule and the place is ready. If you've got time, why don't you go up for a weekend with a friend and check it out for me? See if anything needs to be changed. I've got a pretty hectic schedule for the duration of this quarter and it would be good to know that the place can fit all the kids when the time comes for the camping trip."

She nodded, only half paying attention to his words. Shaking her head, Alyssa opened her desk drawer and pulled out a sealed envelope with a New York City postage stamp. "I believe this is for you. Alan sends his best."

Bernard's grin widened as he took it and slapped it on the desk. "As always it's a pleasure doing business with you."

Alyssa watched his retreating back as he left her office and shut the door behind him.

Taking a seat behind her desk, she flipped through the Rolodex and stopped on Nathan Hughes's business card. Her neatly French-manicured fingertips trailed over the silver-colored embossing. Picking up the phone, she dialed the number to his office.

"Judge Nathan Hughes's office."

"Hello, I need to make an appointment to see Judge Hughes."

"Are you an attorney?"

"No, I'm not."

"Are you from City Hall?"

"No," Alyssa bit out, becoming impatient.

"Where are you calling from?"

"I'm a program director at the Chicago Youth Center; I need to speak with Judge Hughes regarding a funding proposal."

"One moment please."

Alyssa looked down at her watch as the second hand ticked by. After over five minutes of recorded music, the woman came back on the line.

"I can get you in on August twelfth at ten o'clock."

"You cannot be serious." Alyssa sat back with a thud. The date was over four months away. Not to mention the end of summer. She needed approval soon to make the required deposits.

"That's the best I can do. Either take it or leave it."

"Thank you, but I think that I'll have to leave it. Have a good afternoon."

With that she placed the phone back on the cradle, then opened a desk drawer to pull out a train map of downtown Chicago. People changed for better or worse. Lily's death had sent her into a time in her life that she would rather not remember. Instead of dealing with her grief, she'd turned to parties, friends, and complete narcissistic behavior.

But she was no longer the girl she used to be. It was the woman whom she'd become that Nathan Hughes would have to face.

Chapter 6

The familiar sound of absolute silence greeted Nathan as he stepped off the elevator and onto the higher level of the adjacent underground parking lot. At seven o'clock in the evening many automobiles filled the spaces. When he had first taken the position as a judge, Nathan wouldn't leave his office until late in the night.

In the recent past, long hours and heavy caseloads, along with meetings, political functions, and conferences, filled his calendar and had the effect of reducing his personal life to the bare minimum. There had been no special woman in his life, no list of old flames or potential marriage partners, but that would not deter him from his goal. Yet he was of the firm belief that Gillian's rejection of his marriage proposal was a setback, not a failure.

Making a mental note to speak with his mother about potential candidates, Nathan put his career plans aside and crossed the parking deck toward his car. For the next couple of hours he would enjoy catching up with his old friend and Japanese host brother, Satoshi Nakamura.

"Was it my name that did it?" a feminine voice called out to him.

Nathan halted his long stride and turned around. "Excuse me?"

He watched as Alyssa Knight pushed herself away from the wall and moved slowly toward him. The lady didn't just walk; she flowed with a proud carriage and the surefooted grace of a cat. He thought she looked more confident and sensual than the last time they had met. She had pulled her hair back, leaving only a few wisps to trail down her cheeks. His eyes began another leisurely trip that started at the tips of her brown leather sandals and traveled upward over the tan skirt and ivory V-neck blouse, taking in all of her feminine curves.

Her footsteps echoed in the quiet as she pulled a bound document from her briefcase, held it out to him, and pointed to the bottom left section. He followed the downward movement of her finger until it stopped on one name: Alyssa Knight, Program Director.

"The youth center funding proposal."

Nathan nodded. "What about it?"

"You vetoed more than fifty percent of the activities."

"Yes, I did," he replied confidently.

When the freight train upon which Nathan's father was working had collided with a passenger train, Reynard Hughes did not stand idly by and wait for help to arrive. No, he had gone into the twisted and burning wreckage to save lives and in the end sacrificed his own. One of which happened to be a member of a wealthy Texas oil family. To honor his father, the Owenses set up the Reynard Hughes Memorial Foundation over which Nathan had complete control. And so he made time to review every proposal.

"Was it because of me?"

"You believe that my decisions were personal?" he inquired, careful to keep his expression impassive.

"Tell me they were not," she challenged coolly, her light brown eyes locking with his.

Nathan heard the rumble of an engine only moments before he would see the rapidly approaching headlights. Leaving nothing to chance, he took Alyssa's arm and abruptly maneuvered the two of them between two cars as a delivery van came barreling down the parking aisle.

"Not again," Alyssa whispered and clamped her eyes closed as her heart rate sped up and her mouth went dry. From behind tightly closed lids she could see a hand reaching. She began to shiver from the sensation of the stinging cold wetness of snow on her face. Her fingers clamped onto the document in her hand.

"Alyssa? What's wrong?"

The combination of Nathan's deep voice and the pressure on her arms brought her back to the present. Drawing a shaky breath, she said, "I need a moment to compose myself."

"You need to sit down," he corrected, feeling the tremors running through her body. "My car's just over there."

Unable to shake the feeling of panic, she allowed him to guide her away. "Maybe if I sat down for a minute."

Nathan used the remote to unlock the Mercedes, opened the passenger-side door, and carefully lowered her into the seat.

"You're shivering," he pointed out after keying the ignition and turning the temperature control dial to full blast. Nathan turned toward her and softened his voice as though speaking to a frightened child.

He took her hands in his and his brow furrowed. They were cold as ice. "You want to tell me what just happened?"

She managed to conjure up a smile. "We were almost run down by an express mail delivery van."

"That's not what I meant. What happened to you back there?"

"I was just startled."

"No, you were terrified." As an attorney he'd done his fair share of pro bono work. Working with criminal attorneys who assisted people who lacked the adequate resources to hire private counsel, he'd met men and women facing of time behind bars or lethal injection. Their faces had eloquently defined fear in a way no dictionary ever could. The expression on Alyssa's face as he'd pulled them both between the cars had held that same look.

"I'm fine, really," she replied firmly. "That idiot should know better than to drive that fast."

"I'll have a word with the security guards tomorrow morning."

"I hope Henry never allows that delivery guy back in the building," she said fiercely.

Nathan raised a heavy eyebrow. "You know Henry?"

Alyssa busied herself with placing the funding proposal back into her bag. "He let me come down here and wait for you."

His eyes narrowed. "Why would he do something like that?"

Her chin went up a notch, and this treated Nathan to the sight of her doelike eyelashes fluttering up to reveal a defiant gaze.

"I told him that I wanted to surprise you with good news."

"Alyssa." The tenor of his voice deepened.

"I hinted that we were close." She glanced away and looked everywhere but into his eyes. The full truth was that she'd practically declared that they were two steps away from settling down and raising a family.

"He let you stay down here alone?" Nathan swore under his breath. Of all the irresponsible things for her to have done.

"No. He made sure to send someone to check on me."

"How long have you been waiting for me, Alyssa?"

He had asked a simple question, but the steely tone in his voice warned her that lying would not be an option.

"Have you ever tried climbing?" She asked a random question at a perfect time, because she didn't like the way the conversation was headed or the way Nathan's brown eyes bored into her own. She'd stood in front of hundreds and given eloquent speeches, but this one man reduced her to meaningless chatter.

"Climbing?"

"After we closed a rather large leveraged buyout deal, my team decided that we would take a weekend trip to Greece and try rock climbing. We spent one day learning the basic rock climbing techniques. The next morning we took a private boat to the Greek island of Crete. When you reach the top you can look over at the bay. The sunset was magnificent."

"Really?" The doubt was evident in his voice. "Isn't that dangerous?"

"Yes, but you wear a harness and our team was with a professional instructor. However, no matter what the precautions, you can still get hurt." She pulled up the hem of her skirt to show him where there was still a light-colored scar.

"I have never been rock climbing, nor do I intend to." His gaze reluctantly moved from the view of her naked thigh. She wore no panty hose and her supple legs sent heat to a certain part of his anatomy. "How long were you waiting for me, Alyssa?"

"Two and a half hours," she mumbled, more than humbled by his lack of awe.

"Why didn't you come to my office?"

"I tried and that prison warden you call a judicial assistant wouldn't let me through."

Nathan held back a grin, knowing that Liz would not appreciate the less-than-flattering description of her character.

"When did you eat last?"

"I had a muffin and tea for breakfast." She frowned. The news that her proposal had been rejected had taken away her appetite.

"And what time was that?"

"Six o'clock this morning," she answered unthinkingly.

"Where did you park your car?"

Alyssa shook her head in confusion at the seemingly randomness of his questions. "I took the train."

He nodded, pleased that her answer made everything all that easier. "Are you allergic to seafood?"

"Not that I know of. Why?"

Nathan didn't answer; instead he backed the car slowly out of the parking space and turned toward the exit. "Fasten your seat belt."

"What are you doing?"

"I'm taking you to dinner."

After buckling her seat belt, Alyssa bestowed upon him

an arch look. "What if I don't want to go to dinner with you? What if I have plans?"

Turning onto the expressway, Nathan accelerated and merged into the evening commuters. While he negotiated the traffic, his attention from driving never wavered. "Do you?"

"No," she admitted reluctantly. "But a lady needs to be asked. It's the proper way of things."

She glanced over at him and their gazes locked for a brief moment. Alyssa noticed the slight flare of his aquiline nose, the expertly tapered cut of his hairline.

"I take it that your time in London has schooled you in how the British mind their manners. However, you're not in England, you're in my city and my car, so we play the game my way."

Alyssa blinked at the mention of her having lived in London, more than curious as to why he'd kept up with her movements. Ruffled by the commanding tone in his voice, she fired back, "Don't forget Chicago is my home too. Besides, I knew you when you couldn't calculate the hypotenuse of a triangle, Nathan Hughes, so don't try to do that judge thing with me," she admonished him.

As familiar exits whizzed by, Nathan relaxed his grip on the leather steering wheel and sat back. The infectious sound of Alyssa's laughter went straight to his veins. Before he could respond, the gentle beeping of the car information panel announced an incoming call.

Glancing down, Nathan withheld a sigh at seeing his mother's name and phone number displayed on the screen. Reaching out, he hit the send key. "Hello, Mother."

"I had not heard from you in quite a while, my son. Ralph and I just wanted some reassurance that you were still among the living."

Pulling up to a stoplight, Nathan glanced over in Alyssa's direction in time to see her small attempt to hide the laughter that threatened to spill out. Although his mother had her hands full supporting his stepfather's diverse telecommunications and media business ventures, she still had time to meddle in his life.

"I'm fine, just busy."

"Undoubtedly so busy that you were unable to attend last Sunday's family dinner?" The note of disapproval in her voice came clear through the airwaves. "I must say that Sabrina and Karl missed you."

"My apologies."

"Just make sure you arrive promptly at six o'clock next Sunday."

"I'll be there."

"Good. Also please thank Gillian for me. The flowers she sent to your sister's bridal shower were absolutely gorgeous."

"Did Lauren have a good time?"

"I think she was rather pleased with the affair. She adored the present you sent, Nathan. I never would have thought to get her a replica of your father's favorite train engine."

"I'm glad to hear that."

"Are you still at the office?"

"Nope." He cracked a smile, imagining the way his mother's brows would knit together whenever he surprised her. "Satoshi's in town for a medical convention so we're going to catch up over dinner."

"Please say hello for me."

"I will," Nathan promised as he maneuvered the car to the outside lane in preparation to exit.

"Take care."

"You too."

With that he hit the end key and pulled into the restaurant's parking lot. Turning toward Alyssa, he watched as she moved her hand to smother another laugh.

"You can let it out now."

"It's nice to know that some things or people never change."

"My mother is quite a character, isn't she?" Nathan's wide grin prompted her own lips to curl.

"I still can't fathom how our mothers became friends, much less remain friends," Alyssa commented.

"Don't let the accent and the manners fool you. My mother

may have remarried into a wealthy family, but deep down she's still the same woman who packed her bag and left Mississippi with a young college-educated railway-car man who had little money in his pocket and the light of dreams in his eyes."

Well aware of the quiet intimacy of the car as they came to a stop, Alyssa cleared her throat and asked another question. "May I ask who Satoshi is, and won't he mind that I'm coming to dinner?"

"Satoshi Nakamura was my Japanese host brother. I stayed with his family in Tokyo during a yearlong student exchange program."

She blinked and then looked at him curiously. Every moment she'd spent in Nathan's company thus far he'd managed to surprise her with another unknown facet of his personality. "You studied Japanese?"

Nathan turned off the ignition and pulled out the car keys. "As well as law, politics, and philosophy." He watched as she took off her seat belt and moved to open her door. "Don't even think about it."

"What?" She snatched her hand back as her head swung around in his direction.

Aiming a meaningful glance at the passenger-side door, Nathan exited the car and walked around to open the door for Alyssa.

He held out his hand and was rewarded by the touch of her soft fingers.

"Ever the Renaissance man, aren't you, Nathan?" Her generous mouth curved into a smile.

"Times may change, people may change, but there are some things that should remain ever constant, such as the polite manner with which a man takes care of a woman." He closed the car door and keyed the alarm system. "Shall we?"

Gifting him with a beautiful smile, she placed her hand on his extended one. All of her worries melted away and thoughts of the youth center faded.

After stepping through the door of the restaurant, Alyssa

stood to the side while Nathan warmly greeted a man she assumed was Satoshi. The dining interior along with the small alcove was very Japanese. A scent of wood and the color of pine served to accentuate the Asian-style decor. The restaurant, Murasaki, had tatami mats and sliding screens; the gentle sounds of the Japanese koto blended with the murmur of conversation. The kimono-clad hostess greeted them with a smile and a slight bow.

Alyssa stood back watching as the men exchanged greetings in Japanese. She was not alone in her curiosity; other patrons as well as the restaurant's Japanese staff seemed fascinated by their conversation. Several moments passed before Nathan remembered her presence.

"Satoshi, I'd like you to meet a friend, Alyssa Knight. Alyssa, this is Dr. Satoshi Nakamura, my host brother."

She shook the man's proffered hand and was surprised by the firm grip. With his spiked hair, height, and distinguished features, she could bet that he had more than a few unattached female patients. "Nice to meet you, Dr. Nakamura."

"Please call me Satoshi, I hate hearing the word *doctor* after I leave the hospital."

"All right." Her smile widened. "Call me Alyssa."

After they were settled in the private Japanese-style dining room, Alyssa let out a sigh of relief to see that the seating arrangements had been adapted to Western tastes. Underneath the low table was enough space for her to stretch her legs. She took a seat on a cushion atop the traditional heavy straw mats. She turned to her dining companion. "What field do you specialize in, Satoshi?"

"Oncology. So are you in the law field as well?"

"No, I'm a program director at a local youth center."

"That's wonderful. I want to pioneer a mentor program at my hospital."

"I thought most large medical institutions had them."

"I benefited from a mentor program when I interned at

a medical school in Toronto. In Japan, the practice is more haphazard. It is about family ties and favors."

"Sounds like you have an uphill battle on your hands," Nathan said, wiping his hands on the hot hand towel provided by the waitress.

Satoshi broke apart his wooden chopsticks. "Alyssa, if you have any ideas that could help I would be appreciative."

"I'd love to be of assistance but I'm new to my position. I have a colleague who is very knowledgeable about those types of programs. I'll send him an e-mail in the morning."

"Thank you." He turned back to Nathan. "Before I forget to tell you, Mother and Father will be in town this summer for an American Medical Association conference."

"Can't wait to see them."

"They were especially pleased to hear that Lauren's getting married. Although it's traditional to send money, Mother wants to give something more personal so she's already begun shopping for the perfect kimono."

"I'm sure Lauren will be happy," Nathan replied. "I hope you're hungry because I plan on ordering a lot of dishes."

"Starved. They kept us in seminars all day." Satoshi took out a calling card from his wallet. "If you two would excuse me for a minute I want to call the hospital before things get busy and check on some of my patients."

Nathan looked down at his watch and rapidly made the necessary time zone calculations. "Sure the nurses will pick up the phone at six o'clock in the morning, Satoshi?"

"Well, there is this one nurse . . ." He tilted his head and grinned.

"Still got the ladies all over you."

"What can I say?" Satoshi shrugged, giving Alyssa a flirtatious glance. "I have a way with women. It's called courtesy and charm."

"I know," Nathan shot back. "I taught you that."

"I've learned a lot more since those days. Again, please excuse me and feel free to begin eating without me."

She watched as he turned his attention toward her. "Alyssa, if Nathan starts talking about business, have him tell you about our *onsen* adventure."

"I like your host brother," Alyssa said as soon as Satoshi slid the door closed.

"He seems to like you as well."

"If I translate correctly, I believe he said that I was pretty and too smart for you."

"You speak Japanese?"

The astonishment in Nathan's voice matched the degree that his eyebrows rose, Alyssa noticed. Pressing home the point that she was more than his match, she took up her chopsticks and held them with ease. "In business circles it's always to one's advantage to pick up as many languages as one can. I don't *speak* Japanese, but I can understand some of the words, especially should they apply to money."

"You are clearly a woman of surprises, Alyssa Knight."

The sliding door to their dining alcove opened and a waitress deposited plates of Japanese appetizers on the table. Carefully picking up a steamed dumpling and a sushi roll, Alyssa looked up at Nathan. "Surprise me by telling me the story about your *onsen* trip."

"To begin, *onsen* isn't a place but it's the name for the public bathhouses. There was this night after exams and Satoshi and his gang decided that I should experience some Japanese culture."

"That doesn't sound so bad."

"I was drunk."

"I have a hard time picturing you intoxicated, Nathan." She gave him an arch look.

"It happened."

"And . . ."

"You do not wear clothing in Japanese public baths, Alyssa."

"You mean . . ." She blushed.

"I was forced to walk through a crowded room of Japanese men with only a postage-stamp-sized hand towel."

"That sounds . . ." Alyssa began, but her imagination got the best of her and she couldn't help but start to giggle.

Nathan chuckled. "Luckily or unluckily, I only remember bits and pieces of what happened. From what I can piece together I may have made a spectacle of myself."

"I'm sure that wouldn't have been a hard thing to have happened considering that as an African-American, you would have stood out." Alyssa took a sip of water to moisten her dry throat. The wide smile on her face was in no way diminished at Nathan's raised brow.

The arrival of the main courses and Satoshi's return interrupted their shared laughter. Picking up his glass of beer, Nathan took a sip, all the while watching as his host brother regaled Alyssa with tales of their adventures. It was a reunion and a new beginning, he mused, taking a bite of tuna sushi. For the next two hours, Nathan let down his guard and enjoyed the company.

Chapter 7

Later on that evening, after taking Satoshi back to his hotel, Nathan glanced over to look at his silent passenger. He'd watched her all evening. Alyssa Knight not only intrigued and attracted him, she made him laugh. That combination of qualities set the gears rotating in his head. Not ready for the night to end, Nathan lowered the windows and the cool night breeze circulated into the parked car. "So what happened after graduation? For all appearances you disappeared."

"I was given an opportunity I couldn't pass up."

"And that was?"

"A fully funded fellowship to study finance and economics at Oxford's business school."

"I take it that analytical mind of yours served you well."

"That and hitting the books every night."

"And after graduating you decided to stay," he surmised.

Her intense perusal of the car's instrument panel stopped. "I didn't feel like coming home yet."

He lowered his voice. "Your dad's illness changed all that."

"No, more like hastened my return. I was ready to come back."

"Are you settling in at the center?"

"I'm happy. What about you?" Her voice became more animated and she took his hand within her own. "Tell me more about your success story. From regular law school student to judge who speaks fluent Japanese?"

Nathan shrugged. "What can I say? Hard work and luck, I guess."

"And lots of talent. Now is not the time to be shy. I don't remember anyone ever winning an argument against you."

"The year before my entrance into law school, I had a chance to study law as an exchange student at Hitotsubashi University in Tokyo."

"Were the classes difficult?"

"Very. Japan's criminal and legal system is vastly different from our own."

"How so?"

"First it reflects the Japanese culture, and secondly its roots lay with the German, not the American, legal system. There is also a heavy emphasis on mediation."

"I like the sound of that."

"I'm not surprised." He grinned.

"Would you care to practice some of that mediation now?"

He raised an eyebrow while lowering his hand from the leather-encased steering wheel to the gearshift. "And what do you propose?"

"As I see it, we both want what's best for the kids. It's just that we have two ideas on how to accomplish it."

Nathan turned his body to the right and gave Alyssa his full attention. "Go on."

"I think it is easy for you to discount my ideas because you've probably never done any of them."

He paused before responding. "Maybe I don't like to change something that works and accomplishes its goals within an allocated budget."

She met his gaze with a look of confidence he found as disconcerting as it was appealing.

"I've also considered that possibility and can respond by saying that not only is change beneficial but it also broadens the kids' horizons."

"Beneficial in what way?"

"The events I've proposed. You've axed only those that dealt with the arts or were not focused on the business field. Studies and research have found that exposure to the arts, extracurricular activities, and time outside of their daily environment are a tremendous boost to a teenager's confidence, self-esteem, and attitude."

Nathan felt a slight stirring in his loins as she began to toy with the pendant around her neck, and he took a deep cleansing breath while anticipating the cold shower he would endure tonight. Looking away, he wondered how that one innocent gesture would have such an effect upon his self-control. "These kids need to be prepared for life after high school graduation."

Alyssa took the red-marked original out of her bag and handed it to him. "If you'd taken a closer look you would have noticed that I've retained most of the professional skills classes, business seminars, and mentoring events that were held last year."

He flipped to the financial section of the document and looked at the dollars requested. "Your proposal, however, doesn't request additional funding. How is that possible?"

"My events take advantage of many of the free performances and corporate donations. The only event that will draw on the Hughes Foundation grant funds is the camping weekend."

"I have a responsibility to allocate grants that are in keeping with the principles of the foundation that bears my father's name." Not one to easily change his mind or his decisions, Nathan started the car.

"And how is it that allowing these kids to experience a world outside of the city would not be in keeping with that directive?" she questioned.

"You're fighting very hard for this." He turned into traffic.

"Is that surprising?"

"At one point in time I would have said no—"

"I was a college student, Nathan," she interrupted, her voice slightly tinged with exasperation. Not to mention that she'd been dealing with the death of her best friend.

"Then you were old enough to have known better." He pressed a button to close the windows.

Alyssa bit her tongue and turned to look out the window as the city flew by. She was well aware that her behavior had been more than reckless and didn't need Nathan to remind her of that fact. Clearing her throat, she turned to watch him. The relaxed way he maneuvered the automobile, the sense of concentration, the way he gripped the gear shift. The car, with its panel display, leather seats, smooth ride, and powerful engine, suited him.

After giving him directions to her condominium, Alyssa sat back and sighed. "I never told you how sorry I was or how much I regretted what happened that night."

"No, you didn't."

The car slowed to stop as he double-parked in front of her apartment building. Stilling her fingers from playing with the edge of her sleeve, Alyssa asked, "Would you accept an apology now?"

At that moment, filled with good food, having been charmed by the presence of her company, he could have forgiven her for almost anything. Still staring straight ahead, Nathan took a deep breath and regretted it instantly as the sensually floral flagrance of her perfume filled his lungs and added fuel to his already growing attraction. A small grin tilted the corner of his mouth. "Yes."

He turned off the engine and switched on the car's emergency blinkers.

"Thank you for dinner."

"My pleasure, I'll see you to your door."

"You might get a ticket," she pointed out.

"I'll take the risk. Traffic court is just down the hall."

"Nathan, have you ever in your life gotten a ticket?"

"No."

She reached out and put her palm against his brow. The skin was cool to touch. "You don't have a fever."

"Why would you think that?"

"You would never so much as jaywalk when we were growing up and now you plan to disobey city ordinances?"

"I'm not the boy you knew."

She gave him an amused look before opening the car door and flooding the interior with light. "I'm beginning to see that."

Three minutes later, she unlocked the door to her apartment. After putting the keys back into her purse, she reached into a side pocket of her leather portfolio and pulled out a business card with her home phone number written on the back.

"This is for you."

He took the card from her fingers and slipped it into his pocket.

"I guess this would be good night."

"What, no good night kiss?" Nathan mocked softly.

She smiled. "The last time I kissed you, you ended up on the floor."

"And this time?"

Eyes locked with his, Alyssa took a step forward with the intention of bidding him good night in a European way, with a kiss on the cheek. Yet as she leaned forward and her lips neared the side of his face, she found her lips meeting his instead. Her eyes widened in surprise and then she slowly lowered her lids as her mouth opened, granting entrance to his tongue, and her hands, of their own volition, moved to rest on his chest.

Her fingers curled over the soft fabric of his jacket as her pulse accelerated and his tongue leisurely explored, playing hide-and-seek with hers. The kiss ended as naturally and unexpectedly as it had begun.

Taking two steps back, she forwent the temptation to touch her fingers to her lips. Alyssa blinked and then dipped her chin before meeting his eyes. It took her a moment to reclaim the veneer of confidence she'd cultivated over the past years.

"You have my phone number. Call me when you want to talk."

Reaching back, she gripped the doorknob, went inside, and closed the door. As soon as the bolt slid home, Alyssa closed her eyes and sighed because it had been that good. The way the man had moved his tongue in and out of her mouth demanded a sequel and had a girl thinking about a series. Shaking off those thoughts, she slipped off her shoes and shook her head. This time around, Nathan's kiss had affected her more than she wanted to acknowledge to herself, more than she wanted him to know just yet.

The ringing sound of the cordless phone one hour later found Alyssa with her reading glasses perched on the tip of her nose, a book in her lap, and a mug filled with chamomile tea on the nightstand. Reaching out a hand, she picked up the device and pressed the talk key.

"Hello." Her voice was low.

"Did I wake you?"

She straightened and held the phone closer to her ear. In the background she heard the trickle of piano keys, but as soon as she identified the composition, it stopped. "No, I was just catching up on some research. What can I do for you?"

"I've thought over your ideas."

Her eyes brightened with triumph. "You'd like to negotiate?"

"Let's not get ahead of ourselves. I want to discuss it further."

Alyssa bit back a sigh of impatience. Nathan was holding all the cards, and they both knew it. Using her left hand, she reached up and rubbed her brow. "I've got the time and you've got control of the money. So when do you think I could get on your schedule?"

"Dinner tomorrow night. I'll pick you up at seven."

There were no good nights or goodbyes; only a click of the phone. Then she placed the phone down on the hook and leaned back against the headboard. It was a chance to change his mind, Alyssa reminded herself. That's all she'd asked for. Yet as she took off her reading glasses, put the book down on her nightstand, and turned off the light, the memory of his lips whispered across her skin. In that space of time between curling her arms around the pillow and sleep, Alyssa wondered if what she'd asked from Nathan was in truth entirely what she wanted.

Chapter 8

"I want to investigate Lily's accident." Alyssa took the glass from her uncle Edward's outstretched hand and followed him from the kitchen to the front porch. A slight breeze rent the air as the screen door slammed shut behind them.

"Been meaning to get that fixed." He aimed a hard look at the door. "Guess I could go to the hardware store and pick up some door springs in the morning. Have a seat." Her uncle gestured toward a cushioned rocking chair.

Taking a seat in one of the empty wooden rocking chairs, Alyssa placed her glass of iced tea on the small table and waved at a neighbor across the street who was outside cutting the lawn. On the drive down to his South Side home she'd half expected her uncle to pat her on the back and discourage her, but he didn't.

With a head full of black silver-laced hair, straight shoulders, an unlined brow, wire-framed glasses, and a friendly demeanor, Edward Knight didn't look anywhere near his fifty-seven years, or carry the disillusioned countenance of someone who had spent over three decades as a member of Chicago's police force.

He took the chair opposite her and leaned back as Alyssa met his direct gaze. "Have you talked to your father about this?"

She shook her head. "No, I can't have him worrying about me. Especially when he's still not back to a hundred percent from the surgery."

"I've tried never to keep secrets from my family, Alyssa."

She sighed and sat forward. "I'm not asking that you keep a secret from Pop. I just need for this to be kept between you and me for the time being."

"Before you came home, he asked all of us not to talk about the accident."

"Why would Pop do something like that?" She sat back in the rocker and crossed her arms over her stomach. It was one thing for her father to be concerned, but to make that kind of request . . .

"He thinks you'll take off back to England."

Alyssa's gaze wandered toward the potted plants sitting on the porch railing. Her eyes followed the unhurried progress of a bumblebee as it skimmed from one blossom to another. "I need to know what happened that night, Uncle Ed."

"I know what happened." His voice boomed, then lowered. "You could have been killed by some bastard who didn't have the decency to stop. I'll never forget hearing your name come over the police scanner."

He reached up and ran a hand over his head. "I think you gave me my second gray hair."

"Not the first?" she teased.

"No, that belongs to Sara."

"Have you talked to her since your retirement? Maybe . . ."

"Maybe she'll believe me when I tell her that although we're legally separated she'll always be my wife, the woman I love?" he said dryly.

"Something like that." Alyssa had felt the fallout of his separation from Sara all the way in Europe. One season they were the happy couple and then the next, her mother called to relay the news that Sara had gone to the Dominican Republic to help in an orphanage. The woman had returned to Chicago after two years but she hadn't come alone; she'd brought two adopted daughters with her.

"I see her and the girls every chance I get. I think that's about all I can hope for."

"I could talk to her for you."

"Oh, no!" He waved his hand. "Just got back into town and already trying to make mischief. I think you should just take one thing at a time."

"Good point. Will you help me?"

Uncle Edward shook his glass, sending the ice cubes tumbling. "You're not going to give this up, are you?"

"No. If you don't feel right about helping me, I understand. I've been on the receiving end of Pop's ire too many times to wish that on anyone, least of all my favorite uncle."

Edward cocked his head to the side as both eyebrows shot up. "You think I'm scared of your father? Please, I changed his diapers and I was the one that cleaned him up after his bachelor party, not to mention kept him from getting killed by his wife plenty of times."

Alyssa hid a smile behind her glass of iced tea. "He doesn't exactly see it that way."

"When a woman is screaming in pain, about to have her first baby, and her mother isn't around to calm her down, I think that the threat she's going to kill a man is valid."

"Pop says she was upset," Alyssa said with a straight face.

"Is that what he calls it? Upset . . ." He let out a bark of laughter. "Upset, huh? Sweetheart, your mama was in labor." His brows went up. "I could have dropped on the floor from the words my Sara screamed when she had the last miscarriage, but your mama? She called your father every name but a child of God." His chest rumbled. "Shoot, he still owes me for driving them to the hospital and picking him up off the floor after Alan came out."

Getting up out of his chair, Edward picked up his glass. "You'll need a copy of the police report."

Alyssa bit the inside of her lip to keep the smile off her face. "And anything else that you think might help."

"That case has been sitting for a long time. I'm not going to lie to you, sweetheart; your chances of turning up any new information are about slim to none."

"I have to try."

"All right. You just keep sitting while I go make a call. Got some fresh honey buns and fudge rounds hiding in the den, you want one?"

"Still hiding the treats?" Alyssa laughed softly, remembering the times as kids that one of her siblings or cousins would decoy Aunt Sara while the others would search the den for her uncle's hidden sugar stash.

"Old habits . . ." He opened the door and took a step in.

". . . give you a big waistline," Alyssa finished just as the door slammed shut.

"Got things worked out regarding that promotion you told me about?"

Nathan's arm paused as he readied himself to hit the ball. The racquetball court was twenty feet wide, forty feet long, and twenty feet high, with a problematic lack of circulating air. Once a week he would meet his friend to play this offshoot of squash. As sweat dripped down his forehead and stung his eyes, he turned toward Matt. Their friendly racquetball singles match had only lasted ten minutes before transforming into war.

"Not completely." He sprinted forward to hit the rubber ball, only to miss.

Matt crossed in back of him and caught the ball in his left hand. "You must be sick or something. Hughes not getting things done?"

"Not sick, just distracted. Plus I need to get more information." Silently he admitted that he was distracted by Alyssa Knight. Even after hanging up the phone last night, her husky voice had resounded in his head, preventing him from falling asleep.

He adjusted the cord attached to the handle of the racket and wrapped it around his wrist. Having lost the serve, he moved forward to position himself in the receiving zone. "What about you?"

"Everything's good." Matt pushed up this sweatband. "A lot of my patients are taking vacations so my schedule's pretty free. Are you up for a fish fry at the house this evening? I'm pulling together a crew to play cards."

Five minutes and two gained points later, Nathan picked up a towel and wiped the sweat from his neck and dropped it back on the floor. Nathan grinned at Matt's huffing and puffing. In this game, he made it his mission to own center court. The strategy had yet to fail and he had yet to lose a game. "Can't make it. I already have dinner plans."

"Yeah, we can't have Gillian eating off the Tupperware china." You could have cut through Matt's sarcasm with a knife.

Nathan grinned at Matt's sweat-covered back and took his place at the service zone. He raised his racket, bounced the ball on the floor, and swung, putting the ball into play. When the plastic strings made contact, Nathan gave a satisfied grunt. "I'm not having dinner with Gillian," he replied. "I'll be dining with Alyssa."

Matt managed to rally, but in his second attempt to return the ball it touched the floor twice, thus earning Nathan another point.

"You've got a date with Alyssa Knight? Here's another old psychological theory proven." Nathan stood back, enjoying his friend's dumbfounded expression.

"What are you talking about now?"

"Opposites attract."

"It's business," he replied curtly, taking a swing at the ball. He'd more or less told the truth. Sunrise that Friday had found him going over her proposal for the second time. Even he had to admit that the plans were sound and her ideas for the kids at the youth center intriguingly well planned.

After making annotations to his previous critique, he had forwarded the documents to the attorneys for final review and revisions. His motives for approving the funding so quickly were not all that pure.

While he had been watching her throughout dinner the

other night, the seed of an idea was planted and had only continued to grow and blossom as he examined the situation. Beautiful and successful little sister of a national baseball star comes home to help teenagers get a better chance. Alyssa Knight would be a good asset to the community center and to the lucky man who managed to keep her. Once again, the unseen hands that guided his life had custom-tailored a solution to his situation.

"Only you would think of business while eating with Alyssa Knight. So you're not interested? 'Cause if you are you'd better move fast." Matt raised his bottle.

"Why's that?" he asked offhandedly, but Nathan couldn't keep his fingers from tightening on the water bottle.

"Because when she walked into church last Sunday with her folks, you could have mopped up the drool." Matt paused to take a deep breath and wipe his brow. "Both the mama and the daughter looked good. Both had on sleek black suits. Alyssa had half the male choir missing their notes; even the married ones were taking a peek during the sermon. And you have to know the wives and girlfriends were raising hell at Sunday dinner."

"Were you looking?" Nathan raised an eyebrow as his dark brown eyes cooled slightly.

"Please . . ." Matt laughed. "I only have eyes for one woman."

"The perfect woman we all know and love."

"Exactly." Matt snapped his fingers. "Who could compete with my mother?" Matthew finished packing the balls. "She made roast beef, macaroni and cheese, greens, and corn bread for dinner last night."

Nathan struggled to keep a straight face. What made it so amusing was the truth of Matt's statement. Many women had tried and failed to catch and keep the psychiatrist interested. "No wonder you were slow today."

"Now that's a laugh. You're calling me slow when you happen to be having dinner with a smart, Chicago-born, church-raised, beautiful woman who can get tickets to the hottest baseball games of the season, and all you can think about is business?"

"Business before pleasure, my friend." Nathan placed his racket in its case.

"Now that's what I'm talking about." Matt nodded. "I'm hoping that maybe some of that Hughes luck with women will rub off on me."

"Things aren't working out with the pharmacist?" He pushed open the glass door to exit into the hallway.

"Not for lack of trying. Now that I'm thinking of starting a family, it's hard to find a good wife and even harder to find a woman who wants a lot of kids."

"How many kids you want?"

"Give or take the possibility of twins? Five."

Nathan jerked open the locker door. "That's quite a few."

Matt shrugged and pulled out his duffel bag. "Hey, I'm an only child and I'm entitled to a big family. I want three girls and two boys."

"You don't want a family, you want to start your own tribe." Picking up fresh towels, they headed to the shower room and the sound of their laughter filled the room.

Later on that evening, Nathan parked his car on the corner and sat for a moment before taking off his seat belt, exiting the automobile, and stepping onto the sidewalk. The ten-story newly built luxury condominium with its brick walls stood out in the neighborhood filled with older, more established houses and apartment buildings. Nathan paused to look down at his watch. Right on time.

The first set of glass doors automatically opened to his footsteps; looking into the security camera, Nathan dialed the number to Alyssa's residence and watched as a chime sounded and the second set of glass doors opened, admitting him into the open lobby. It took mere seconds for the elevator to deposit him on the fifth floor. Crossing over the plush carpet of the hallway, Nathan pressed the buzzer to Alyssa's apartment.

"I'm not exactly ready yet," she said in apology, waving him inside. "I was so into my softball game with the kids that time got away from me."

Nathan's fingers clenched as his eyes traveled downward from her towel-covered hair, lower to the revealing V of the silk robe . . . down, down to the shapely legs that would haunt his dreams that night. "Good evening."

"Come on in." She moved back and opened the door wider, then pointed to her attire. "As you can see, I'm running a little behind."

Nathan walked through the door to Alyssa's apartment and waved a dismissive hand. "Our reservations aren't for another hour."

"Good, I'll be ready in ten minutes."

"Take your time."

"Make yourself at home but be careful of the crates." She turned and headed down the small hallway to the left. "There's plenty to drink in the refrigerator."

Nathan crossed over the hardwood floor and came to a stop in the center of the living room. After a moment, he perused the space, making note of the arched windowed doors that opened out to a plant-covered balcony. As the noise of the hair dryer intruded upon the muted sound of the music from the small home stereo, he wandered around, nodding with silent approval of the apartment's layout, with the kitchen and living room closer to the main entrance, and the more private living quarters toward the back.

The apartment still had an air of temporariness about it. Pictures leaned against the walls. Crates decorated a corner of the room; and the furniture was placed for expediency versus design, yet, from his first breath, inhaling the scent of sandalwood, he knew that if given more time, the condo would become a home. He walked around and inspected everything from the haphazardly arranged statuettes on the shelves, to the knickknacks, to the magazines spread about the kitchen table.

"Thank you for waiting."

Nathan's expression did not change when he turned to see Alyssa standing in the doorway.

"You're fast," he commented. While the women in his family possessed a great number of virtues, speediness at dressing was not one of them. Nathan forced back a grin, recalling the countless number of times before his mother's remarriage that he'd bickered with Lauren over the use of the shared bathroom.

"I've had to be." She took a dozen steps to stand beside him. "Business doesn't wait for one to do one's makeup or change into a fresh pair of stockings."

Alyssa toyed with the small diamond and sapphire heart pendant around her throat. Although too casual for a corporate business dinner, she'd chosen to don the orchid flounce skirt and matching wrap top because they made her feel more feminine.

"You look nice tonight."

A soft blush colored her cheeks at the appreciate tone she heard in his compliment. Alyssa had received compliments all of her life and had learned by her mother's gracious example how to respond. Yet this time was different. It was Nathan who said them and for that reason they meant *more*.

"Thank you," she replied. A soft smile curved her wine-tinted lips upward. She took a moment to leisurely survey and appreciate Nathan's sense of style. With his black polo shirt pulled just right over his chest, trousers of acceptable length, and a two-button sport coat draped over broad shoulders, she would have sworn he had a woman at home. Just as the suspicion entered her mind, she pushed it away. She had no right to be jealous. Yet the logical thought did nothing to keep her teeth from clenching. "You're not looking so bad yourself."

"Shall we go?" Nathan took her light jacket off the couch and held it out for her. She turned around and he drew in a rough breath as the play of muscles underneath the velvet of her skin at the line of her neck mesmerized him.

Alyssa stood still waiting for his hands to move away, but enjoying the touch of his fingers on her slender shoulders. The nonchalant expression on her face was a charade that could be ended by a glance at the pulse fluttering wildly on the left side of her neck.

Preparing to step away, she said softly, "Thank you."

"Wait." His voice was soft in her ear. Before she could move, Nathan freed her thick hair from underneath the coat collar. An involuntary gasp escaped her lips at the surprise of his cool fingers grazing her neck.

"Apologies," Nathan mumbled, taking a step back.

The mood shifted subtly between them as her gaze rose to the fullness of his lips. An insane desire to kiss him flared through her, and to mask the emotions, Alyssa busied herself tying together the belt of her coat and gathering her purse. By the time she'd locked the front door and stepped into the elevator, she had regained control of her accelerated pulse.

It wasn't until after Nathan had tucked her into the secure confines of his luxury car and they were well on their way to some unknown destination that Alyssa allowed herself to ponder what was taking place between the two of them.

She had been a friend, not a girlfriend, to many of her handsome, charming, and intellectual male university classmates and colleagues. Blocking out the pain of Lily's death, she'd thrown herself into her intensive and intellectually demanding business studies. Although London was less than two hours away by train, she rarely ventured far from Oxford, even opting to remain at school over the Christmas holidays. Instead she preferred to spend her time among the precious books housed with Oxford's world-famous Bodleian Library.

All of her hard work resulted in lucrative offers and solicitations of interest from some of Europe's top financial houses. It was only after she began working in London that she started to date, and it wasn't until Harrison that the lure of ardor and power had conquered her resolve to remain unattached. At his skilled fingertips, she'd exchanged her innocence for a sexual passion that burned more fiercely than any dance she could ever imagine.

She hadn't thought to find that manner of attraction again for a long time, but all it had taken was one kiss from Nathan to light the fire she preferred to keep banked.

The closer they came into downtown Chicago, the more the traffic grew. For the most part, Nathan, content to enjoy the feel of the powerful engine, the soothing blues melodies drifting through the precision-placed speakers, and the presence of the beautiful woman by his side, had been reluctant to disturb the quiet ride through the busy downtown streets.

He glanced over at Alyssa as she sighed and settled into the supple leather seat. "Tired?"

"No, just coming down. Competition is one of life's natural highs."

"Did your team win?"

"No, but we put up a fight to the end," Alyssa replied. "I'm sure that I'll be sore tomorrow. I'm not quite as in shape as I used to be." That was not all she would have in the morning; the lingering questions regarding the night of Lily's accident would still be there.

"You look just fine to me, maybe a bit on the skinny side as my mother would say."

"Your host brother was right."

"About?"

"Your current lack of politeness where women are concerned. That was one of the most backhanded compliments I've ever heard."

"But truthful." Nathan swallowed a grin at the hint of reproach in her voice. Turning into the restaurant parking lot, he continued, "You don't eat enough."

"Maybe you should watch the road and not my waistline. Anyway, how did you find this place?" Alyssa not so subtly changed the subject.

"I lost a bet."

That caught her interest. "Isn't it against the law to gamble in Illinois, Your Honor?"

"This was a private wager between friends."

"You've piqued my curiosity. What kind of bet was it?"

"Nothing too exciting, Matt and I played a round of golf. Loser paid for dinner."

"I imagine that you didn't lose by much."

"True, but I learned about this place so it wasn't a loss after all, now, was it?"

"Good food?" she asked.

"Only the best southern soul and jazz in Chicago."

Alyssa's lips quirked. "That almost sounds like a boast, Nathan."

"Just speaking the truth."

"Pop might disagree with you on that. He and Mama spend almost every Thursday night at Buddy Guy's Legends," she said while aiming a challenging look in Nathan's direction. The jazz and blues club located in the South Loop, with its Southern cooking and live blues, attracted both nationally renowned musicians and talented local artists.

"I'll let you decide, but I'm fairly confident that you'll like the restaurant."

"I have pretty eclectic tastes and high standards." She affected a proper British accent. "As I'm sure you'll discern well. Appearances are deceiving and I haven't tasted the food yet."

Chapter 9

Some time later, Alyssa unbuckled her seat belt and took a moment to pull down the mirror to check her reflection before the passenger-side door opened and a hand appeared to assist her from the car. *Always the gentleman,* she mused. Without hesitation, Alyssa placed her hand in his and was comforted by the strength.

They stepped onto the sidewalk and turned toward the blue canopy emblazoned with two words: JAZZ NOTE. As they walked, Alyssa was well aware of the warmth at the small curve of her back from Nathan's hand; aware in the way a woman was of a man: the nearness of his body, the scent of his aftershave.

All of that changed as soon as Nathan pushed open the door of the restaurant. A stylish sign hung over the doorway and the decor within was sleek, with mahogany tables, plush seats, and low glass fixtures. The crowd was a mixture of old and young.

The air was permeated with the scent of barbecue, mesquite wood smoke, and corn bread as the high-pitched sound of the cornet rode over the low, rhythmic sound of the bass and murmur of voices. Waiters weaved through packed tables carrying platters filled with succulent-looking fare. Eight musicians packed the center stage while off to the side a young woman's fingers trailed over the keys of a black baby grand piano.

On the way to their table, Alyssa glanced over the numerous photos and memorabilia that lined the walls, recognizing many of them from Pop's record jackets. Only when Nathan came to a stop next to a small table in a partially secluded corner and pulled out her chair did her attention come back to the present.

"What do you think?" Nathan asked after he took his seat. He wondered if she knew how many eyes had trailed after her as she moved with an unconscious sensuality across the dining room.

She gave the room another sweeping glance before responding, "So far I like it."

"Still not convinced?" Nathan's dark brown eyes fused with Alyssa's amber gaze. The candlelight made her features all the more lovely.

She smiled, placing the cotton napkin in her lap. "I'm only kidding, Nathan. I already know that Pop would like this place. I'm sure he'll come if only to get a good look at that picture of Joe King over there."

"I keep forgetting about how familiar you are with jazz."

"I know about music," she corrected gently. "I like to dance and I'm not too picky. I like all kinds."

Picking up her menu, Alyssa perused it only for a moment, and then placed it back on the table.

"Made your decision so quickly?"

"Yes."

"What are you having?"

"I'd like you to choose for me." She pointed a lightly buffed fingertip toward his menu. "Impress me."

Nathan saw the hint of challenge in her eyes and lifted his menu to signal the waiter. He gave the order, complete with appetizers and a bottle of wine. It wasn't until the waiter had filled their wineglasses with the rich Cabernet that he spoke.

"I looked over the proposal again last night."

He watched as her expression became blank and he had to admit that Alyssa Knight could have been one heck of an attorney. "After revising my comments, I had it delivered to the attorneys for review. Once they make the changes, you should receive a check for the full amount of your funding request. But before all that I have a request to make of you."

"What . . ." Her voice trailed off.

Nathan enjoyed the way her eyebrows rose as her bottom lip dropped toward the carpeted floor. On the surface his decision may have been business, but in reality it was purely personal. In following his instincts, he wanted whatever deals were made between them to be purely personal, intimately physical, and none too soon. He knew he had to do something to capture her attention. "I would like you to take me camping this weekend; show me what it is about being in the great outdoors that will have such a profound effect on the kids."

Alyssa reached out and took a sip of water to moisten her dry throat. "What changed your mind?"

"You changed my mind."

"How?"

"As you previously stated, I haven't met the teenagers you work with and I don't know the latest effective teen programs. What, or more who, I do know is you. I know that you start what you finish and that you believe in measurable success."

"I don't know what to say," she started after setting her glass on the table.

"Is that because you expected me to give you a hard time?"

Alyssa chafed a little inside as she'd thought herself somewhat skilled in her abilities to read a person. Nathan, however, had just ripped a hole in her confidence. "I had expected that you would not be so agreeable," she admitted.

"How about we have a toast?"

"Yes." Her slender bracelet-clad wrist reached forward to take the glass held in Nathan's hand.

"To the success of the youth program."

She tapped it against his and then drank deep. The dryness of the wine brought tears to her eyes, but the warmth of it going down numbed the surprise ricocheting through her body. Although she was far from being unhappy at the change in fortune, this was not how she had expected the evening to pass.

"Is there anything that I need to purchase for our camping trip?"

After savoring the taste of a stuffed cherry tomato appetizer, Alyssa wiped her mouth. "Whoa, slow down. I haven't agreed yet."

"But you will?"

The thought of spending time alone with Nathan excited as well as frightened her. Some innate warning system was flashing a red light in her head, but all she could see were the expectant faces of the teens as they discussed the idea of camping. "Of course."

"Good." His eyes lightened. "This weekend looks good for me."

"But not for me." She shook her head. "I have commitments on Saturday. It will have to be next weekend."

The arrival of the food and a visitor cut the conversation short.

"Nathan, I thought I recognized you," came a woman's voice. He put down his silverware and turned toward the source of the call. Petite and powerful, Sabrina Jackson could easily give a person the impression of delicate helplessness. Nathan shook his head; his stepsister had never in a day of her life been helpless.

Completely ignoring his dinner companion, Sabrina dipped down and gave him a hug. Nathan smothered a curse. He loved her not out of obligation, but unconditionally as a sister. However, no one in the family was blind to the fact that Sabrina could be the nicest person in the world to family and deadly when crossed or jealous. "I missed you at the dinner last week, Nate. How are you?"

"I'm good. What are you up to?"

"We're having dinner with friends."

"I'd ask you to join us but we're already eating. Sabrina, you remember Alyssa Knight."

"I most certainly remember Alyssa," Sabrina replied.

Nathan placed his napkin on the table and moved to stand

beside Alyssa's chair in preparation of introducing Karl. "And this is her husband—"

"Karl Jackson," Alyssa lifted her face politely, giving the older handsome gentleman her cheek, which he leaned down and kissed. It was the devil in her that made her lips curl upward and her eyes linger slightly on Karl's face. Everything about him whispered of power and respect while Sabrina's designer label shouted elegance and privilege. "I haven't seen you since the conference in Munich. Have you taken over any other European telecoms recently?"

"No, just busy dealing with the ones I have. What brings you to Chicago, and is Harrison with you?"

Alyssa's smile slipped, not because of the mention of Harrison's name, but at the spark of tension she felt from the man at her side. She'd learned early on in her relationship with Harrison to be aware of his moods. The intense moodiness and jealousy that hid underneath the cool and cultured British exterior had at first surprised and later frightened her. The telltale signs of tension were all too apparent from the set of Nathan's jaw and the way his fingers tensed on her shoulder.

"Actually, I've moved back home."

"Alyssa and I graduated from the same high school, dear," Sabrina explained. "Rosemarie and her mother are close friends."

Karl raised a bushy eyebrow. "I'm surprised no one let me know that you were opening an office in Chicago."

"I've also left the firm." Alyssa's brisk tone left no room for further questions.

"I'm sure he . . ." He paused, looking from her to Nathan. "Excuse me, *they* were sorry to see you go."

"Their loss is our gain." Nathan inserted himself into the conversation after taking his seat. "Alyssa is the new program manager at the youth center."

Karl's brows rose in surprise. "That's a rather dramatic change."

"It's a challenge." Alyssa nodded her head. "But there is no other place I would rather be than helping the community."

"Speaking of helping the community." Sabrina moved closer to her husband.

Alyssa suppressed the urge to roll her eyes to the ceiling. She had no designs on the man in front of her. No, not while she was busy trying to figure out the man across the table. Nathan's sudden approval of the new programs in addition to the way he looked at her throughout dinner had caught her off guard.

Sabrina continued, "Are you coming to the auction, Nathan? Gillian personally sent the invitation and is wondering why she hasn't heard from you yet."

"I plan to be there, but I need another invitation."

Seeing the look of puzzlement on Sabrina's face, he elaborated. "I would like an extra invitation for Alyssa."

"I'm sorry, but I sent the last out to Karl's business associates. I'm sure Gillian will have a few at the door."

Pasting on a bright smile to hide her mounting anger at Nathan's presumptuous behavior, Alyssa tipped her wineglass. "No need, I already have an invitation."

She was slightly rewarded as her statement garnered surprised glances from both Nathan and his stepsister. "My parents won't be able to attend, so I will be taking their place."

"Will you be coming alone?" Sabrina asked.

"I'm not sure. I've only recently come home and my social schedule hasn't been a high priority on my list."

"Well, we'll have to change that," Karl replied. "Sabrina's always involved with something."

"Honey," Sabrina interjected. "Our party's arrived."

"Well, it was good seeing you again, Alyssa, and I'll see you on Sunday, Nathan."

Sabrina grabbed her husband's arm and not so discreetly pulled him away.

Despite Alyssa's diminished appetite, the pan-fried breaded catfish still looked good. She returned her attention to her plate and took a bite. The fish was perfection alone, but dipping it into the small dish of mustard sent it over the top. The taste brought back happy memories of summers spent helping her mother at the church fish fry.

Nathan noted the satisfied expression on Alyssa's face and was pleased that she'd liked his menu choice. Sabrina's arrival had been an untimely interruption, but her having introduced the subject of the charity auction gave him the opening he needed. He was attracted to Alyssa both physically and mentally. Her self-assured demeanor, passionate nature, and lightheartedness would complement his laid-back personality.

"I will take you to the auction, Alyssa."

"I might not be going." Her fork paused midway to her lips.

"The answer you gave Sabrina was quite firm."

She swallowed the garlic mashed potatoes before replying, "I could have changed my mind."

"Change it back."

"All right, enough of this." She placed her silverware down. The undercurrent of tension that had arrived with the visit of his stepsister should have but hadn't left with her. "What is the matter with you, Nathan?"

"Is there someone in your life?" he asked.

"If you are asking if I'm committed to someone, Nathan, then the answer is no." She met his hard stare with an impassive one of her own.

Nathan sliced through his steak. "And the man you left in London, this Harrison?"

Alyssa hesitated for several seconds. "He and I dated for a while."

"Did you love him?"

"At one point I could say that I was in love with him."

"What happened?"

She toyed with the stem of her glass for a moment before answering. "On Saturday afternoon, I closed a five-million-pound deal and got the stamp and seal of his father's approval. On Sunday evening, Harrison asked me to marry him."

Nathan finished his meal and returned his full attention to the woman across the table. "You declined the offer?"

"Yes."

"Why?"

Alyssa tilted her head and moved her gaze from his eyes to the candle flame. She thought her reason for leaving Harrison rather obvious. "Because I won't be second in a relationship, especially not to business or ambition. Now it's my turn at the twenty questions."

"Go right ahead."

"Are you seeing anyone?"

"Not at the moment."

"Why?"

"I'm looking for that special lady."

"Good luck," Alyssa said through tight lips. She then sat back as one waiter cleared the table and another deposited two scrumptious-looking desserts on the table as well as two cups of coffee.

"Luck is chance, a play of the odds. I don't believe in odds or coincidences, Alyssa." Nathan put neither cream nor sugar into his coffee. Just raised the porcelain cup to his lip.

"Then what do you believe in?"

"Blessings, opportunities, and careful planning. Your return home is all the proof I need."

Catching sight of the intent gaze Nathan was aiming her way, Alyssa decided that now was the perfect time to duck and cover. Putting cream and sugar in her coffee, she avoided acknowledging the implication of his words.

Chapter 10

It was after eleven o'clock when Alyssa turned to unlock the door to her apartment and invite him in.

"Thank you for dinner tonight." She took off her coat, placed her keys on the side table, and flipped on the lamp.

"It was my pleasure." Making sure to keep his hands by his sides, Nathan watched as Alyssa swept her hair behind her ear. The darkness of the rest of the apartment lent an air of intimacy to the entrance alcove. In the soft light of the entranceway, the shadows played over her face, making her all the more beautiful to his eyes.

"Did I mention earlier that you have a very nice apartment? Did you decorate it yourself?"

"Thanks for the compliment, but this is a work in progress. I just received my last shipment of crates last week."

Two pairs of dramatically arched double doors allowed light and fresh air to flood into her cozy living room. On the wall, an extended iron hook provided support for a hanging plant. On the floor, prayer rugs with the pattern of a Moorish arch warmed the room.

While the open apartment with its high ceiling, tall windows, state-of-the-art kitchen appliances, and oak floors was inherited from her aunt, the mixture of furniture along with the unpacked crates and boxes was the sum of all the things Alyssa had collected over the years.

She gestured toward the kitchen. "Would you like something to drink? Tea, water, coffee?"

"No, thank you." He stepped forward only to become still when they were six inches apart. "I don't make decisions lightly."

Years ago he'd had a boy's crush. Now he had a man's desire. He wanted to make love to her, he wanted her laughter, her smiles, the husky voice whispering in his ear, he wanted to feed off the vibrant energy she seemed to glow with.

He reached out and trailed a fingertip over the softness of her cheek. His piercing gaze slid over her body from head to toe, then settled upon her face. "I want to see you."

She deliberately misunderstood and guided her chin so he could see her eyes. "You are right now."

"You understand my meaning perfectly, Alyssa."

"You want to date me?" she asked quietly. *Date*. The word sounded safe, simple, calm. Something completely unlike the sparks going off in her stomach or the warning bells in her head.

"In the beginning. Yes."

Her eyes widened, curiosity shimmering in their depths. "And the end?"

"We'll decide that once we get to the middle." His fingers left her chin, sliding down to trail over the soft skin of her neck with the gentlest of touches, and he leaned closer to her and pressed a soft, hot kiss against the hollow of her exposed collar. "Just a friendly warning: I don't anticipate there being an end."

"You don't mince words, do you, Your Honor?" Alyssa was surprised that she could speak, much less ask a coherent question. The place on her neck that had been a recipient of his kiss seemed to pulse with heat.

"I try not to."

"And what about the rules?" she inquired unsteadily in an effort to cool the flames before she ran the risk of getting burned.

"I follow many rules. Which rule is it that you wish to discuss?" The muted laughter in his eyes and the hint of a grin on his lips let her know that he wasn't serious.

She drew a shallow breath. "The one about not mixing business with pleasure."

He bent down and gave in to the impulse that had been hammering ever since she'd opened the door to her apartment earlier that evening. Nathan inhaled the heady scent of her skin as his lips grazed the corner of her mouth. "I haven't broken any rules . . . yet."

She struggled to keep hold of her wits as the rational part of her mind ceased to function. "You're a judge. Aren't you supposed to always follow the rules?" she disputed.

"Yes, I suppose I am." As his fingers brushed over her breast, she let out a small gasp that ended with a moan.

"Even now, Nathan?" She struggled to sound out the words.

"Before was business." He drew back slightly to stare into her eyes. Heat pooled in his lower body when her tongue darted out to run over her lips. "Now is just pleasure."

That was all the warning she got, before his mouth covered hers. Her lips parted of their own accord to allow him entrance. Alyssa's lids drifted downward as her arms wound around his waist. Caught up in the silent dance of their tongues darting in and tasting each other, she felt her nipples hardening against the solid warmth of his chest, as a sense of wonder wrapped around her and the sweet tingling of passion stirred in the apex between her thighs.

As in dance, most of her life she'd striven for balance. She reserved most of her passion for music, the melding of movement and rhythm, and her logical mind for work. Yet in all ways she thought first and acted later. But now as his fingers caressed the skin above the crevice of her breasts, she wanted to immerse herself in the heat that flowed from Nathan's touch. Alyssa moaned low in her throat at the feel of his mouth upon hers, one hand pressing upon the sensitive curve of her back while the other brushed over the exposed skin of her neck.

Nathan lifted his head slightly as a ragged groan escaped him as he huskily whispered in her ear, "Damn, woman, do you know what you do to me?"

Alyssa opened her eyes and took a deep breath, yet did not make a move to leave the circle of his arms. Swallowing a nervous giggle, she met his glance and deliberately looked down toward the slight bulge in his pants. "I have a good idea."

Nathan lowered his head into the top of her brow and inhaled the floral scent as laughter rumbled in his chest.

"Minx." He gently tugged a strand of her hair. "Spend the day with me Saturday."

"Not one to waste time either, are you?" Alyssa pulled back slightly and tilted her head to look at him.

"I'll pick you up at noon. We'll have lunch on the pier and a cruise for dinner."

Alyssa waited until they had come to a stop in front of her apartment door. She leaned against the wall and crossed her arms over her chest. "Did I mention, Judge Hughes, that I don't take kindly to orders? Not to mention, I already informed you that I have a *date* for Saturday."

Swift, hot anger knotted in Nathan's stomach, causing his grip on her shoulder to automatically tighten until Alyssa's wince of pain caught his attention. Abruptly he let her go. "I take it Harrison is back in town?" he questioned, his dark eyes showing the barest flicker of anger.

"It's not with Harrison." Alyssa bit the inside of her cheek to keep from smiling.

"I was under the impression that you didn't play games, Alyssa."

"I don't with people my own age," she replied cryptically, thoroughly enjoying watching him lose his trademark unruffled demeanor. Nathan's seemingly endless supply of confidence was goading her to tease him. "If you can swim, you may join us if you like," she said innocently. "I'm sure his mother won't mind."

"His mother?"

"Yes, I believe you know her."

Nathan's brow wrinkled in confusion. "What are you talking about?"

Deciding to put him out of his misery, Alyssa walked over to the coffee table and picked up a handwritten note.

"Sophie's son, Curtis, is having a parent-child swimming lesson at the pool this Saturday. Since she won't go near water unless it's in a bathtub or a sink, I volunteered to go in her place."

"I don't take well to being teased, Alyssa."

"So I've noticed. If you're serious about spending time with me, Nathan, you'll just have to get used to it. So you want to come?" she invited with a soft smile in her eyes.

"Are you sure he won't be upset?"

"Why would Curtis mind?" Alyssa imagined her friend's face as she pulled up in front of her home not only driving her new Jeep but with the man she'd nicknamed Old Reliable in the passenger side. The thought was amusing, but it wouldn't happen, as much as she was tempted to change it from impossible to actual. She had an appointment later that afternoon with her former dance instructor. Not only would it be nice to see Dame Limón after all the years, but she could also gather more information about the night of Lily's death.

"Males no matter what the age don't like to share." His gaze involuntarily dropped to the outline of her breasts underneath her blouse.

Not bothering to hide a gasp of incredulity as her cheeks flamed, Alyssa opened the door and then looked back to Nathan as he stood grinning down at her. "Good night."

"No good night kiss?"

Alyssa balled her hands on her hips and refused the invitation to take a swipe at his face. Instead she grasped the door handle and smiled sweetly. "Men don't share, remember? And don't forget your swimming trunks on Saturday."

Nathan shook his head in bemusement as Alyssa closed the solid oak door. He reached into his pants pocket and gathered his car keys. Only when he heard the click of the lock sliding into place did he walk down the hallway and press the elevator button. By the time the doors to the elevator had opened,

Nathan had gone back and forth as to whether he should knock on her door again. Only the sight of the nameplate of her apartment stopped him. She was home and home for good. He would make time.

Nathan tossed his car keys up and down. It had been too long since he'd wanted a woman in his life, too long since he'd spent any time outside of judicial chambers or in his study. In the short time since Alyssa Knight had tapped him on the shoulder at the coffee shop, he'd come to the conclusion that she was the one: the woman who would be his wife, his partner, the mother of his children. He would do everything within his power to make that come true.

"Sure you don't need backup?" Nathan inclined his head toward the legion of children standing in the shallow end of the swimming pool. Curtis's head was barely visible amongst the group. Nathan had spent some time chatting with him after Sophie had dropped him off. The boy was smart, outgoing, and crazy for his mother's good friend. Nathan's interest sharpened as he looked at Alyssa. The woman had a knack for collecting admirers.

"I think I can handle it. Plus you're the honorary lifeguard, remember?"

He took a step forward and toyed with the goggles hanging around her neck. "I'm still not sure about what it is I'm supposed to do."

"If a child looks like he's having trouble, you dive in and help."

"It might be a little difficult."

Her brow creased. "I thought you told me you could swim."

"I'm an excellent swimmer, Alyssa. It's just that I might be distracted." He moved to take a few strands of her hair in his fingers. His warm brown eyes locked with hers.

She raised both brows at that, turned, and lowered a mesh bag she was carrying to a nearby lounger. Then she calmly untied her robe and draped it over the bag. His body tightened as her slender body was revealed, clad only in a sleek blue racing suit. She lifted her hands and tied her hair back, slipping off her sandals as she did so. He swallowed hard at the way her breasts thrusted out against the thin swimsuit.

Then she walked to the edge of the pool and shot him a knowing look over her shoulder before diving into the melee of shrieking children occupying the water.

"Your wife is a very good swimmer," one of the fathers commented. Nathan's lips curved into a proud grin as he watched her across the pool with the kids following her like baby ducks.

"Thank you," he replied, not bothering to correct the man's erroneous assumption. Should things transpire as he planned, Alyssa would rightfully bear his name and his children.

Standing next to the white lounge chair, he placed his towel in the armrest and watched her teach with the other instructors.

The hotel's heated indoor Olympic-sized swimming pool had been carefully divided so that the kids couldn't wander into the deep section. Even given the extra precautions, the chance of a child getting hurt was lowered by the presence of parents both in and out of the water.

He raised his eyes to look out the glass walls and caught a glimpse of Chicago's landmark building, the Sears Tower.

The splash of water on his feet drew his attention.

"Are you coming in?" Alyssa called.

"That depends. Are you planning on ever coming out?"

"Yes, unless you'd do me the favor of passing me a pair of medium arm floaters over there."

Bending down close to the pool's edge, Nathan smiled and widened his eyes innocently. "I wouldn't be able to tell which is which."

He watched as she moved over to the ladder and quickly rose from the water. His admiring gaze lingered on Alyssa's shapely legs. He recognized the swimsuit from a famous women's fashion catalog his assistant had left lying on her desk one afternoon at lunch. However, the waiflike image of the model had not stirred any interest in him whatsoever. The flush to Alyssa's face, her hair pulled back into a ponytail, with only a few damp strands clinging to her cheek made the picture she presented all the more delightful.

The sight of water droplets on her brown skin sent blood rushing to the lower part of his anatomy and made him grateful for his foresight in having not taken off his sweatpants.

"Curtis is having a great time. Too bad Sophie couldn't be here. Maybe one day she'll be able to get near water again."

Nathan picked up a large white towel from the lounge chair. "Because of her husband's accident?"

"Sophie won't go anywhere near water."

"Yet she let Curtis join in today."

"She may not be able to conquer her fear of water yet, but she won't jeopardize her son's safety." It hadn't been easy for her friend to come to that decision. She'd been in the room when Sophie dropped by the center to deliver Curtis's permission slip.

"It's been a while since I've been swimming." Nathan unfolded the towel and wrapped it around Alyssa. He took his time molding the towel into her skin.

"Sure you can manage a lap by yourself, Your Honor?" The humor underneath her smooth alto voice was unmistakable.

"Is that a challenge I hear?"

"I do believe it is."

"Too bad I can't clear you of your misconceptions."

"Why is that?"

"The pool is a bit too crowded for that at the moment."

"Uh-huh, I remember you don't like to share. Most of the kids will be leaving at 4:00 P.M. and I've been told that time has been reserved until 5:00 P.M."

"Is that so?" He grinned down at her. The morning spent watching the children play had rubbed off on him. "Want to have our own little race later?"

"Sounds good. How about we add a friendly wager to that?"

Alyssa raised her chin and looked into his face. She liked it when he had a twinkle in his eyes. "What are you willing to lose?"

Nathan let out a laugh at her response. "I do admire a woman with confidence."

Seeing the rising cloudiness of annoyance in her eyes, he tugged a strand of her hair. "I seem to remember that you didn't like the water when we were in junior high school."

"People change."

"I've seen."

"The stakes?" Alyssa prompted.

Nathan blinked, pulling his eyes from the swell of her breasts. "A bet?"

"Loser pays for dinner."

He grinned confidently into her sparkling eyes. "I've been curious to sample some of the bread and butter pudding little Curtis said you make so well. Loser cooks dinner."

"You're on," she agreed, laying her towel on the chair. Alyssa turned to head toward the bathroom, took two steps, and turned around in time to see Nathan's lingering gaze at her backside. "And, Nathan . . ."

"Yes?"

"I like my Caesar salad extra crisp, my steak medium well, cheese on the baked potato, and my dessert chocolate."

That said, she turned and, knowing that he was watching, put an extra swing in her walk.

Two hours later at lunch while the kids gathered in an adjacent room watching a Disney movie, Alyssa sat at a table sipping a mixture of fresh-squeezed orange juice with a dash of cranberry juice and wearing a beach wrap she'd purchased dirt cheap on a layover in Bangkok.

She looked down at the plate on her table and swore she'd gone to heaven. The large cheeseburger topped with lettuce and tomato was only part of the gourmet love at first sight.

It was the onion rings that sent her back to the days when Pop would hustle the family into the car for a weekend treat at Hackney's. The hamburger restaurant was a Chicago institution; she and her mother would split a half-pound burger on rye bread while she'd shared a plate of onion rings with Alan.

She ate a ketchup-dipped onion ring and bit back a groan. It was almost caramelized and was greasy enough to satisfy her junk food yen.

"That good, huh?"

Alyssa looked up, noticing Nathan's eyes were twinkling with humor as he looked at her plate.

"Swimming gives me an appetite."

"Is that all?"

Alyssa popped another onion ring in her mouth and shook her head while chewing. Covering her mouth with a napkin, she mumbled, "No, it's been a long time."

Nathan studied her with shrewd eyes. "You're not on some fad diet, are you?"

"Would I be about to consume half of a charcoal-grilled cow if I were on a diet?"

"Sabrina was on a high-protein diet two months back, I believe. She raved that she could eat hamburgers."

Alyssa ignored him and took a bite of her cheeseburger, savoring the taste of well-done beef. "I hadn't heard of that diet. I may have to check it out." She put her burger back down on the plate. "Can you eat burritos as well?"

"Are you forgetting that I'm a judge, Alyssa? Answering a question with another question is an often-used tactic to avoid an answer."

Alyssa took a sip of her seltzer water. "No, Nathan, I am not on a diet. I eat what I want when I want. It's just that many of the people I associated with in London were vegetarians, and mad cow disease gave my meat-eating friends the will to swear off beef." Not to mention that Harrison hadn't been the pub-going type and the only place to get a decent burger in London was the local tavern.

"You're really good with kids. They like you."

Alyssa shook her head. "It's that favorite aunt vibe I give out. They're my clients. I make it a point to know their wants and speak their language. You don't seem to be doing so bad yourself."

He smiled. "I'm studying for my future children."

"Plural? As in more than just one?"

"I wouldn't like for my son to ever have to say he was an only child. And you?" His gaze sharpened.

She shifted slightly in her seat. "I'd like to have children one day, once I find the right partner, but in the meantime I have my little crew. Curtis called me Auntie in the pool."

"Now that Alan's getting married you could soon have that title officially."

"Yes, and you could soon have the title Uncle Nathan." Alyssa waved a ketchup-tipped onion ring. "Hmm, has a nice ring to it, don't you think? I wonder who will be first."

"Knowing Lauren, I don't think it will be too soon in the immediate future."

"Knowing Alan, having met Cassandra, and having listened to my mother coo over baby clothes in the mail order catalogs, I don't think it'll be too soon after the wedding that there will be a new diaper-wearing member of the Knight clan."

"You'll be in the wedding?"

"Absolutely, being the sister of the groom. I have to call Cassandra about the dates for the fitting and bachelorette party. I'll stay with Alan for a little while as well."

"How long has it been since you've seen him?"

"We talk at least once a week; usually he calls to check on me. But I have to admit that it will nice to spend more than a few hours in an airport lounge with Alan."

Nathan's dark eyes lowered to the table and then rose. "If I had only one regret, it would be that I haven't spent enough time with my sister. I would know her more as the woman she has become than as Nicholas Randolph's wife."

Alyssa leaned forward and placed her hand on his. "You still have time. The wedding isn't until autumn."

"Very true. I plan on visiting Lauren soon, but first I have to make it through our camping trip."

Alyssa playfully swatted his hand. "Have you no faith?"

"I have all the faith in the world in you."

Her eyes narrowed at the twitch in his lips.

"But I'd also like fish and chips to complement that bread and butter pudding."

At five o'clock, Alyssa left the swimming pool area and went into the dressing room with a smile on her face and a confident swagger in her walk. She had gotten the last laugh and the last lap on Nathan. Swimming was the best exercise for dancing and she'd done it as much as possible. One of the unexpected perks of her former job was that traveling allowed her access to luxury hotels with only the best facilities. She'd had to pull out all the stops, but she'd beat him and couldn't remember when she'd enjoyed herself more. In fact, she hadn't wanted the afternoon to end. Only the knowledge that they would be spending the entire weekend together alleviated the immediate desire to see him the next day.

After showering and putting on a change of clothes, she pulled out of the hotel and turned the car north toward the Chicago's northern suburb of Highland Park.

Alyssa turned up the stereo and tapped her finger to the rhythmic sound of the radio. Her new toy purred and she enjoyed the wind whipping around the tendrils of her hair. It had taken her less than fifteen minutes to fall in love with the canary-yellow Jeep Wrangler, but after taking the top off that morning, she loved the vehicle even more. The sun's soft rays on her skin, the breeze, the music, and knowing that she wouldn't be spending her weekend on a plane or in a hotel room were exactly what she needed to end any remaining doubts about leaving her life in London.

She'd spent the past three days trading answering machine messages with Anna Limón. The dance teacher had found time to squeeze Alyssa in for an hour-long chat before she rushed off to a recital. The woman had spent the past forty years being a dancer, a teacher, and codirector of a dance troupe. From the sound of her messages, she had not altered her fast pace in retirement.

Alyssa slowed the Jeep as she turned into the parking lot of the five-story Tudor building, which matched the address written in her notes.

When Anna Limón opened the door, a smile formed on Alyssa's mouth as her eyes widened in surprise. The woman had not aged a day; in fact, with a pixie haircut accentuating her delicate features, she seemed to have grown more stunning.

"I'm pleasantly surprised to see you. Many years have passed, have they not?"

"I apologize for not keeping in touch, Dame Limón."

"Quite all right. When I joined my first dance troupe after leaving Juilliard we traveled the world and I formed many friendships but lost them all because I was never in one place long enough to correspond. Of course, this was before the age of e-mail and mobile phones. Are you still dancing, dear?"

"Not as much as I'd like and much less than I should."

"Why the heavens are you not? You can join my group." She looked her up and down with a critical eye. "We can get you back in form."

"I haven't been able to dance with a group since Lily died."

"It's been that long?" The other woman's dark eyes widened.

"I managed to take private lessons in London."

"You have such a talent, dear. It's not for dancing alone but for sharing with people."

"It feels wrong to dance without her, Dame Limón."

"It is wrong for you to stop feeling the joy of dancing with others, Alyssa. Lily would not have wanted that for you." Dame Limón took her hand and led her into another room. "Please have a seat. I'll go and make us some coffee."

"Thank you." Alyssa looked around the modestly decorated living room, admiring the watercolor paintings and photographs of notable dancers.

"I appreciate you taking the time to talk with me," she said, taking a seat in one of the living room chairs.

"Of course, what did you want to talk about, dear? Your messages were rather vague."

"That night, the performance, the accident. Could you tell me everything you remember about the night Lily died?"

"Ah." She sighed and sat back, making the sign of the cross. "My poor *bebé*."

"The performance . . ." Alyssa prompted.

"The performance went off without a hitch. I was very surprised, very surprised."

"Why?"

"Andrés was very tense that night and not himself. At one point, I thought he would come to blows with another dancer during the warm-up."

"He was upset about another dancer?" Alyssa flipped to a clean page in her notebook.

"Not really, he apologized immediately after the incident and explained that he was just nervous. But afterward . . ." She shook her head and exhaled loudly. "I feel so sorry for Andrés. To have fought with one's sister before her death. I wouldn't wish that burden on my worst enemy, much less my star pupil."

Alyssa's eyes narrowed. "They fought?"

"Yes, or something like that. She was very distraught when she left the dressing room and you took off after her." The dance instructor frowned. "Don't you remember? You were there."

Unconsciously, her fingers tightened on her pen. The psychiatrist she'd seen after the accident had diagnosed that deep trauma caused her to block out the memory of Lily's death. There had been the option of hypnosis, but the procedure had been vetoed because of the risk that added stress might upset her fragile state and send her into depression. "No, I lost my memories of the entire event. The doctors called it disassociative amnesia."

"I understand." The woman gave a sympathetic nod. "The sadness, you see. Grief does things to us all."

"What about after the performance, can you tell me more about Lily's behavior?"

"She seemed fine until after the party. You'd both changed clothes. I was working with the stage director to arrange shipment of the props back to the school, when you both popped into the office to say good night. You mentioned needing to go back to the dressing room to get your bag and Lily went with you.

"It was about thirty minutes later when I was doing a final check to make sure we'd taken care to clean up the mess after the party that I saw Lily running down the hallways toward the back exit."

"Did she say anything to you?"

"No, she was crying, you were following her. Andrés was standing in the doorway yelling that the conversation wasn't over."

"Do you have any idea what they could have been arguing about?"

"I'm sorry but no, I don't."

"Was there anyone else nearby who might have overheard the conversation? Another dancer, perhaps?"

"No, everyone had already had gone. Wait."

Alyssa watched as the dance instructor's brow wrinkled, her lips pursed.

"There was a tall blond gentleman standing behind Andrés."

"A dancer?"

"He wasn't a member of the stage crew or a dancer. I remember because he didn't fit."

"Fit how?"

"He was rather European in his dress. Plus there was the fact that he was older. Maybe late twenties or early thirties."

"Could Lily have argued with him?"

"There's always that possibility."

"What happened next?"

"Andrés and the stranger followed you and Lily. I was about to intervene when I was called back out to the stage to sign papers. Ten minutes later one of the stage crew ran into the building and yelled for someone to call an ambulance.

"When I made it outside, I found you unconscious near the sidewalk and Andrés cradling Lily in his arms."

Dame Limón placed her teacup on the table and breathed heavily. "It was a long time before I could sleep at night without hearing his screams."

"Did Andrés ever talk to you about what happened?"

"No." She shook her head. "He came to see me a month after the accident to say good-bye. Although he had been accepted into the Alvin Ailey Dance Troupe, he decided to stay close to his family and join the Hubbard Street Dance Company while studying modern dance. I was very sad to see him go."

They chatted for a few moments more, each inquiring about the other's family and former students. It was after eight o'clock in the evening before Alyssa got on the road back to her apartment. Luckily she was driving against the flow of traffic leaving downtown Chicago, so she spent very little time at a standstill. With her turn signal on in preparation of exiting the freeway, the repetitive blinking reflected her mental questioning. What had Lily and Andrés fought about?

Chapter 11

Nathan Hughes definitely had a thing for Asian interior design. Alyssa raised her eyes from the front room where sliding doors with silver handles made an elegant contrast to the polished wood floor, then looked down the hallway toward a tall antique chest of drawers upon which rested a glass vase with a single white orchid. It had been fewer than three days since they'd walked along the lakefront holding hands and a little under forty-eight hours since they'd last dined together.

However, the mere whisper of his name, the thought of his voice, or an innocent reminder of his generous gift to the youth center was a reminder of his growing presence in her life.

The living room's abundant wood tones along with cream-colored walls and uncluttered Asian aesthetics lent the space a warm and welcoming feel. Yet in all Alyssa's wandering, it was the small things that caught her eye. Always the small things that made a house a home. The hint of a glass water circle on the otherwise perfect round coffee table, a rumpled sage-colored pillow with an indentation fitting the dimensions of Nathan's head. She noted the jacket tossed over a chair and the photographs on the fireplace mantel.

"My word," she whispered as she turned toward the right, and instead of a wall or doorway, her eyes encountered a small ocean. The large aquarium with a myriad of fish, coral, and plant life took up the entire wall. It was a thing of wonder and the large aquarium's inside illumination brightened the walls with waves, which made Nathan's home less a showroom and more of a private retreat.

When Nathan returned downstairs with a duffel bag in his hand, he stopped in the doorway, taking in the tranquility of the scene, and took a moment to watch her trail her fingers over the glass as she stood in front of his pride and joy. The recessed two-hundred-gallon in-wall aquarium could be seen from both the kitchen and the living room. He had planned, designed, and filled the delicately balanced ecosystem with the vibrantly colored tropical fish, flora, and fauna. With his feet making no noise he moved to stand beside Alyssa's side.

"You have a nice home, Nathan."

"Thank you."

"Did you do all of this yourself?"

"I would love to take all the credit. But most of the rooms were decorated by Lauren and my mother."

"This aquarium as well?"

"That I did on my own."

"Won't they get hungry while you're gone?" Her voice was low and husky.

He looked down into her eyes and checked the urge to trace the gentle curve of her face from her small earlobes to her pert chin. Their closeness and the silence only interrupted by the gurgling water running into the aquarium from the filter made the low-lit room more intimate.

"The aquarium serves as a model saltwater environment complete with potentially carnivorous inhabitants. If they're not fed on schedule, some of the more aggressive angelfish have a nasty tendency to take bites out of their smaller neighbors. I installed an automatic feeder after learning the importance of getting them fed on schedule."

She gave him an arch look. "That sounds like the voice of experience."

"Late hours at the courthouse had some unfortunate consequences."

"Fishicide?" she joked.

"Cannibalism." He grinned. "Let me turn out the lights and grab my keys so we can get on the road."

"How about we take my car?"

"Alyssa." The patronizing tone in his voice was unmistakable.

"Honestly, Nathan. Your luxury car, no matter how wonderfully German-built, isn't likely to appreciate the rocks, mud, and dirt. Besides, I'm itching to take a drive out of the city."

"Why don't I take a look at your car and then we'll talk?"

"After you."

She enjoyed watching him stride down the hallway. The sight of his backside in the jeans was lovely indeed. She shook her head as a smile curved her lips; he had a lot to thank his mother for.

"Two days." Alyssa stopped the grocery cart that Nathan had pushed into her hands. She'd planned to make a quick stop and pick up some basic supplies, but what she hadn't planned on was Nathan. The man was going to drive her crazy.

Nathan had taken one look at the Jeep Wrangler, raised an eyebrow, and silently conceded that in this instance hers was the better vehicle.

In the past half hour, they'd gone up and down most of Dominick's aisles. Chicago's first two-story grocery store boasted a marvelous selection of gourmet foods, fresh produce, and choice meats, but she was only interested in the frozen food and cereal sections. A full ice chest in the back-seat would keep everything nice and cold.

Bernard had assured her that the cabin had a microwave and she planned on putting it to good use. How could you have a relaxing weekend if you had to spend most of the time slaving over a hot stove?

"Did you say something?"

"No," she bit out, coming to an abrupt stop in front of a massive array of condiments.

"I could have sworn I heard you speak."

"Have you been working too much lately, Nathan? Maybe you're starting to hear voices in your head."

Alyssa tried deep breathing in the canned goods section, grabbed a bag of chips and salsa in the snacks section, counted in French in the dairy section and Italian in the pasta aisle. Finally as she pushed the cart around another corner and he tossed in an oversized bag of chocolate-covered raisins, her patience ran out. "Nathan, we're going for two days, not forty days and forty nights. Why are you buying all of this food?"

Even if somehow her Jeep got stuck in the mud, the trees fell over the road, a flood washed away all means of travel, they'd still be able to survive for at least three weeks.

Nathan placed a package of chicken in the cart. "Are you hungry, Alyssa?"

"No, I ate earlier this evening."

"What did you eat?"

Her brow wrinkled. "Salad and a grilled cheese sandwich."

"Do you plan to enjoy that same menu this weekend?"

"Maybe I did think that I'd spice things up with frozen lasagna. I love Stouffers."

"You do know how to cook, don't you?" As he moved away, Alyssa was forced to push the cart to follow him.

"Better than that." She grinned brightly. "My mother taught me how to read a cookbook."

"Oh." Those nut-colored brown eyes of his held a suspicious twinkle.

"Yes, but I hadn't planned on cooking."

"That works out because I planned on cooking for us."

"You know how to cook?"

"Yes, I have a fairly large repertoire."

"Let me guess. Grilled chicken, grilled steak, ribs, pizza, and popcorn?" Alyssa knew few men that knew their way around in the kitchen. Most, including her father and older brother, needed explicit instructions and adult supervision in the kitchen.

"Teriyaki-grilled salmon steak, breaded mussel shells, mesclun salad, roasted red potatoes, asparagus spears, and for dessert . . ." His voice trailed off. "Marble cheesecake."

Her stomach, although full, woke up to the tantalizing image his words conjured in her mind. "You're going to cook all that?"

"Sadly, no." Nathan lowered his gaze after glimpsing the look of disappointment on Alyssa's face.

"Tease." She pushed the grocery cart forward and bumped him on the rear end.

"One more insult and you may not be getting that victory dinner until the next millennia," he warned after picking up two sirloin steaks. "I don't know what kind of setup Bernard has, so the menu will be a little more basic."

"I know that the appliances and gas grill were delivered on Monday, and the decorator purchased cooking utensils, pots and pans; after that your guess is as good as mine."

"That should be more than adequate. Now let's get going. Just two more aisles and I'll have all I need."

Performing a bow that the queen herself would have approved of, Alyssa affected the pulling up of her overfull skirts, and bent her knee until it nearly touched the floor.

"Lead on, Your Majesty." She grinned with a highbrow British accent. Her eyes, twinkling, met Nathan's and as she rose to stand on one side of the cart, he curled his arm around her waist. Together they walked down the aisle looking every bit the married couple.

Once they'd securely stowed the groceries in the back of the Jeep it took them less than thirty minutes to get out of the city and on their way. As the vehicle sped southbound upon a straight stretch of I-90, she took a quick peek over at the sleeping man in the passenger side. The shadows under his eyes spoke volumes, but so did the fact that he'd been knocked out by the time she turned onto the Chicago Loop.

Lowering one hand from the steering wheel, Alyssa inched up the volume on the car stereo. The husky voice of her favorite

French chanteuse combined with the rhythmic movements of the automobile erased the tension she didn't even know she'd had.

At 9:00 P.M. the highway was clear of traffic, and according to the directions it would be less than two hours before she got to Bernard's weekend retreat in Union County, Illinois. The clear two-lane highway was a welcome change from London's usually crowded motorways.

The farther away from the city she traveled, the darker it became and the brighter the stars seemed to shine. *It's been too long,* she mused, settling into her seat for the drive. Stretching out her hand, she pushed a button and the smooth sounds of the orchestra filled the Jeep.

She'd agreed to Nathan's request to go camping impulsively. As bad as she wanted to close the loop on getting the funding so that she could concentrate on pulling the event together, the real reason behind why she should have postponed this trip lay nestled inside her briefcase on the backseat. Uncle Edward had left a copy of the accident and investigation reports with the concierge desk in her building. Somehow she'd find a moment alone to read it. After having left three messages on Andrés's voice mail with no response, she needed to pursue other avenues of information.

The digital clock on the stereo read 11:15 by the time Alyssa turned onto the unmarked road that led to Bernard's newly built country retreat. Slowing the Jeep, she turned onto a dirt and gravel road, and then following the instructions that the car salesman had given her, shifted the Jeep into four-wheel drive. The complete darkness except for the bright beams of her headlights and fog lamps had her driving slowly up an incline and around a few curves.

As she came to a stop in front of the abode, Alyssa pursed her lips and let out a silent whistle. Bernard never failed to surprise her. His "cabin in the country" turned out to be a house. A beautiful two-story house surrounded by trees and miles away from the main road.

Alyssa had been aware of Nathan from the moment his breathing evened in sleep to the point that he stretched before opening his eyes. Looking into the rearview mirror, Alyssa had a very strong suspicion that if it rained, a minibus could have a fairly difficult time negotiating the dirt road and the short hills. Alyssa turned off the engine and took off her seat belt.

"This isn't exactly what I expected." Nathan stepped down from the Jeep.

"What exactly did you expect?" She pulled the keys out of the ignition. Her thoughts mirrored his own; Bernard had been vague in terms of describing the place. It had never crossed her mind that he would build a full-fledged year-round living abode.

"Small wooden cabin with outside plumbing. Something along the lines of *Little House on the Prairie.*"

Stepping out of the Jeep and onto the freshly planted grass, Alyssa threw her head back and laughed at the thought of the ex-commodities trader and current youth center president using an outhouse. Her glance caught on the sight of a mid-sized satellite dish anchored to the side of the roof and she laughed harder, yet the sound was muted in the quiet of the surrounding wooded area. Only Nathan's chuckle and the repetitive sound of crickets met her ears.

"Now that I think about it, I knew that Bernard wouldn't last a day without access to the financial news, hot water, telephone, and computer."

"Point taken." Nathan removed his hand from the Jeep.

"If you're disappointed," she commented while getting her purse and briefcase from the backseat, "I'm sure we can grab some blankets and camp out."

"No, thank you. How about you get the door and I'll grab the bags?"

Alyssa took the keys out of her pocket and walked up to the house. With its brown stucco, the custom-built home blended in with the outdoor environment. After unlocking the heavy wooden front door, she pushed it open only to draw back at the sound of a shrill beeping noise. She reached out blindly and felt against the wall until her hand encountered a light switch.

"That sound cannot be a good thing," Nathan commented after joining her with their bags

"It's okay, I've got the alarm code." Alyssa punched in Bernard's phone number and let out a sigh of relief when the red light turned to green.

"That's pretty sophisticated for such a secluded location." His eyes scanned the room.

Nathan's raised eyebrow spoke louder than words. Alyssa shrugged. *Different people, different lives.* The Brandells' summer house in Tuscany could comfortably house an entire Olympic team. "There are a lot of luxury vacation homes in the area," she commented offhandedly. "Bernard also mentioned that the local security company will be coming out to check on the house."

She put the keys on a side table. "Shall we grab the groceries?"

"I'll get the groceries, you find the kitchen."

Alyssa's eyes narrowed at the commanding tone in his voice.

"Find the kitchen," she repeated, mimicking his tone while placing a hand on her hip. "You should go find a cave. Better yet, go find a hole to crawl into."

"Only if you come with me."

Rolling her eyes toward the ceiling, Alyssa picked up her weekend bag, then raising her chin, looked at Nathan. "Since we need to get up early and check out the hiking trails, I will be finding a bedroom. Good night."

"See you in the morning. And, Alyssa?"

She took a few steps. "Yes?" One hand was poised on the banister of the steps leading to the second floor.

"Sweet dreams."

She looked at the suggestive grin on his handsome face, and a familiar warmth started in her insides. Pushing it down, she turned and walked slowly up the stairs as the back of her neck tingled like a lover's caress. He did that, damn him. She knew he was staring at her. Her fingers tightened on her bag. It would be an interesting weekend.

Later as Nathan finished putting groceries in the spotless refrigerator, he closed the door and his thoughts returned to the woman upstairs. The women he had dated in the past, with the exception of Gillian, had expected him to do everything, be everything. It was not one-sided, for he'd been raised to care for women. Yet with Alyssa there were no expectations, no questions, no need for his presence, and it relieved as well as annoyed him. He would have her to himself for less than forty-eight hours. Nathan turned off the overhead lights and headed upstairs. He'd make each and every minute count.

The next morning Alyssa was torn from sleep by a persistent knocking on her door. Fighting the urge to bury her head under the pillow and go back to the wonderful dreams of chocolate sundaes, and Nathan Hughes wearing nothing but a chef's hat, she opened her eyes, then shut them tight against the intense sunlight pouring through the windows. Glancing at the alarm on the bedside table, she groaned. She hadn't overslept in a long time. "Come in."

"Rise and shine."

Rolling over, she looked straight at the object of her unconscious lust and struggled to keep from blushing. Nathan stood fully clothed in the doorway. If she were anyone other than Marva Knight's daughter, Alyssa would have cursed. Usually, she did not need an alarm, because she'd had the luck of having been born with an internal clock. But every clock eventually needed to have its batteries changed and she needed to oversleep.

Alyssa gripped her pillow tighter. It should have been a sin for the man to look good that early in the morning, and it had to be early. Dressed in jeans and a charcoal-gray turtleneck, he could easily have been taking up residence in a courtside basketball seat rather than trampling through the forest.

"Come on, angel." He gifted her with a full grin. "Breakfast is almost ready, the birds are singing, and daylight is wasting."

Pushing her tousled hair back from her face, she lifted the light coverlet and stretched as a yawn escaped her. "Lord, you must be one of those morning people."

"I take it you are not too fond of my kind?"

She nodded her head. She loved the quiet of the early morning; it was when she did her best work. But to be so cheerful to get out of a warm and comfortable bed at the crack of dawn? "It's unnatural," she said, swinging her leg off the bed and standing up. Her lips involuntarily twitched upward in response to the grin on Nathan's face.

"The only thing unnatural about this morning is not waking you with a kiss."

"Why didn't you?" she boldly asked.

He chuckled and moved from his perch in the doorway. "Chances are that no matter how appealing you look in the morning, you are a carrier of morning breath and I have to check on breakfast."

Taken aback, Alyssa didn't respond verbally, but physically. Nathan barely managed to duck the incoming pillow.

"They say the early bird catches the worm."

As she pictured Nathan trapped underneath the metal hinge of an oversized mousetrap, a silly smile curved her lips. "But it's the second mouse that gets the cheese." She aimed a meaningful look his way before heading out into the hallway toward the bathroom.

"Morning breath," she repeated. Not this woman. Alyssa looked in the mirror as she dragged dental floss between her teeth. Before sticking a toothpaste-filled brush in her mouth, she held up a cupped hand, exhaled sharply, and checked. There was nothing to be embarrassed or ashamed of.

After showering, combing her hair into a ponytail, and pulling on a pair of jeans and a shirt, Alyssa returned to her bedroom. She was still annoyed by their previous conversation. It only took her a minute to make the bed and fluff the pillows.

Instead of taking a direct route and following her nose to the kitchen, she decided to explore the first floor. The house was built with stone and wood, yet on the inside its open-beamed ceiling was far more rustic than the newly constructed outside had led her to believe.

She caught the scent of freshly cut wood as her toes sank into the soft carpet. She eyed the overstuffed sofa and imagined herself just spending the day lounging there bathed in warm sunlight from the curtainless windows that dominated two of the walls with a good book and a tall cup of tea. A stone fireplace that served as the focal point in the living room looked somewhat out of place when her eyes landed on the digital readout of the temperature-control system.

In the fairly large living room a wide-screen television and audio system complete with an extensive video and audio selection took up the wall opposite the fireplace. It looked like Bernard had spared no expense in building the country retreat. One of the two doors led to a small study complete with a cordless telephone, fax machine, printer, and computer monitor. Soon after her tour, the smell of pancakes wafted through the air and started her stomach growling.

"I'm impressed," Alyssa said as she stepped into the kitchen area.

Nathan Hughes hadn't just made breakfast, he'd put together a feast, Alyssa observed while surveying the various plates and bowls on the table nicely situated by the window in a breakfast nook.

"Good, I hope that you're hungry as well." A smile crinkled Nathan's eyes at the sight of Alyssa barefoot in a pair of well-worn blue jeans. He gestured for her to take a seat and then pulled out one for himself. After filling her plate with a few choice selections and then his own, he took her hand and said grace.

"What's the story with the luxury vacation home?" Nathan picked up a glass carafe of freshly brewed Hawaiian-blend coffee and filled their cups.

"Last year, one of Bernard's relatives passed away without having children. The man left him the land in his will. Bernard drove down with the intention of putting it up for sale but took a look at the property and decided to build a cabin."

Alyssa paused as her gaze took in all the interior decorating. "Since his taste seems to lean to the extravagant and perfectionist side, it was just completed last week."

"And he has generously agreed to allow fifteen teenagers to stay?"

"Only for two nights, then we move to a campsite and pitch our tents." Alyssa cut into a blueberry buttermilk pancake. Steeped as it was with syrup and the perfect shade of brown, she thoroughly enjoyed the bite.

"What did you have to do to wring that promise?" He had only met Bernard Shaw three times, but like recognized like. No matter how much he desired to serve the community, a man didn't allow entrance into his castle without a price.

She used her napkin to wipe syrup off her lips and sighed. "Four seats in a first-row box behind home plate at Yankee Stadium." She watched him pause before taking a bite of fruit.

"My father used to love to cook Sunday breakfast when he was at home. Mom and Lauren always appeared like magic when he was finished. It was as if they had a sixth sense. They would sit down at the table in their church dresses."

"This." She pointed to the sausage, pancakes, fruit, coffee, and yogurt. "This is unbelievable. Pop and Alan can't cook to save their lives. Mama had to straighten out some family business and went out of town for a few days. We would have starved if it hadn't been for frosted corn flakes, school lunch, and Aunt Sara. She'd leave cooked food with detailed heating instructions for Pop every day."

Alyssa resisted the urge to pat her stomach after finishing her last pancake. The meal, the company, the mood hit the spot. As Nathan reached for her empty plate, she put her hand on his, halting the movement. "I'll do the dishes. In our family, we have a saying that the cook can't be the maid."

She caught his look of surprise, then he leaned back with a grin. "Be my guest."

Picking up the dishes, she carried them into the kitchen and placed them in the stainless steel sink. Taking a moment before her next trip to clear the table, she glanced around the room and got her first good look at Bernard's dream kitchen.

Induction-heating stove top, every appliance straight from a Williams-Sonoma catalogue, in-wall refrigerator, double oven—she shook her head in disbelief. The ultramodern kitched had to be just for show; Bernard couldn't cook to keep from starving. The man had over thirty restaurants in his mobile phone's speed dial.

It was ten minutes later that Alyssa had rinsed and stacked the last dish into the dishwasher.

"Ready to go?"

She whirled around in surprise; Nathan was standing a mere foot away for her. The man was quiet as a cat and could be just as sneaky when he wanted something.

"Not yet." She closed the door to the dishwasher, picked up a cloth, and dried her hands. "I just need to make some sandwiches for lunch and throw in some snacks for the trail."

"Already done." Nathan took her by the shoulder and gently led her out of the kitchen. "Get your shoes on and let's go."

"For a big-city guy, you're in a rush to get outside."

He abruptly stopped and turned her toward him. Fixing his hands around her waist, Nathan pulled her close, bent down, and kissed her hard on the lips. He'd wanted to grab and kiss her as he'd watched the early morning light filter through the blinds and cross her face. It was a long night lying in the same bed and holding her, but being unable to touch her as his body demanded. Remembering his frustration, Nathan cupped her buttocks and was rewarded when she moaned in his mouth. He let the kiss linger before pulling back. "Either we can go outside, get in that Jeep, and go for a hike, or finish this here and now. You choose."

Without saying a word, she turned around and left.

Chapter 12

After parking the Jeep in a small parking area at the base of the trail, Alyssa stepped down into the warm sunlight. Located in western Union County, the Bald Knob Wilderness covered over 5,800 acres, making it the largest designated wilderness area in Illinois. Their goal was to hike the six miles round-trip on the Godwin Trail.

Knowing that it would be much cooler on the tree-shaded trail, she pulled on a fleece jacket and a nylon windbreaker. She looked to the other side and was happy to see Nathan doing the same. Checking the skies, she noted a few gathering clouds and made a mental note to include rain gear on the teens' packing list. Perhaps she should schedule an extra meeting with the outdoor expert.

Three and a half hours later, they reached the end of the trail and found a grove of trees to sit under for lunch of sandwiches and chips. She was delighted more by what was than what wasn't, the silence broken by the buzz of a flying insect and the shrill call of a bird in the nest, versus the sounds of cars and trucks.

As they'd hiked, Alyssa had made it a point to steer the conversation into safe waters that included family, sports, and food, but excluded relationships. They stopped for lunch near the top of a hill and took a seat underneath the trees. Nathan said, "You take dancing class, go camping, are well traveled, and swim like a fish. What other secrets are you keeping?"

While hiking, Nathan had caught a glimpse of Alyssa he'd

forgotten existed. She'd begun to whistle a tune he remembered from childhood. It blended with the shrill calls of birds and crickets. With her lips puckered and arms swinging, she looked sweet, sexy, carefree, and to his eyes perfect.

"I knit badly when I'm nervous, I burn my fingers every time I bake, and I cry while watching old Humphrey Bogart movies."

She finished off the last of her sandwich and started on the chips. "So are you excited about giving your sister away at the wedding?"

"I'm happy for Lauren and I approve of her choice. Nicholas Randolph is a good man."

Alyssa licked the salt off her fingers from the chips before responding. "I always had the idea that Alan and Lauren would get married and there would be two Knights and Hughes couples in the family."

"Are you disappointed in your future sister-in-law?"

"No, not at all. I like Cassandra. It's just that the wedding held here in Chicago might have given Aunt Sara and Uncle Edward the kick they needed to think about reconciling."

"It can still happen." Nathan gave her an intent look.

"With who?"

"You and me, Alyssa."

Although the sixth sense, which had thus far kept her from getting burned, wasn't sounding the alarm, common sense told her to take the foot off the gas and apply pressure to the brakes. She shifted on the tree trunk. They'd brought a blanket but left it in the Jeep; the ground was still damp from last week's rain showers.

"Married people sleep together, Nathan."

"Amongst other things."

"What about my morning breath?" she joked, crumbling up the potato chip bag.

"As long as you use my toothpaste, I don't think we'll have a problem."

"I'll be your friend as I always have, but I can't allow for there to be more than that," she stated firmly. Alyssa was well aware that she was backing away from her earlier attitude of less than innocent flirtation.

For long moments, Nathan looked at her, his thumb moving slowly over the apple in his hand. He liked it here, just the two of them. The wind through the trees reminded him of the rustling of paper that accompanied a search through old state code tombs and federal files. Nathan noticed her gaze faltered before his as she buried her hands in the pockets of the jacket.

"I wonder if you're motivated by fear or comparison. Is it guilty until proven innocent? And if so, do I get to know the charges?"

"What?"

"You're intent on punishing me for another man's foolishness."

"No, that's not it," she denied.

"Then why the change?"

"It's just that I've just gotten home. I've got other things on my mind than getting into a relationship."

"Such as work."

"That would be one of them," she answered vaguely.

"And . . ."

"Look, Nathan, at the moment I have priorities to take care of."

"So does the U.S. Postal Service."

Alyssa let out an impatient sigh and shifted on the tree trunk.

His eyes gleamed with amusement. "You can stop dodging any time."

"What will it take to get you to stop pushing?"

My wedding band on your finger, your presence at my Senate confirmation hearing, my son suckling at your breast would have been the best response. Instead, Nathan leaned his head against the tree and replied, "When you spend more time in my home than at your condo. When your smile is the first thing I see in the morning and your lips the last I taste at night."

Alyssa held her tongue as her body warmed at the thought of waking up in his bed. No matter where her eyes wandered, they always came back to him. She was in full view of his splendid profile. When dressed in a suit and tie the man was handsome, but now as he relaxed, the right side of his face catching little sparkles of sunlight that managed to slip through the overhead canopy, he was so endearing he made her heart ache. For several moments, she wondered if she'd developed some kind of freak split personality.

Raising her gaze from the apple in his hand, Alyssa gnawed on the inside of her lip. Half of her wanted to crawl into his lap and indulge in an illicit fantasy and the other half . . . The half with an ounce of self-preservation calculated that she had a better chance of surviving a walk through Death Valley with nothing but a Coke and a smile than getting emotionally and physically involved with Nathan and coming out with her heart intact.

"I don't have room in my life for you," she claimed. Her usually quick-thinking mind had turned to mush. Must be the food and the air, Alyssa mused. It had nothing to do with the compelling urge to curl up in his arms.

"Move into my place. I have plenty and an empty bed." He tossed her half of the apple and she caught it easily. Growing up with a star baseball player in the house had its benefits. "You can even sleep on the right side of the bed."

"No, thank you." She bit into the apple. "I like sleeping on the left." In truth she usually slept on the right side but woke on the left.

"Is that so?" His eyebrow rose. "I could have sworn you slept on the right last night."

"You came into my bedroom!" Birds that had once been sleeping took to the air. Alyssa inhaled deeply, counted to ten, then released the air from her lungs.

"You cried out in your sleep last night," he stated gently.

The words blew away the storm of words that had threatened to pour out of her lips.

"Want to talk about it?"

"No." She brushed away a flying insect and then put the rest of her uneaten apple in a plastic bag.

"Do you have nightmares often?"

"Only when I sleep in a new bed, in a new place, with a man who has a habit of entering a room unannounced."

Nathan grinned as the shadows left her eyes to be replaced by anger. Fire. That's what he wanted, needed. Time wouldn't affect the emotion coursing through his body. Nathan was absolutely certain about few things in his life, yet this was one of them. He'd spend the rest of his days wanting only her, like his father, like all the past men in the Hughes family. They knew how to treat, were taught how to keep their women. The only broken lines in the family tree that sat protected in his mother's home were in death. Divorce was not an option.

"Why didn't you wake me?"

He shrugged and placed a small knife in its leather sheath. "No need, you settled down." He didn't mention that she'd quieted after he'd lain beside her. It had to have been the most exquisite and painful night of his life. She fit him perfectly.

Ignoring the hand he held out, Alyssa got up, dusted off the backside of her jeans, put on her backpack, and headed down the trail. Attraction was one thing, but arrogance another. She didn't want to talk to him.

She made it all the way back to the house before disaster struck. She'd kept her mouth shut when he'd brushed her breasts while reaching into the backseat of the Jeep. She'd even managed to ignore his comments and meaningful glances during the half-hour drive back. Yet it was within thirty feet of Bernard's weekend house that things . . . no, *she* went south.

Heading toward the front door, Alyssa slipped and fell. The ground didn't hurt her body but the damp sensation of dirt clinging to her face about killed her pride. Turning over, she bit back a curse word as she looked up into Nathan's face.

"Are you all right?"

"No," she mumbled.

"Where are you hurt?"

"My pride and my backside," she replied.

"Here."

She lifted her dirt-covered fingers and put them into his outstretched hand, to be abruptly pulled up. She recovered her balance only to have her face mere inches from his, pressed against his chest. She stared at his upwardly curved lips. Yet she could see the flare of hunger in his eyes and guess the direction of his thoughts.

"You don't want to do it," she warned, yet didn't pull away.

"Yes, I believe I do, and you know what?"

"What?"

"So do you."

"No, I don't," she retorted.

"Afraid?" he taunted.

"Of what? A kiss? I've kissed many men."

"I know," he replied dryly. "I was one of them and I remember it well."

"I don't."

"Doesn't matter." His fingers clenched on her waist. "You may have kissed other men, but mine you will never forget and you still owe me."

"For what?" She was so wrapped up in the moment that she didn't feel the cooling of the temperature, so close to the scent of aftershave mixed with male sweat that she missed the damp breeze that served as precursor to a rainstorm.

"For that graduation night kiss."

"Do I still owe you?" She angled her head. "I don't really remember the kiss and I'm sure it wasn't so terrible that I left a debt."

"A debt must be paid. Honor among friends."

"What are the terms for repayment? Is there interest involved?"

"Oh, there's plenty of interest, but we'll negotiate that when the time comes." He wiped away a swatch of smeared dirt off her cheek.

"When do you plan on collecting?"

His wide smile revealed perfect teeth. "Now."

"You wouldn't." Alyssa's pulse skittered to a halt and then revved to sixty.

He did.

Nathan pulled her close and all she could do was wrap her mud-slicked arms around his shoulders to keep her balance. Without warning he'd wrapped her in his arms, her tongue tasting his mouth, and at the moment the clouds, after taking their sweet time to roll in, started dropping their payload of sun-warmed rain. But nothing mattered but the strong fingers cupping her rear, the swelling of her breasts, and the vibration of his groan on her lips.

"I could take you here and now. In the rain, in the mud. You're playing havoc with my self-control, Alyssa."

Raindrops fell on her face and she licked them off her lips. The temptation was there, the attraction, the heat, but not the necessary final ingredients of trust and love.

"Cold shower?"

Nathan nodded.

"Me too." She sighed into his chest.

"One day I won't stop," he warned.

"One day . . ." She pulled away and bent over to pick up her backpack. "One day I won't want you to."

"But not today?"

"No, Nathan. Not yet."

He took his time in the shower, then dressed in chinos and a long-sleeved shirt. Finally relaxed and anticipating the pleasure of Alyssa's company, he went back downstairs.

Alyssa joined Nathan in the kitchen and helped him prepare a meal. In fact she'd contributed to her own celebration dinner. It seemed that working together in the kitchen had made the meal all the more delicious. Something about watching him patiently peel, slice, and chop was inordinately attractive. Maybe it was something about seeing a man who knew his way around the kitchen, she added. The sight was a rare and welcome treat.

After eating, they sat on the sofa in front of a small fire, watching the flickering flames and listening to the crackling of burning pinewood.

Alyssa sipped the brandy-laced coffee, letting the room soften a bit as she sat back on the sofa. They gazed at each other until Nathan turned toward the low coffee table in front of the sofa. She watched, curious, as he deliberately placed his cup on its flat surface, then took her cup from her hand and set it next to his.

"How about a dance?"

As he curled his arms around her and they settled into a comfortable, slow rhythm in front of the flickering fire, Alyssa realized what it was that made her want to tell Nathan everything. It was his presence, so much like her father, like her older brother, Alan. It was the listen-first, act-later manner, along with meaningful silences and complete acceptance.

Unlike Harrison and the other career-driven men whom she had issued temporary visas into her personal life, he didn't try to change her, mold her, move her, or manipulate her. Music, shadows, smoke, and dance set the scene. But it was his musky scent that turned her nipples hard, the brief contact of his thigh upon hers, the sensation of his large hands on the small of her back that led to her raising her face to his and inviting his kiss. The movements of his lips upon her own, slowly, gently, exploring, made her knees weak.

It was only the popping sound of the wood that broke the spell and had Alyssa opening her eyes and pulling in a deep gulp of air. "We should stop."

"We should, shouldn't we?" Nathan whispered against her mouth, only to place his hand against her pelvis.

Alyssa gasped at the contact, only to have it cut off by his tongue rolling in her mouth, sending chills over her skin and setting fire to her blood.

"Nathan," she whispered against his cheek. "Just because we can doesn't mean we should. This is too fast."

"We're not strangers who met in a bar or club. We were friends and we will be lovers."

The lure of a confident man would be her downfall. She liked it all. The way his voice vibrated across her skin. The way he took the lead, giving her body no option other than instant response.

Alyssa pulled her hand away and put some distance between them. She believed him when he said they would be lovers. The attraction that flowed between them was something that could not be denied or decreased.

"Sleep in my bed tonight."

"Where will you sleep?"

"With you."

Alyssa went completely still. "Why would I do something that crazy?"

"So I can get a good night's sleep."

"What?"

"Last night you woke me with your nightmares. Why don't you sleep in my room tonight? I promise nothing will happen."

"Nathan . . ." she started, not sure how to respond to his offer.

"I won't lie to you. It's been a while since I've been with a woman, but know that you will be safe. You have my word."

Alyssa lowered her eyes. He was asking her to trust him. The thing was that she already did, but did she trust herself to merely sleep with the temptation inches away? "All right."

Alyssa took that moment to yawn.

"You go on ahead. I'm going to step outside for some air."

After she'd slipped into a pair of lightweight Egyptian cotton pants and a top, she tied up her hair. Nathan's bedroom still smelled of clean, crisp sheets. She turned down the bed and fluffed the pillows.

You're just going to sleep with the man, she thought. Then why was she so nervous? As the day's exertions and the brandy caught up with her, she lay down on the left side of the bed and drew a light coverlet and sheet over her shoulders.

She was still awake when Nathan entered the room and joined her on the bed.

"Maybe this isn't the best idea," she said, her voice reduced to little more than breath and anticipation.

His hands gently turned her around and pulled her into his chest as his arms wrapped around her. "Close your eyes, Alyssa."

She reluctantly acquiesced. It was a short time before she fell asleep.

Alyssa awoke the next morning from a nice dream only to find an even better reality. Forgoing the urge to reach out and run her hand over the slight stubble of Nathan's chin, Alyssa eased out of the bed and went over to the window. Her hands rubbed her arms up and down to ward off the morning chill. Pulling back the curtains, she looked outside. The rain, which had started yesterday evening, showed no signs of letting up.

She was about to let the curtains go when she caught a movement out of the corner of her eyes. Close to a border of the grass and the trees stood a man in a green rain slicker. A prickle of unease crept up her spine and she debated whether or not to wake Nathan.

Remembering Bernard had mentioned the possibility of visits by the local security company, Alyssa turned from the window and intended to go take a shower, but instead paused and stared. Nathan lay on his stomach, an arm stretched across the bed where she had been lying moments before. His face softened in sleep, begged her to wake him with a kiss. Instead, she tiptoed out of the bedroom and into the bathroom. Turning on the warm water, she stepped inside the shower stall and the spray washed away the residual sleep, yet the shadow of unease remained.

It was only after breakfast when Nathan had ensconced himself in Bernard's computer room to make a phone call that Alyssa got a moment to herself. Pulling the case files, she curled her legs underneath her on the couch. She flipped open the file with Lily's name on it and began to read.

Thirty minutes later, she leaned her head back over the lip of the sofa and sighed with frustration. Rubbing her brow, she closed her eyes to the open-beamed ceiling and mentally went over what she'd just learned.

First investigation team: two transferred, one left the department. The notes and typed letter began to mimic a pattern of neglect a mere two months after the accident: lowered priority, lack of follow-up, officer reassigned to new police precinct.

Case reassigned, reenactment sketches missing, paint evidence lost in transit to new precinct.

The word *missing* was going to make her scream: forensic evidence, witness reports, scene reenactments. Everyone who had ever touched the case had subsequently left, been reassigned, promoted, the like went on and on. The interviews were a waste of reading time and lacked crucial details of the events that took place before the accident. How could her interview with her dance instructor have yielded more information than the professionals? The facts so frustrated her that she wanted to say to hell with all of it. In business she could be relentless, but in this personal quest she had little by way of connections and less to go on.

"Something I can help you with?"

Alyssa opened her eyes and looked into Nathan's upside-down face.

"Not unless you can wave a magic wand and give me my memories back."

"What's this?"

Before she could move, he'd picked up the manilla folder from out of her lap and opened it.

"Give that back."

Nathan flipped open the folder. "A police file? This doesn't look like youth center business."

"Very good observation. Now hand it over." She made a grab for the file but only ended up landing with her face flat on the sofa. Sitting up, she pushed the hair from her eyes and shot Nathan a dirty look as he settled into the chair across from her

"You're investigating Lily's case?"

"That's the plan."

"I want to help."

"Why?"

Nathan moved from the recliner to take a sear beside Alyssa on the couch. "Because I can."

The expression on her face let him know that his response had not been enough. Placing the folder on the table between them, he stood up and moved to take a seat beside her on the sofa. "More than that I want to help because I care about you."

She lowered her head while her eyes remained locked on the sole item resting atop the walnut-colored coffee table. "I had nightmares for months after Lily died. Even in the middle of summer, I remember waking up shivering with cold. For months afterward the joy went out of my life. My first love was dance but I couldn't step into the studio."

"I don't recall that you were injured."

"I only had a slight bruise and concussion. The injury was mental. I could only dance if I was alone or with an instructor."

"Maybe you shouldn't think about it." Nathan looked into her eyes and they spoke of a sadness tucked away in her heart. The warm gold brown of the richest honey, they revealed a depth of emotion.

"That's exactly what Lily's brother, Andrés, advised me to do." She shook her head. "But I'm not so sure.

"I couldn't handle her death so I ran, Nathan. I used friends, parties, and alcohol in college. After graduating, it was business school and work. I don't want to run away this time."

"Then stay and see this through."

"Easier said than done," she said wryly. "The police never found the person responsible for the hit-and-run."

"No witnesses?"

"According to the police, I was the only possible witness and I couldn't remember anything after the performance. It was all a blank, but now maybe I'm getting that info back. I can't help but wonder what happened that night."

"Do you feel you can accomplish what the police could not?"

"I thought I could. But maybe Uncle Ed was right. It's impossible," she said.

"Nothing is impossible as long as we work together. Tomorrow I'll call in a favor and see how to go about getting the case reopened."

"We?" She gave him a curious look.

"Call it doing my civil duty." No, it was more. Something long dormant in Nathan's heart roared to life and he knew that one of his missions in life was to protect the woman across from him.

He reached out and took her small hand within his own and gave it a gentle squeeze. "Alyssa, I'm a judge. But first I was your friend. Years ago someone not only broke the law but almost broke your spirit as well. I will not let that go unpunished."

"Thank you." She leaned over and rested her cheek against his shoulder. She wasn't too proud to accept assistance, or too stubborn to go it alone. She would accept Nathan's help but would make sure that he understood that she would take the lead. Even with the rain outside, Alyssa's heart felt lighter. No matter the obstacles, they would succeed.

"We should get started back toward the city," she whispered. "Traffic . . ."

"One more hour shouldn't matter." He settled his arm

around her and placed a kiss on her hair. "Now, did I ever tell you about the time Lauren and I pretended to be the Sundance Kid and his common-law wife, Etta? We held my father's favorite train for ransom."

"No, you didn't." She snuggled closer, listening to the richness of his voice as Nathan shared childhood memories of his father and his passion for the railways. She learned about the African-American connection to the rails and discovered they were largely responsible for developing the railway system. The blood, sweat, and lives that built the first overland link between the East and West.

Rain continued to roll down the windows as he rubbed her back. Looking down into her curious eyes, he felt something catch in his heart and he held her tighter. They talked for hours, strengthening the bonds between them that had grown loose over time and distance.

Chapter 13

"Alyssa, there's a good-looking man with a funny accent here to see you."

She frowned into the telephone. "Funny?"

Instead of a quick reply, Alyssa overheard a voice from her past. "Please pass on that Harrison would like a moment of her time."

"Did you hear that? Is he from the islands?"

Alyssa shook her head with a smile. "Yes, a North Atlantic island. Harrison is British."

"Oh," Carol drawled.

Alyssa bit the inside of her lip to stifle a laugh. She knew at that exact moment, Carol was subjecting Harrison to a thorough visual examination. "Could you let him back please?"

"All right."

"Thanks." Alyssa hung up the telephone, straightened her desk, and finger-combed her hair.

By the time the door opened, she had moved to stand next to the window. Entering her office, Harrison immediately flashed his perfect white teeth in a smile, while the corners of his eyes crinkled. The charcoal pin-striped suit fit perfectly, a feat only an Oxford Street tailor with Italian fabric could accomplish.

"A million heartfelt apologies and I've missed you terribly."

Alyssa remembered the last time he'd shown up at her office with an offer. "Throw in an 'I'll never act that way again' plus a little groveling and I'll take it."

With his hands in his pockets, he took a few steps in and stopped to look around. "So this is your new office?"

"Yes," she said cheerfully. It hadn't come with the perks of state-of-the-art equipment, a corner office with sought-after views, or a dedicated personal assistant, but she loved getting up in the morning, enjoyed walking through the doors to be greeted by her coworkers, and most of all she loved working for the kids.

"It's quite . . . how shall I say?" He paused. "Different."

"Thank you."

"What exactly is it that you do?"

"I'm a program director. I organize events, activities, coordinate funding, and sometimes I teach classes."

"I'd like to hear more."

Alyssa glanced at the watch on her wrist, then back at Harrison. "How much time do you have?"

"The car's outside and my next meeting will not begin for another three hours."

"It's a beautiful day. Why don't we talk outside?"

After they'd taken a seat in the courtyard adjacent to the center's playground, Alyssa noticed how out of place Harrison looked dressed in a suit and tie. "You can take off your jacket. I promise not to tell the boys back on Lombard Street," she teased.

He stood up and took off his jacket, laying it over the back of the bench. For several moments, an uncomfortable silence reigned. They had been colleagues and friends; they had been lovers. Despite the fact that they were no longer any of those, Alyssa leaned back into his arm, then stretched out her legs. She was unsure of how to classify what they were to one another if not by what they had been to each other.

"So when did your flight get in?"

"About three hours ago. The arrival procedures in this country are absolutely barbaric. It took me over an hour to run the gauntlets of customs and immigration. I slept over the Atlantic, but I'm still knackered."

She slowly raised her chin and stared. *Knackered.* Harrison's use of the British slang for exhausted made her take a second look at the man sitting by her side. Slang was common and that was one thing Harrison's strict upbringing would never allow him to be.

His smoke-colored eyes examined her from head to toe. "You've changed already."

"How so?" she asked, lifting her face into the afternoon sunlight.

"More relaxed and if I dare say it, more beautiful. Are you happy here?"

"Very." She looked away, slightly uncomfortable with his compliment. "You look more relaxed as well."

Discounting his usual attire, Harrison sported a tan and the taut skin over his cheeks had loosened, possibly brought about by the repeated act of smiling.

He looked around the tree-enclosed area. "You used to drag me to parks whenever we arrived into a city during the daytime."

"And you hated it."

"No, I just didn't understand. I didn't understand you, then. I still don't. I would have bought you anything your heart desired and in most cases it was souvenirs and pastries. In Prague, I would have taken you to the castle; Monaco, I had a table reserved at Le Saint Benoit. The night that you dragged me from a nine-hour flight from London to Singapore only to sit in a tram to see animals at the Night Safari."

She tapped him on his shoulder. "If I recall correctly, you were the one who volunteered to walk back to the car so that you could get a better look at the rhinos."

"Yes, I did. I enjoyed myself that night. I guess it's one of those paradoxes of attraction that makes me want Caitlin."

"Caitlin?" she gently prodded.

"I've met someone."

"Oh." Alyssa smiled, in no way jealous. "Is she demure,

polite, and British?" she asked with the same casualness of inquiring about the time or the weather forecast for tomorrow.

"No." He paused. "She reminds me of you."

"Let me guess." She eyed him shrewdly. "She's American?"

"Exactly. She's from Texas. I don't know what it is about women from the States." His masculine grin reminded her of a very pleased wolf.

"Did she get Sir Brandell's approval?"

"No, I'm not taking her within a hundred kilometers of my father. To be completely candid, we haven't spoken since you left the company. He continues to think that I should have made a better offer."

"Did you tell him it had nothing to do with money?"

"Nothing matters except that I didn't succeed. Bloody hell, it was like blinkers came off my eyes. I was no better than one of his prize thoroughbreds and I hadn't won the Royal Ascot."

She'd had a close-up view of the blinkers he'd mentioned, the plastic cups that sat a few inches from the horse's eyes and kept him focused straight ahead.

Alyssa shook her head delicately, remembering the first time she'd met Harrison's family. The formal introduction had not taken place over dinner at an exclusive London restaurant but at Britain's most popular horse racing event. She'd spent two of the five days of racing ensconced in the hospitality facility discussing fashion and the latest royal scandals with his mother, health management with his younger brother, the surgeon, and equity restructuring with Harrison's father.

As required by racing customs, she'd been a designer-label and flamboyant-hat-wearing nervous wreck, a condition that wasn't helped by being unexpectedly cornered by one of Sir Brandell's inebriated business associates who happened to believe that his wealth and social ranking could secure him a night in her hotel room. An ice-cold club soda delivered to his face had resolved the issue.

"I'm sorry it turned out so badly."

"Don't be." He rubbed the back of his neck. "For some men

wisdom comes at the bottom of a tall glass of Guinness, but after one of many arguments with my father, I promised myself that I wouldn't make the same fatal mistake with Caitlin that I made with you."

"What was that?"

"I let you walk away."

"You couldn't have stopped me," she said, confused.

"But I could have gone with you. I could have talked with you. I could have asked you to give me the opportunity to change instead of letting pride gain me a sore head the next morning."

Alyssa had to admit he made a good point. Once she made a decision, nothing could change it. That was an aspect of her personality that ensured her career success, but did not work well in her personal life. "You could have done all that but what we had . . ." Her voice trailed off.

Harrison interjected. "I know that what we shared wasn't love but I could have listened and put your needs above those of the company. Your resignation was a red flag that I could not ignore."

"I'm glad."

"In fact." He crossed his legs and looked up toward the sky. "Your leaving was the best thing that could have ever happened to me."

"So I should have left sooner?" she asked dubiously.

"No, you silly goose."

He tweaked her cheek and Alyssa almost fell off the bench in shock.

"It's just that thanks to you I'm a better man." He grinned and squeezed her shoulder.

Alyssa let out a soft laugh and playfully tapped him on the shoulder again. Another first in her life and a contribution to the universal sisterhood. Her mother would be pleased that she'd helped some future woman to a better husband.

She'd seen the changes in him from the moment he'd walked into her office, the relaxed set of his shoulders, the slight tan, but the most telling of them all was the lack of formality to his bearing and the casual displays of affection. It had been drilled into him from birth that public displays of any emotion were strictly forbidden.

"I'm glad, Harrison, so now that we've got that personal business out of the way, what's the real reason you showed up at my doorstep?"

"Why not just to see an old friend?"

She gave him a direct stare. "I've been on the receiving end of more than a thousand of your e-mails, been privy to your daily diary, and a willing partner on cross-continent business trips. Tell me the truth."

He roughly loosened his tie and cleared his throat. "I have a leveraged buyout in Hong Kong that I wanted to help the Singapore office with. It's just a one-off situation. You recall Mr. Goi?"

"Yes." She nodded. Born in the Fujian province of China, the plain-speaking businessman had impressed her with his combination of business knowledge and street smarts. "Is he well?"

"He's in excellent form. In fact, he's planning on retiring within the next year and handing the reins over to his eldest son. Only one thing is giving him trouble."

"What is that?" Alyssa felt the small leap of adrenaline as an old excitement came back, but she suppressed it. During her tenure at Brandell's PLC, she'd led a group of investment banks in putting together a deal for Mr. Goi to acquire a Malaysia-based semiconductor maker. It had been her biggest challenge and the pièce de résistance of her career.

"He's quite keen on pulling a Taiwanese electronics company into the fold. It was a pretty standard buyout until a few weeks ago. Negotiations stalled when an American company by the name of Worthington Enterprises made a counteroffer."

"I left you all my files in excellent order. A look at their debt structuring will give you all the information you need to pull together a team."

"I didn't come here to ask about your previous business

deal. I'm here because Goi personally phoned to request that you come and help with the negotiations."

Alyssa's eyes locked on the empty merry-go-round and estimated that in the next thirty minutes it would be filled with elementary students while the high school kids crowded into desks to get help on their homework from local community residents and college students. Tomorrow she was scheduled to meet with the teen representatives to discuss the outdoor event. *Next week.* Her mind ticked through her ever-growing to-do list and appointment book.

No, she couldn't cancel or reschedule her responsibilities, she couldn't leave, and she didn't want to go. She was home, buying real plants, paying a mortgage, cashing in on her frequent flier miles, making some progress on Lily's case, and she was falling in lust. "I can't do it, Harrison. I'm sorry but I have commitments; not to mention that I don't want to leave when I'm just settling in."

He sighed and toyed with his Rolex. "Mr. Goi will be disappointed, but how about dinner tonight?"

"So you can ply me with food and wine with hopes of getting me on a plane?"

He reached over and toyed with a lock of her hair. "Exactly."

"So this is where you've been hiding. Carol has been searching the entire center for you, sweetheart," Nathan commented, making his way over to the two people sitting on the bench.

When he'd closed his car door and gone into the community center building, nothing seemed out of sorts, yet the sight of a suit-and-tie-clad silver-haired white man leaning against a new-model Cadillac caught his eye. Shaking his head, he had opened the center door and entered. He needed to see Alyssa. Nathan had spoken with the police chief earlier that afternoon and the man had emphasized that the case could not be reopened unless new, concrete evidence was discovered.

The decline of Harrison's dinner invitation died on her lips as they both stood quickly. Alyssa took a step forward and then stopped when Nathan came to a halt at her side. Standing between the two of them as each took the other's measure was as if she were standing in the midst of a silent battle. Harrison was the first to move, extending his hand.

"Harrison Brandell."

"Nathan Hughes."

"Well, Alyssa, I see that my time is up. It was nice chatting with you."

"You too." She pasted a smile on her face while trying to ignore the band of steel that wrapped around her waist.

Harrison's eyes went from Alyssa's to Nathan's and back to hers. "If you should have a change of heart, you always know how to reach me. I can find my way out."

Her lips thinned at the deliberate innuendo, but she nodded politely. "Good luck."

"Who is he?" Nathan inclined his head toward a departing Harrison.

"I believe I mentioned Harrison to you before."

"You told me what he *was*," he corrected. "But I want to know, who *is* he to you now?"

Her lips compressed into a thin line. She didn't like his frown and she didn't care for the sharp tone of his voice. If it hadn't been for something else shining in his eyes she might have walked away. Of all the matters that sat on her plate, Nathan's jealousy wasn't a side dish she needed to deal with at the moment.

"Hey, Ms. K!"

Saved from having to answer his question, Alyssa turned from Nathan and waved to a group of students that just walked onto the basketball court.

"Hey, guys." Alyssa smiled as the group sauntered over.

After introducing Nathan to the teenagers, Alyssa took a step back and watched him work. His presence drew respect and trust from everyone. She noted that he had a way of meeting their eyes and that his manner of speaking changed. In one instant he went from the judge to the older brother on the street. By the time Nathan had finished giving a basketball history lesson, the smile on her lips could have formed the St. Louis Arch.

"Good luck with your calculus test tomorrow, Mark," she said as the boys were walking away.

"Hold up, fellas," Mark called out before turning back to her. "Almost forgot. Ms. K, your brother was on fire last night. Never seen the dude hit that good."

"Thanks, I'll have to tell him," she responded before stepping toward Nathan. "I have to get back to my office."

"That's fine. It would be better for us to talk there."

Alyssa frowned. "What is there to discuss?"

"You didn't answer my question," Nathan said as soon as she'd shut the door to her office. His voice was filled with the lingering anger he'd felt at the sight of Harrison's hand on her cheek.

She paused from gathering her things. In front of a cold fireplace while watching the raindrops roll down the cabin window, she had laid her life bare to him, spilling secrets, goals, and dreams. To have him question her so sharply at this juncture in their relationship was too much.

"You have neither the grounds nor the rights to take that tone with me, Nathan Hughes." Alyssa turned around and eyed him coolly. The dark tenor of his voice reminded her too much of Harrison's the night he'd attacked her dance instructor.

"I'll ask you one more time." Nathan didn't care much for the icy tone, even if he partially agreed with her observation. He took off his sunglasses, dropped them in the nearby chair, and met her stare. He had no claim on her yet, but she would soon be spiritually and legally his wife.

"And I'll give you the same answer." Her brows knitted together and her chin lifted in challenge only to gasp as his fingers brushed across her breasts and his hands grabbed a hold of her crossed arms.

"This gives me the right." Nathan pulled her tight against him and kissed her hard. It was unrelenting. He wasn't sure whether it was to make his claim, put his mark on her, or

Angela Weaver

exorcise the remnant of another man's touch on her skin. He turned his head slightly to the side, almost bruising her mouth as he opened his mouth against hers and slipped the tip of his tongue over the swell of her bottom lip. He paused in surprise when Alyssa opened her lips and met his tongue with her own. He released her arms and slid his hands around her sides and lowered his palms to cup her rear.

Moments later, he pulled back and was rewarded with the sound of her soft moan. "Now, should I be concerned about your British visitor?"

Alyssa looked up at him from underneath her long lashes and struggled to regain her breath as well as keep the smug smile off of her face. She'd never been shy in regards to members of the opposite sex. That kiss and all those before had only served to whet her appetite. She was playing with fire and the heat of it ignited a fierce passion that surprised her.

"No, Nathan. Harrison was just stopping by to say hello and wanted to invite me to grab a bite to eat later." She kept the real reason for this visit a secret, having a sneaking suspicion that telling him about the job offer would make a delicate situation worse.

"Share dinner with me tonight."

Alyssa rubbed her thumb on the back of his neck. "I'd like to go home first."

"I'll take you." He nodded.

It was only when he pulled onto the interstate heading in the opposite direction of her apartment that she laughed softly. "I guess I should have specified my home."

"You are right." He grinned while weaving confidently through traffic. His housekeeper, Mrs. Earls, usually cooked a nice meal when she came to take care of his home. It would be a pleasant change to share the table with Alyssa instead of eating alone. The car responded to his directions perfectly as his mind formulated the perfect seduction. Yet first he would get business out of the way.

"I spoke with the police chief this morning."

Alyssa studied his face. "Not good?"

He gave her a detailed version of the meeting, and then covered her hand with his own. One thing that he left out was the statute of limitations. The case would have to be reclassified as murder if they wanted to have it tried in criminal court. He figured they would cross that bridge when they came to it. There was always civil court.

Chapter 14

After eating a satisfying meal and dessert, Alyssa eyed Nathan over the rim of her glass as he finished placing the last of the dishes into the dishwasher. He'd insisted that she sit and relax instead of helping to clean up. Uncrossing her legs, she smoothed down the hem of the silky cotton dress. No stranger to the dangers and the pleasures of attraction, she took a sip of the sweet red wine and then stopped. She would seduce him with natural, not alcohol-induced, courage. All evening they had both been on a razor's edge as unspoken words and checked emotions filled the air.

The dinner had but satisfied one hunger while intensifying another. He'd touched her both physically and mentally since she'd stepped into his home. He'd placed a hand on her knee at the dinner table, fed her spoonful after spoonful of ice cream, and kissed her neck as she leaned down to pick up a dropped napkin. He'd spent the evening taunting her, toying with her, and now it was her turn. Each conversation, whether about something as trivial as the weather, politics, or sports, had been peppered with innuendo. "Would you like to have coffee in the den or outside on the deck?" he asked while drying his hands on a kitchen towel.

While impatience warred with anticipation, Alyssa placed her wineglass on the table, stood, and moved toward Nathan. The sound of her sandals slapping against the terra-cotta tiles echoed in the large room as she rounded the kitchen island to stand in front of him.

"No," she answered, tilting her face upward slowly, so that he would meet her gaze, and see her desire. "I don't want coffee."

Not breaking eye contact, she raised her hand and ran a finger over the side of his cheek, slowly lingering over the slight roughness of his jaw. Her other hand came to rest on his shoulder.

His voice deepened. "Then what do you want?"

"I want you," she murmured before pulling his head down and kissing him. Catching his bottom lip between her sharp little teeth, she sucked it as she slowly began to stroke the nape of his neck.

After a minute, Nathan drew back and held her hand within his own. "Are you aware of what you're inviting, Alyssa?"

"Maybe. Maybe not," she answered. But the smile that graced her lips was slow, deliberate, and enticing. She knew from the flare of his nostrils and the way he licked his lips that her actions had spoken louder and clearer than any words of invitation. They had danced around each other for far too long and Alyssa was caught up in the moment. The knowledge that she affected him so strongly was a powerful aphrodisiac.

She inhaled sharply as Nathan's hands locked onto her shoulders, pushing her back toward the kitchen sink. The countertop was hard against her back for an instant, then forgotten in the feel of his lips, his tongue surging deep inside her mouth. She slipped her arms around his neck and her body molded to his as her neck fell back, inviting him to explore the curve of her throat.

Passing up the invitation to linger there, he moved upward. His teeth nipped her ear and his voice whispered so softly it sent all other thoughts scattering. "This is not a game and I am not a boy to be toyed with." His warning was more of a growl than a statement.

"I don't play games." She turned her face from side to side, gasping for breath as her pulse throbbed to keep up with the rapid pace set by his lips and hands. "Not anymore and never with you."

Nathan inhaled and the sweet, subtle scent of her body raced down the back of his throat and brought his thighs into full contact with hers.

He took her hand and drew her out of the kitchen. Wordlessly he led her through the living room toward the steps leading upstairs that curved slightly, the late evening sun falling from the overhead skylight.

Nathan didn't bother to switch on the light as they entered the room and only released her hand when they came to a stop in the center of the master bedroom. This was the only room in the house other than that basement study over which he'd exerted any influence.

He'd had a hand in everything from the battleship gray on the walls, to the tribal rugs scattered around the room, to the carved stone mantel over the fireplace. The heavy damask curtains framing the windows could be loosed from their ties to block out the outside world. He'd even purchased the African walnut sleigh bed from a furniture gallery on Oak Street.

He looked into her burnished gold eyes and saw longing staring back at him. Needing to ground himself in the reality that the woman he'd dreamed about for months after his undergraduate graduation was in his arms, he traced his finger along the smooth contours of her face, caressing her lovely high forehead, the corners of her crescent-shaped eyes, her upturned nose, the hollows of her sculpted cheeks, and finally the delicate bow shape of her full mouth.

"Exquisite," he whispered, his finger lingering on the supple, sensitive bottom lip. It took everything he had to act the gentleman when all he wanted was to push her against the wall and put out the fire she'd started the day she strolled back into his life. Her tongue darted out in temptation and that was all he needed, and more.

"Alyssa," he groaned, as he bent and sought to taste her lips with his own. Her mouth opened for him, and his tongue surged inside, tasting the fruity, slightly spicy taste of red wine. His hands wound tightly in her hair as he kissed her with a fervor that surprised even him. Her hands moved from his shoulders to his chest and then lower to his washboard abdomen.

"I've thought about doing this for a long time."

"Touching my stomach?"

"Well." Her eyes twinkled. "Judges aren't known for being physically fit, now, are they?"

"Not all judges are alike," he started before turning to trail his lips across her neck as he slid his hands around her buttocks and up the curve of her back to deftly unzip her dress. Her startled gasp was echoed by his mumbled curse.

Pulling back, Nathan drank in the sight of her feminine curves covered solely in lace panties and a matching bra. The softness of her brown skin begged for his touch.

"Would you like me to take it off?" Alyssa questioned softly. Her eyes locked with his and the desire she saw sent a heady sense of hunger through her as she began to unbutton his shirt. Her breath caught in her throat as his fingers traced around the delicate midnight-black lace of her bra, further stimulating her nipples.

"I believe I can manage when the time is right," he murmured against the hollow of her neck while running his thumbs across her nipples, feeling the weight and shape of her breasts in the palms of his hands.

Before she could respond, Nathan kissed her again, his lips tasting hers as he murmured against her mouth. She leaned into the kiss, their mouths parting, tongues darting in and tasting each other. The feel of his hand on her skin made her dizzy with need. Alyssa moved her hips against his, deliberately rubbing against the evidence of his arousal.

Taking a shaky breath, she pulled back and boldly reached down, her nimble fingers catching hold of the buckle on the slender leather belt he wore. She tugged it apart easily, then unbuttoned and unzipped his pants. Before she could push them down, she found herself turned around and looking at the bed instead of Nathan's smooth chest.

Too fast. Nathan cursed inwardly and positioned her so that her back was to him. He trailed his fingers over her back and, marveling at the muscle, unclasped her bra and slid it down her arms. As he did so, he leaned down and trailed his lips over her neck, satisfied as she leaned her head to the side and released a husky moan.

"I have dreamed of doing this every night since the cabin. Kissing you." He nibbled the top of her ear. "Undressing you, holding you in my arms, running my hands over your body."

His hands cupped her breasts as his sex jutted into her backside. "You have beautiful skin, Alyssa. Soft. Full."

He held her closer and the contact of her rear with his groin was as much a pleasure as a pain.

"Take me to bed, Nathan." Alyssa shivered at the heat burning from his tongue as it swirled slowly on her shoulder, his teeth grazing her neck, his hands massaging her aching breasts. Her knees threatened to buckle at the touch of his hand on her inner thigh. Would the man reduce her to begging or drive her insane first?

She didn't have to ask twice as Nathan swept her up into his arms and gently placed her upon the bed. Seeing the desire in his eyes, Alyssa lay back, content to relinquish the lead. The contact of the cool sheets against her bare skin sent a shock through her system. Yet the sight of him undressing wiped all thoughts from her mind as her eyes paid appropriate homage to the image of male perfection. God had spared no expense when He created that mold, some irrational part of her mind observed as he dug into the nightstand.

After placing on the latex condom, he lay back down beside her and took her face between his hands. Nathan slid his hand down her back, his fingers curling, locking onto the swell of her buttocks. All the while he watched her face for signs that he pleased her, that she wanted him, that she was ready.

He touched her in all the places that made her arch, licked

all the spots that made her purr and twist. Yet when the time came, Nathan paused. As if she could hear his thoughts, her passion darkened, eyes opened. "This night is for us. I need you to tell me what you like."

Alyssa thought it sweet for him to ask although she had no thoughts of not finishing the dance they'd started so long ago. She wanted him hard and fast, long and slow. She just wanted *him* inside filling the hollow need. Her answer came not in the form of a vocal response, but instead she ran her hands down his back and cupped his buttocks. She pulling him down, arching her back upward only to have him stop at her entrance.

"Nathan," she started with a gasp that ended in a moan as his fingers traveled up her inner thigh and settled upon her most sensitive spot. Alyssa closed her eyes, blinding herself to everything but the sensations sweeping through her body.

"Look at me," he commanded, positioning himself above her.

He needed her to see him. He wanted to see her eyes as he entered her. They were nose to nose, and he stared into the darkness of Alyssa's eyes where the core blazed with a fire of a different color, and she placed a hand on each of his shoulders.

"I have never forgotten that first kiss," he said. "I imagined having you in my arms like this. Tasting your skin, breathing in your scent, loving you." His lips moved over her bottom lip and Nathan drew in a harsh breath as her golden eyes met his and she nipped his bottom lip with her teeth.

Nathan transferred his attention to her breasts and sucked her nipple gently, his eyes still holding hers, then he gripped it lightly between his teeth, teasing the tip with a series of butterfly-light flutters of his tongue.

Moment later when her body trembled uncontrollably underneath his, Nathan raised his head. "Say it," he ordered hoarsely. "Say you want me. Only me." His fingers withdrew from her, rubbing against the most sensitive place of her womanhood.

"Only you," she moaned. "Please, Nathan."

As if some spell commanded her, she met his look of

possession and unable to think of anything but putting an end to the yearning, she nodded. He leaned down and kissed her and then he slid inside her with a single graceful thrust. She cried into his mouth, arching her back at the sensation. Advance. Retreat. Again. He came in hard and the fullness of him rocked her to her core.

"Nathan." Alyssa wrapped her arms around his shoulders and buried her face into his neck, her eyes closed as her chest rose and fell in hard little breaths. Nathan's lips were close to her ear, his breathing harsh and raspy, and she moaned again as the warm pressure built first in her back, then worked its way down, then out. Over and over, wave after wave racked her as she cried out with full release only to feel his pulsing moments later.

With a sigh, he slid an arm under her and then rolled over, carrying her with him so that he was still inside. He would never get enough. He looked at her dilated pupils, swollen lips, and flushed face and felt her skin against his as her breasts rubbed against his chest and invited his touch. Bending his head, he kissed her deep as he grew hard again. "Once more."

It was much later that Nathan pulled the satin sheet over both of their bodies and wrapped his arms around Alyssa's bare stomach. Gently pulling her into his embrace, he sat his chin on her shoulder. He had glimpsed a piece of heaven that night and knew he would no longer be satisfied without the touch of her hand, the kiss of her lips, the melody of her sighs, and the possession of her body.

He tightened his grip, feeling her unsteady breath upon his skin. He would not be satisfied until he had her heart. "Stay the night."

Alyssa opened her eyes and stretched like a cat and winced at the delicious soreness between her thighs. Twice they'd made love, the second time more intense than the first. She could stay in his arms forever. The thought slipped into her mind as she relaxed against the cushion of his chest. Yet the ever-present voice of experience, which sounded suspiciously like her mother, pointed out the possible consequences of staying where she was.

"Nathan." She lifted herself up and turned toward him. "I know this is going to sound strange but I'd like to take baby steps."

"Baby steps?" His lips curved into a smile that shot straight to her heart.

She regarded him seriously as he reached out to brush a stand of hair from her cheek. "I don't want to rush this or rush us," she said slowly. "I think it would be best if I went home tonight."

"I'll allow it for now."

"Allow?" Her voice rose along, with an eyebrow.

"You know what I want, Alyssa. I'm old-fashioned and male." He had a gleam in his eyes.

"How's that?"

"I like my woman to be by my side all night."

"Then I suggest you pack an overnight bag next time," she replied flippantly before sitting up and pushing her hair back. Taking a moment, she slipped out of bed and began to gather her clothes. She would shower in her own home and sleep in her own bed.

"You acknowledge that there will be a next time." Nathan sat up and leaned back against the headboard with a confident grin on his face.

Alyssa looked at his powerful upper body and then strolled back over to the bed. "I'm cautious, not foolish."

With her free hand, she trailed the tips of fingers lightly across his chest, enjoying his indrawn breath. "If you play your cards right, there will be many."

"Minx." He grinned. "Get some clothes on before I forget about my good intentions."

Her neighborhood was only parked cars and empty sidewalks when Nathan brought the car to a standstill in front of her building and turned on his blinkers. It was only after they had entered the apartment building and stepped out onto her floor, that Nathan broke the comfortable silence. "I look forward to tomorrow night."

Alyssa's brow creased momentarily. "The charity auction?"

He reached over and gently picked up her hand and stroked the inside of her slender wrist. The jump in her pulse pleased him.

"I'll pick you up at 6:30."

"You may be knocking on the door of an empty apartment, Nathan Hughes. Didn't we have a talk about asking versus making assumptions?"

Nathan took her keys and unlocked the door. Placing them in her outstretched hand, he kissed her on the lips. "Good night, Ms. Knight. I'll see you on the morrow."

Chapter 15

Chicago was a beautiful pearl nestled in the middle of America. And tonight after a hard rain, it showed beautifully in the evening twilight, Alyssa decided, tearing her eyes from the elevator's windowed walls. The hotel was situated in the center of Chicago, and on a clear day a view from its many suites saw the lazy waves of Lake Chicago, towering buildings, soaring airplanes, and a sprawling, diverse city teeming with life. Noting the appearance of many of the other passengers in the elevator, she concluded that both the black-tie de rigueur for after-eight events and the hotel's gilded elegance set the hotel apart from all others.

She surveyed her appearance in the mirrored elevator doors. Her single-sleeved low-cut dress was burgundy silk and clung to the shape of her body all the way down to its above-the-knee hem. She had wanted to be beautiful tonight, a match for the distinguished man at her side. She snuck a peek at Nathan's clean-shaven jaw and regretted the absence of the short goatee that had tickled her skin.

Alyssa mentally shook her head and suppressed the jolt of heat in the vicinity of her garter. She wanted to take Nathan home and make her daytime fantasies into nighttime pleasures. For a moment, she averted her gaze and wondered if her desire for him exuded from her skin like a perfume. Did it rise from her skin and could the other occupants of the elevator catch its scent?

She caught his glance and smiled as his hand came into

contact with the center of her back. "That dress should come with a warning label," he whispered in her ear.

"Why is that?" she asked as they arrived at their destination. The gray-sheened door slid back, opening to a large reception area. Alyssa adjusted her grip on the small beaded purse, which matched her dress. She'd spent the morning in a salon getting her hair relaxed and styled. After a quick soak in the tub, she'd skillfully applied makeup to her face before painting her nails.

His eyes moved slowly over her neck, gazing at the soft wisps of hair at her nape. If possible the soft, warm illumination of the sunset made her more desirable. "You are hazardous to a man's health."

"You don't seem to be in such bad shape." She tilted her chin and her bronze-tinted lips curled into a smile that sent a surge of lust through him.

"I was referring to other men who might be foolish enough to approach you."

She didn't respond, but her eyes took on a gleam that might have been amusement or annoyance. Taking no chances that it would be the latter, Nathan placed a firm hand on her elbow and pulled her close as they followed the other guests toward the registration tables.

After securing two brochures imprinted with their individual bidding numbers and elegant gift bags, they strolled across the marble-floored, crystal-chandeliered lobby and down the stairs to enter the midsized ballroom. Because of its reputation and exclusivity, the event was attended by a well-heeled and moneyed set.

For the next thirty minutes, she sampled various gourmet canapés, sipped wine, previewed the variety of donated artworks, mingled, and chatted with people that came up to Nathan. While he was deeply involved talking with a fellow justice, Alyssa scanned the room and her eyes widened to see her friend Sophie wearing a stunning ruby dress proudly escorted by her glowering boss.

"Sorry about that."

"No need, I was enjoying the show."

"You are a lover of classical music as well?" Nathan looked over toward the live orchestra.

"I appreciate classical music but I was referring to the sight of Bernard's face when Sophie was approached by yet another man while her escort went to get her a drink."

Bernard had spent the most of his time neglecting his own date. Alyssa easily recognized Irene Leonards, the former basketball cheerleader turned morning news anchor.

"I'll go say hello and you can catch up with your stepsister." Alyssa patted him on the arm before stepping away.

She had to tap Bernard on his arm to get his attention.

"Alyssa, you look lovely." He gave her a quick grin before returning his attention to the other side of the room.

"Thank you, but don't you think pink bunny slippers would go better with my diamond tiara?"

"What?" Bernard's neck performed a 180-degree turn.

"You're staring at Sophie, Bernard."

"Alyssa . . . look at that. She's flirting with a boy her son's age."

"He's nothing of the sort. You're jealous."

"I'm just worried. I don't want her getting hurt by these young bucks who don't know how to treat a lady like Sophie."

"Well, did you tell her that?"

"In not so many words. I asked her if Curtis was comfortable with her seeing his gym coach."

"How did she respond?"

"Told me to mind my own business."

She shook her head and chuckled. "You can catch more flies with honey than you can with vinegar, Bernard."

He turned his glowering look in the direction of Sophie's date as he put his arm around her waist. "Bug spray works just as good."

Alyssa raised an eyebrow and was about to comment when the lights dimmed slightly and a chime rang. Sparing Bernard one more look of amusement, she rejoined Nathan. "Ready to find our seats?" he asked.

"Of course. Have you seen anything that you want to bid on?"

"I have all I need, right here and right now." Nathan looked at her with a calm and knowing eye. Alyssa would have had to be deaf, dumb, and blind to mistake his meaning.

The entered the adjoining room and took their places at the assigned seats.

"Thank you for coming. The proceeds of this event are to benefit the United Nations Children's Fund."

The auctioneers proceeded to introduce the staff, explained the rules of bidding, and then gave the order of the upcoming sales.

Their proximity to the stage made it possible for her to get a good view of the array of art pieces, both traditional and avant-garde, antiques, valuables, and jewelry that were brought out and bid upon.

Bernard purchased a bracelet, while Sabrina picked up a pair of silver candlesticks. Yet nothing struck Alyssa's interest until a picture of a dancer was unveiled. The artist had done the impossible by capturing all of the ways in which the woman danced: the emotion, the movement, the flow of music, and the grace.

"Graciella de la Ferie, painted by Italian-French portrait painter Giovanni Boldini, estimated value forty thousand. Bidding will begin at two thousand."

Alyssa raised her bid brochure.

"Twenty-five hundred." Someone else raised a card.

"Three thousand."

And so it went on. It was only when the bidding reached the five-thousand-dollar mark that Alyssa stilled the urge to lift her hand.

"Do I hear six thousand?"

"Six thousand."

Alyssa blinked as from the corner of her eyes she saw the

movement of Nathan's arms and the auctioneer pointing in his direction.

"What are you doing?"

"Bidding."

"Well, stop it," she hissed.

"I like the painting."

"No, you don't."

"Seven thousand."

"I want it for the dining room."

"Eight thousand," the auctioneer called out.

Nathan raised his hand again and pressed his lips together to keep the grin off his face. He had seen the way Alyssa had gazed at the painting. Having never seen her dance, he imagined that she would look very similar to the woman in the picture.

"No."

She couldn't stop him at ninety-five hundred.

"Do I see ten thousand?"

Alyssa snatched the brochure out of his hand and then sat on it.

"Give it back, Alyssa."

She crossed her legs at the ankle and sat up straight. "Try and take it."

"This is not the time or place for such foolishness."

"You can add male ego as well."

"One hundred thousand." A raspy voice from the back of the room shattered the otherwise silent live auction proceedings. Like in the movies, everyone turned toward the back. Yet it was only Alyssa who felt the hairs on the back of her neck stand on end. The two men she'd seen the day she visited Lily's grave were positioned near the door. A woman dressed in a nurse's uniform stood to the left of the wheelchair-bound man.

"One hundred one thousand?"

The auctioneer waited for a brief moment, then tapped the gavel. "Sold to patron forty-one for one hundred thousand. Ladies and gentlemen, we will have a brief recess."

As people began to leave their chairs, Alyssa remained seated. "Who is he, Nathan?"

"Are you okay?" He turned toward her and cradled her cold hands within his own.

"Yes, it's just that he seems familiar."

"Charles Worthington. He is the former mayor of Chicago. He was elected for two terms."

"Is he ill?"

"It's just been released to the public that he has terminal cancer."

Alyssa studied him, trying to figure out why the sight of the man, who had an emaciated shape, scared her. When he met her stare with a searching one of his own, a chill crept up and down her spine.

Disturbed, Alyssa turned around, eyes locking on the painting. Her desire to own it had disappeared, as well as her desire to remain in the room.

"You're shivering," Nathan observed.

"Just feeling a little jittery. Maybe too much excitement."

"Or disappointment?"

"No, I was more into the thrill of bidding than the satisfaction of winning."

They stood up, and as she collected her bag from the chair, Alyssa glanced toward the back of the room. Worthington was still looking in her direction. Concentrating on Nathan's handsome face, she fought the urge to look over her shoulder as they walked past the former mayor on their way out of the room. The man disturbed her more than she wanted Nathan to know. Relieved to be leaving, she slid into his waiting arms and let him lead her away.

"Sure you want to go?"

"Positive." She shook her head and mustered a smile. "Could we call it an early night?"

"Would you be up for a small nightcap at my place?"

"Maybe, but I think I'm going to need some extra sleep for tomorrow," she hinted.

"Why? We're just going to the family dinner." Nathan kissed her on the cheek after the door opened and they stepped into the empty elevator.

"Which will be at whose house?"

"Sabrina and Karl's," Nathan said as his finger paused from pressing the button for the lobby.

Comprehension dawned in his eyes as a look of understanding passed between them. Alyssa watched as Nathan sighed and looked skyward. The sound of their mingled laughter followed the elevator on the ride down.

While waiting for Nathan to open the door of the Mercedes, Alyssa fingered the spaghetti strap of the cotton asymmetrical dress she'd picked out of her closet that morning. They had talked about many things during the drive out to Chicago's exclusive northern suburb of Lake Forest. Alyssa welcomed the time to talk and share her thoughts and feelings about simple matters. It also helped to keep her mind off the coming afternoon engagement.

Although she had grown up knowing his mother and step-father, she was Lauren's friend, Alan's little sister, but now what was she?

She flipped down the mirror, checked her makeup. Not satisfied, Alyssa reached into her purse and reapplied her lipstick and then froze as her eyes came into contact with the neatly trimmed bushes decorating the front walkway.

"Alyssa?"

"Sorry." She took Nathan's proffered hand and stepped out of the car.

"Are you nervous?"

"A little," she admitted.

"There's no need. You've known my mother for years."

"I haven't seen your mom in years and this is different. I'm not greeting her as your friend or as Mrs. Knight's daughter.

I'll be . . ." Her voice trailed off as her mind struggled to find a word that fit her new role as it related to Nathan.

"You're meeting her as my lady." He reached over and trailed his fingertips over the side of her face.

"Am I?" She arched an eyebrow and her lips. "Funny, you know a girl likes to be asked."

Not bothering to forgo the temptation, Nathan bent down and kissed her.

"Now you've gone and messed up my lipstick."

"Actually I think it looks better." He flashed a crooked smile that was downright sexy.

"Hmm, you may be right. Caramel is your color." She flashed him a smile, thoroughly enjoying the sight of glossy brown on the bow of his upper lip.

"Minx. Come on. Let's go and brave the lion's den."

"That sounds positively horrible, Nathan."

Amusement lit his face. "At least we're together."

"Remember that and don't leave me."

He brought her hand to his lips and kissed it gently. "Never."

He took her hand and gave it a quick squeeze before opening the trunk and taking out a bag filled with wine and gourmet cheeses, crackers, and smoked salmon. They walked up the front stairs of the colonial brick building. Before Nathan could reach out and ring the doorbell, the iron and glass doors opened inward.

Alyssa found herself pulled into a tight bear hug and released. Ralph Phipps then turned to pat Nathan on the back. "Come on in. We're eating out back, so I hope you've got appetites because we've got barbecue and grilled everything."

"What's the occasion?" Nathan grinned at his stepfather.

"It's not every day you introduce a pretty young gal to the family."

Sabrina took Alyssa's arm and Rosemarie's, then turned them in the opposite direction. "We'll join you in a few minutes. I just finished decorating the exercise room and I've got to show it to someone."

"I thought you were working with a decorator on a children's room."

"That's next on the list after I get my closet renovated."

"Sabrina," Mrs. Hughes drawled.

"I don't have enough room for my shoes and Karl won't let me have real estate in his closet."

"You have more shoes than the law should allow, not to mention a twenty-square-foot walk-in closet."

"Oh, look," Sabrina whispered. "Muffin's asleep on the treadmill. Don't want to wake her. Poor thing, she just had her shots yesterday. I threw up at the sight of the needle."

"Muffin?" Alyssa questioned, then blinked twice as the object she'd thought was a small rug twitched and resolved itself into a puffy white canine.

"Ralph bought him for my birthday. He's a purebred Pomeranian. Muffin doesn't like getting shots and I don't like them either."

"Honey," Nathan's mother drawled. "You might want to get used to them. I hate to tell you this but the medication the doctor will give you during childbirth is in a much longer needle."

"Mama."

"What? I'm not going to sugarcoat the truth like your daddy. I went through labor twice. All he did was watch once."

"I'm going to a prepregnancy class next week." Sabrina began to twist the ring on her finger. "Karl told me it's a piece of cake."

"Karl is a man, sweetheart. They have little concept for the ritual of childbirth, but you'll learn." Rosemarie's tone was laden with meaning.

"Oh, Alyssa, I'm sorry. We didn't mean to ignore you."

"That's quite all right." She pinched herself to keep from bursting into laughter. "I was enjoying the conversation." And she'd discovered that she liked Nathan's stepsister.

Sabrina led them toward the sliding doors that faced the

grounds. Alyssa looked at the workout equipment guiltily. It had been a while since she'd seen the inside of a gym. "Well, here's the Stairmaster I bought Karl," Sabrina said.

"Didn't you give it to him as a Christmas present?" Nathan's mother commented.

"Yes, one of his vice presidents mentioned that it was a good stress reducer. But I really bought it for myself, Alyssa. I declare, after seeing Lauren at that awards banquet, I wanted to work on my backside. Why do you ask, Mama?"

"It looks brand-new and unless I need stronger contact lenses it still has the tag on it and is not plugged into the wall socket."

"He wanted to wait until I had the room together. Now that both the flat-screen TV and surround-sound stereo system have been installed, he can keep track of the market or I can watch a movie while working out."

They finished a short tour of the upstairs and future children's playroom, then went out a sliding glass door onto the elevated garden terrace. While Sabrina went inside to change clothes, Alyssa sat at the table with Nathan's mother.

"I already thanked Marva and your father after the service this morning."

"Mrs. Phipps, why did you thank my parents?"

"Please call me Rosemarie." She smiled. "Why did I thank your parents? Because I'm grateful, Alyssa," she said solemnly. "I haven't seen my son so happy since his father died."

"You think this is because of me?"

"I know so. After George's death, Nathan tried to be the man of the house. Then Ralph and I married. Instead of enjoying being a privileged teenager, he strove to be the perfect student. Even after graduating at the top of his class in undergraduate and law school, he had to be the sharpest attorney and then the best-qualified judge. Lauren, Sabrina, and I tried to get him to relax. We even went so far as to trick him into going to Disneyland. Nathan may have gotten on the plane but he didn't get on a single ride. That son of mine spent the whole week in the hotel suite on the phone or in front of the computer."

"Why am I not surprised?" Alyssa murmured.

"I could have strangled him."

"A good throttling every now and then wouldn't hurt the big fellow." Alyssa laughed.

"Anyhow, now he's laughing, going away for the weekend, playing with kids, and calling *me* on the phone." A bemused smile lit Mrs. Hughes' features.

"I can count on my two hands the number of times he's called me last year. Oh, Alyssa, you're good for him."

"I'm trying to be."

"Now that the two of you are together I feel less guilty about just leaving him and going down to the house in the Bahamas."

"Why would you feel guilty?"

"With his nomination to the federal bench, I thought he'd need Ralph and me for support, but now he has you."

"Nomination?" Alyssa repeated, careful not to sit forward.

Rosemarie shook her head. "He didn't tell you?"

"Probably slipped his mind," she speculated.

"Well, pay it no mind. I'm always the last to know things in this family. I wouldn't have found out if my husband hadn't said anything. That boy waited until the day before graduation before telling us he'd be the class valedictorian."

Alyssa turned to look over the terrace's railing just as Sabrina's husband lifted his beer bottle toward Nathan in a toast. "I wonder what that's all about," she began.

"Don't worry." Rosemarie narrowed her eyes. "I'll find out."

"When will you tell Alyssa that one day she'll be the wife of a Supreme Court justice?"

Nathan closed the lid on the gas grill and put the tongs down on the utensil tray. "After the wedding."

Karl laughed and patted him on the back. "Yes, sir. That's the right answer, sounds like you're a married man already."

"Well, Nathan," his stepfather said after both of the men raised their bottles in a mock toast. "I'm taking your mother down to the Bahamas for a few weeks, but I'm sure she'll be overjoyed to help plan an autumn wedding. She's almost finished making arrangements for Lauren."

Nathan shook his head and watched as Alyssa laughed at something his mother said. "I don't believe in long engagements."

His stepfather's brow wrinkled. "Well, how soon are you planning on wedding the girl?"

"Once Karl gets her ring size for me this afternoon and Mother joins me at the jeweler's on Monday, Alyssa will wear it to work on Friday. I don't want her to get settled into her condo when she has a home."

Karl raised a bushy eyebrow. "I like that. You don't mess around. That's good."

After eating more than her fair share of grilled shrimp, baby back ribs, and sliced fruit, Alyssa was more than ready to trade the patio table outside for the card table in the den. The stereo kicked out a mix of old school jams.

Was it love? she wondered, returning her attention to the cards in her hand. Utterly pleased with the family dinner, comfortable with their relationship, happy with Nathan, and impossibly content with life, she whispered in his ear, "Nathan?"

"Hmm?" He looked up from the playing cards in his hand.

"When you're a federal judge, can I still call you Your Honor?"

Blinking, he looked over at Alyssa as she arranged her cards according to number and suit. Leaning close, he whispered in her ear, "Sweetheart, you can call me whatever you like."

Two rounds later he said, "I take it that Mother told you about the nomination."

"She's worried about not being here to support you."

He looked over to the woman who gave him life and unconditional love, and mentally counted another blessing. "I'll be fine."

"I told her that."

Her confidence in his abilities swelled his heart. "Are you comfortable with my nomination?"

"Why shouldn't I be?"

"There will be publicity."

"As long as it's good, that's all that matters."

"Your support would mean a great deal to me." Nathan touched her cheek.

"You have it. I know you're doing this for the greater good but also because you're a good judge. You deserve it."

Nathan absentmindedly played a trump card. "How do you know so much?"

"I'm afraid that's top secret." She peeked over at Rosemarie just as her husband kissed her on the cheek. "Have to protect my sources."

Chapter 16

Yawning after a day full of seminars, Alyssa opened the door to her apartment and put her keys on the table. She slipped off her shoes as the corners of her mouth turned upward. Smiling was something that she'd been doing a lot of since she started seeing Nathan.

Yet, her grin slipped and all signs of sleepiness disappeared at the sight of the large wooden shipping crate sitting in the middle of the entranceway floor.

She approached the box and walked around it looking for some clue as to where it had come from and what it contained. All of the belongings she'd had shipped from Europe were present and accounted for. Not possessing any of the tools necessary to open it, she went into the kitchen and picked up the phone.

"Maintenance. How can I be of service?"

"Good evening, this is Alyssa Knight in 510. There is a crate in my apartment."

"Yes, ma'am. It got dropped off special delivery this morning. Took two of my guys to bring it up."

"Did you sign for it? Or did a letter come with it?"

"No, ma'am. It was just two delivery boys and a man in a nice suit," the super said. "Is something wrong? Is it broken?"

"I'm not sure. I haven't been able to open it."

"Would you like me to come up and get it open for you?"

"I'd appreciate it."

"Well, it'll be a few minutes. My wife just ran to the store and I can't leave the baby alone."

"I understand. There's no rush. Take your time." She hung up the phone and took one more look at the mysterious crate before going into her bedroom to change clothes.

It was a little before 6:00 when there was a knock on the door. She opened it and stood back, letting the large overall-wearing man into her apartment.

"This should only take a minute." The maintenance man took out a crowbar from a metal box.

"Can I get you something to drink?"

"I appreciate the hospitality, but I'm good. You just step back a little. Don't want you getting hurt."

He only needed to make four pulls on his crowbar before a pane came down. "All right, here you go."

If she'd been holding a glass, Alyssa would have dropped it. Nestled within layers of bubble wrapping was the painting of the Italian dancer.

"Are you okay?"

Alyssa snapped out of it. "I'm fine."

"It's a beautiful painting. Must have cost you a pretty penny."

"I didn't buy it."

"Oh, well. Gotta get back to the kids. Baby's teething."

Alyssa closed the door and went over to her desk. Turning on her notebook, she was instantly connected to the Internet and proceeded to search the local directory for last names starting with Worthington. The ex-mayor's address was surprisingly easy to find. Alyssa wrote down the information on a sheet of paper, gathered her purse, and turned to leave.

It took her half an hour to drive out to Chicago's northern suburbs and talk her way into the Worthingtons' estate. Once she made it through the security gate and past the large entrance doors, a uniformed maid showed her into what appeared to be the modern version of a Victorian drawing room. Having spent time at Harrison's family estate, the trappings of wealth were not new to her, but even after visiting some of the greatest estates in Britain, she preferred the simple cozy space of her apartment to the lofty and often drafty mansions.

"Tea and biscuits, ma'am?"

"Thank you."

"You're welcome."

Alyssa took a seat on a high-backed, Victorian-styled chair.

Three butter cookies, an antiques magazine, and a sip of tea later, the doorknob turned. She stood up with her purse in hand.

"Hello, Ms. Knight, my name's Chad Worthington."

"Mr. Worthington." She shook his extended hand gently.

"Sorry to have kept you waiting. Please have a seat."

She scrutinized everything about him from the open facial expression, to the designer suit and tense body language. He could have just walked out of a boardroom meeting. His clipped silver-blond hair and patrician features were startling enough, but it was his intense blue eyes that sent a shiver snaking down her spine.

"Are you all right?"

Alyssa realized she was staring and summoned up a sufficient blush. "I'm fine, Mr. Worthington."

"Please call me Chad." He extended his hand and she shook it weakly. Up close she noticed his slight tan and silver cuff links with monogrammed cuffs. The fine quality of the shirt's tailoring couldn't be missed.

"Chad." She searched his face. "Have we met before?"

His thin lips curled into a smile that didn't reach his eyes. "I'm afraid not. I'm sure I would remember a woman as beautiful as you, Ms. Knight."

He took a seat while the maid refilled the teapot and poured him a cup. "I hear that you are here to see my father?"

"Yes. I apologize for dropping in unannounced and at such a late hour, but I need to talk with Mr. Worthington."

"Of course." He paused to drink tea. "Are you with the cancer foundation?"

"No, I'm a program director at the Chicago Youth Center, but the reason for my visit is personal."

"If I may ask, could you tell me what about?"

"Yesterday I received a very expensive Italian oil painting of a dancer."

She saw the confusion on his face.

"I'm afraid I don't understand what this has to do with my father."

"Your father purchased it at a charity auction."

"I was unaware that he'd gone out."

"I'm here because I want to know why he had it delivered to my apartment and to tell him that I cannot accept such a gift."

"Well . . ." He paused. "As my father has grown more eccentric as of late I have no idea why he would do such things."

"May I see him?"

"I'm afraid that his health has taken a turn. His doctor has asked that he not have any visitors. My children have not seen their grandfather for over a month."

"If it is not too impolite, what is your father's illness?" she politely inquired, although she knew already.

"My father suffers from terminal cancer. It's in its late stages. Some days are better than others, I'm afraid."

"I would really like to speak with him."

"I'll talk to the physician."

"Thank you. In the meantime, could you arrange for the return of the painting? I feel uncomfortable accepting an expensive gift from someone I don't know."

"It's rare and quite refreshing to hear that. Most people wouldn't be so concerned." He stood so close to her that she could smell his aftershave, and for some reason it upset her stomach.

He reached out and touched her shoulder. "I apologize for

any upset this may have caused you. If it's okay I'd like to make it up to you."

"Really, it's no inconvenience."

"How about we continue this conversation over dinner? I can have the chef whip up something and we could discuss a business proposal I would like to make to you."

Alyssa took a step toward the door. Her subtle movement did not go unnoticed. "We aren't engaged in any dealings."

"Not yet. I know talent when I see it and as it happens I'm looking to fill a community public relations position in our New York office."

Alyssa blinked and smiled with her mouth but not her eyes. "Mr. Worthington, thank you for both of your offers, but I'm afraid that I have to decline. It's late and I really need to be going."

"Please wait, one moment longer." The man moved to stand in her path, blocking the door. "I need to apologize. I have a tendency to forge ahead. While this is successful for me in business, I'm not too sure it works with human resources matters."

"I commend your enthusiasm, but I'm happy where I am."

"Tomorrow is another day and you never know what can happen. How about I give you my card?" He pulled out a slim silver case and extended the card toward her. Alyssa noticed the gold wedding band on his left hand. "The position allows for a great amount of flexibility and a generous compensation package."

Since it was the only polite thing to do, she took the card from his manicured fingertips. "I'll give it some thought."

"Good, I'll have someone in the New York office give you a call."

He showed her to the door and stood in the entranceway watching as she got into the Jeep. Alyssa could see him in her rearview mirror. It wasn't until the iron gates had automatically closed behind her that she remembered Anna Limón's account of the man backstage the night of Lily's death. Her instructor described a man who was blond, tall, distinguished with European-style clothing: a man very similar to Chad Worthington. She pressed the gas and turned onto the street.

Chapter 17

"Welcome, stranger."

Alyssa opened the door and took the overnight bag Nathan held in his hand while inviting him in with one of her most seductive looks. That evening, with the thunderstorm outside, they would have a picnic.

The eating spot had been set with china in place of paper, chilled rosé wine in crystal goblets, French silverware, not heavy-duty plastic, and a patch blanket complete with Turkish cushions over hardwood flooring. Cotton napkins complemented the smell of incense and candles and the sound of jazz. To set the mood for romance, Alyssa covered the lamps with silk scarves.

It had taken her twenty minutes at the grocery store, a half hour digging in unpacked crates stowed in the kitchen pantry, five minutes rearranging the living room, twenty minutes decorating, an hour to cook, and thirty minutes to dress. All the time and energy and effort equaled a man's ultimate fantasy.

Giving thanks to Harrison's mother for encouraging her to take intensive half-day cooking classes, she had prepared a variety of dishes from three countries. A Middle Eastern appetizer of vegetable hummus with sun-dried tomatoes atop fresh pita bread. The salad she prepared with black olives along with baked lamb, which was so tender it melted in her mouth. Last but not least, she'd prepared a spicy Indian curry. For dessert, Alyssa whipped up chocolate and banana crêpes.

They ate leisurely, sometimes feeding one another, sometimes talking, sometimes letting the beauty of the music speak for the both of them. At the end of the meal, Nathan was uncorking the second bottle of wine and she was unbuttoning the third button of her blouse.

"What is the occasion?"

"Couldn't it just be spontaneous?" She raised her glass while lowering her eyes. She took a small sip of the cool fruity scent that flooded her taste buds and senses.

"Dinner out, yes, different woman, yes. But this"—he swept his hand to encompass the room—"has meaning."

"Maybe there is something more to this." She stretched until her toes touched the cuff of his pants.

"That you are going to share or—"

She shook her head, pushing back her hair. "Or what?"

He had never seen her more beautiful or more frustrating. Not for the second, third, or fourth time did he wonder how he could not have fallen for Alyssa. The curve of her neck, the bow of her lips, the sparkle that never left her eyes. The truth of his heart was that he loved her, the woman who took his breath away when she walked into the room, the woman who pulled him from the lonely world of legal justice, the woman who loved him but had yet to admit it.

Like a snake Nathan struck out and grabbed her foot. Alyssa gasped but managed not to spill her drink. "Don't you dare!"

Nathan suppressed a chuckle at the tempting sight of her cute pink toenails, smooth soles, and soft skin. He ran a finger down her instep and held tight she tried to pull away.

Alyssa shouted in laughter. "Let me go and I'll tell you."

"You wouldn't lie to a judge, would you? Especially one who's got you by the toes." He wiggled a finger dangerously close to her foot.

"No, I wouldn't," Alyssa responded quickly. She watched as a slow smile curved his lips, looking both sexy and dangerously handsome as he sat there, one arm stretched across the sofa cushions and the other toying with the empty wine bottle. She'd planned everything inclusive of the after-dinner activities, even going so far as to tuck a condom underneath the book on the sofa's end table.

He let her foot go and watched as it disappeared underneath her skirt. "Tell me."

"Just a moment." She put her drink aside, along with the empty bottle of wine and Nathan's glass. He raised an eyebrow and she drew her feet under her, and, on her knees, moved in closer.

"Going back on your word?"

"No, Your Honor." A thrill coursed through her body. Alyssa moved closer, watching his mouth as his tongue slipped out to catch a droplet of wine. "I promised to tell you but I didn't promise *when* I would tell you."

"I see."

"Oh, yes," she murmured, inching closer so that the cotton fabric of her skirt covered his pants. Alyssa reached out and pressed his legs together so that she could place her knees on either side and straddle him, positioning herself directly over the hardening mound in the crotch of his trousers. She ran her hands over his shoulders, and then toyed with his collar before moving to release all the buttons on his shirt.

"Are you trying to distract me, Alyssa Knight?"

She continued to unbutton his shirt as the music flowed slow and intimate. "Is it working?"

"You know it is."

"Then I am so very happy, but that wasn't my intention." She pushed off his shirt and admired his chest in the warm glow of the candlelight.

"What was your intention?" He reached out and took hold of her waist, setting her upon his lap.

Lowering herself onto the cushion of his thighs, Alyssa traced the corners of his lips with her tongue before slipping it into the crease where his tongue came out to greet hers. After several moments she pulled back and ran her hands all over his chest, lightly scratching him with her fingernails to drive home her point. "You can't tell?"

"Why don't you tell me?" His hands moved up her legs, bunching her skirt, until they came to a stop at her lace panties. He brushed his fingers over a wisp of fabric and groaned.

She was wet. He was erect.

Alyssa leaned back just a little and unbuttoned her last remaining buttons. The lightweight blouse fell from her shoulders and she tossed it to the side with a flick of her wrist. Without a bra, she sat half nude apart from two glimmering pearls in her ears.

"I wanted to tell you about a job offer." In truth there were two; she had not forgotten Harrison's offer and the fact that Worthington Enterprises, a company run by Chad Worthington, had been behind the takeover bid made her suspect that the man wanted her out of town.

"When?" Nathan's gaze shifted from her lips to the dusky brown of her nipples, which were the same shade. His fingertips ran all over her body, barely touching the skin and making her shiver.

"Two days ago." Needing to regain her concentration, she took his hand and held it in her own. The plan had been to seduce, but as her body responded to his touch, she wondered who was the seducer and who would be seduced.

"Harrison Brandell?" His jaw tensed.

Their eyes met and she saw the flare of hunger and anger. She returned her gaze to his hands, admiring his long fingers and the contrast of their skin, the rich reddish brown of his fingers intertwined with the deep yellow of her own.

Raising his finger to her lips, she licked the tip gently, then put it in her mouth and sucked. His dark eyes closed and his groan of pleasure warmed her a thousand times hotter than the heat of the sun. After she had administered similar treatment to all of his fingers, she drew back and placed a slow kiss on the palm of his hand. "No. An American firm. The position would be more corporate community relations."

"Tempted?" Nathan skimmed his lips from her neck to her breast to suckle her nipple gently, his eyes still holding hers, and then he gripped it lightly between his teeth, teasing the chestnut tip with a series of butterfly-light flutters of his tongue.

Eyes half closed in pleasure, Alyssa shifted on his lap, bringing her trembling limbs within closer contact of his sex. Her head swirled from the sweet and woody scent of his skin, the wine, the food, the feel of Nathan's heated breath upon her skin. "Oh, yes," she murmured. "But I would have to leave—"

"The youth center?"

"No," she panted. "Chicago. The position is in New York."

His fingers pushed aside her panties and found the center of her sex, rubbing against her curls and moving farther downward to touch her center and feel its hot moisture. He licked her nipple and blew gently. "Would you be adequately compensated?"

"I imagine it would be a lucrative package," she mused, letting out a throaty purr.

His eyes followed her arms as she leaned away only to reposition herself with a foil packet in her hands. He watched her fingers as she opened it. Nathan wanted to question her further, but lost all of his concentration as her hand unzipped his pants and administered an intimate and daring caress. He gritted his teeth as she skillfully drew out the agony of placing the condom on his member and rolling it down over the sensitive skin.

"It doesn't matter," she whispered low into his ear.

His fingers withdrew from her, deliberately rubbing against the most sensitive place of her womanhood with his thumb. "Damn you. It does."

"No," she moaned and arched forward, her body searching for the continuation of the delicious pleasure his touch had wrought. Of all wonders between heaven and earth, she wanted this man. The smiles, the anger, the gentle warmth of his laughter, the heat of his frowns. Her heart ached and her body yearned for the love of him.

"I'm home, Nathan," she whispered in his ear while quivering with desire. She positioned his hardness and closed her eyes, savoring the feel of him gently rubbing her inner folds, anticipating what would come next, yet not wanting the waiting to end. "And I intend to stay."

Triumphant, he tightened his grip on her waist and pushed his hips upward, pulling her down, burying his hardness inch by inch into the wet, heated flesh. He moved his arms to wrap around her, bringing her close. The feel of her slick skin upon his. Her breath on his skin. Her moist tightness wrapped around him. He caught her moan within his mouth and quickened the tempo.

Reaching the pinnacle and taking control, she stopped at the tip and caught her breath. Then with excruciating slowness she moved downward, to wrap her legs around his torso, kissing, biting, sucking, breathing, loving.

She dug her nails into his shoulders and released a guttural moan. The sharp score of her nails coupled with the sound of her release only pushed Nathan to thrust harder and faster, and then he too gave a soft groan and held her closer to him, her breasts pressed to his chest, his lips on her neck, his body softening slowly.

Much later after the candles were gutted and the music had ceased to play, Nathan touched his lips to her neck and gently nipped the skin to gain her attention. "Who made the offer?"

Alyssa breathed a sigh as her eyes fluttered open. She loved him. That fact didn't make the world brighter, solve all of her problems, or erase her irritation at Nathan's bossiness. But it was a certainty; she settled her cheek on top of his shoulder and eyed the back of the couch. He would complicate her life. He would fill it up and nothing could ever be the same.

"It's a long story." She looked up. His eyes were clear and focused.

"I've got all night and I'd like nothing better than to hold you."

Before answering his question, she filled him in on the painting, the meeting with Worthington's son, her suspicions, her discoveries, and the report.

The information she'd gathered about Chad Worthington read like a typical chief executive officer's bio. He had attended a top prep school, received an Ivy League education. Star pitcher on the baseball team. Graduated magna cum laude, then went to Harvard Business School in Boston. After that he joined his father's company just before his father was elected mayor of Chicago. Chad took over as CEO, married a New York socialite, and had three kids. Everything she'd managed to dig up painted a picture of the successful businessman with the perfect family.

"According to Uncle Edward he didn't so much as have a parking ticket. But I know that he's involved in Lily's death, his company funded my fellowship to Oxford, is a primary contributor to my former instructor's dance troupe, and renovated the former warehouse that houses Andrés's studio."

"Why didn't you tell me?"

She shrugged. "You were busy, Nathan."

"Never too busy for you." He held her face. "Remember that always. I need to know these things."

"And I need to be able to act independently without giving you a checklist of all my movements."

"What else haven't you told me?" He gently guided her chin upward so he could see her face.

"According to a criminal psychologist, vehicular homicide is in most cases an emotional act. What if Lily was the object of Chad Worthington's obsession?"

Nathan processed her statement for a moment. "Were they lovers?"

"No, Lily would have told me," Alyssa said firmly. "I would have known."

"Secrets among friends are not unknown." Nathan tightened his arms around her as his own words hit home. "If they were having an affair and the wife found out, wouldn't it be more likely that she hit Lily?"

"I thought about that, but it was Chad Worthington backstage that night, not his wife. I looked through the newspaper pictures taken at the performance and only Mayor Worthington, his wife, and his son were in attendance."

Nathan massaged her shoulders and pulled her toward him. "All of this is speculation, angel. It's not enough to build a case."

"I tried to contact Andrés but he's not returning my calls. It's imperative that I find out what he argued with Lily about that night."

Nathan grunted at the hardness of the floor underneath the carpet.

"Am I too heavy?" Alyssa questioned, wiggling slightly as he rested inside her.

"If I said yes, what would you do?"

"Beat you senseless." She giggled.

"Then it's a good thing that the answer is no. What do you plan to do next?"

Alyssa pulled her scattered wits about her and thought for a minute. "What I should have done long ago: talk to Andrés. He's been avoiding me."

"Going to hunt him down?"

She snuggled closer to him and twirled a finger around the sparse patch of hair on his naked chest. "I'm going to join one of his dance classes while it's in session. That way he'll have to talk to me."

"Are you ready for that?" He squeezed her gently, knowing why she danced alone.

Alyssa sighed. If she were going to make peace with the past, she needed to make peace with herself as well. So much of her childhood had been wrapped up in dance; she still spent her adulthood enjoying the activity. "Yes, I get tiny knots in my stomach at the notion, but it's past time for me to get over that fear."

"You are an amazing woman, Alyssa Knight."

She shifted slightly in his lap, feeling a stirring of his sex within her. His fingers clamped on her thighs and moved slowly up to their apex. The movement caused her to draw a deep breath, tightening, and drawing her forward to his chest. She wrapped her arms around his shoulders and whispered in his ear, "I made my bed for you."

He picked her up and carried her toward the bedroom. "And so we shall lie upon it."

Although it was unplanned on her part, fate had stepped into her life yet again. When Alyssa emerged from the women's changing room with the class, it was to discover that she would be joining the Spanish dance class. Her eyes locked with Andrés's as he stood at the front of the room.

She watched as he faltered in his stretching routine. Without missing a step, Alyssa raised her arms as twin sets of light brown eyes stared into each other. One set in determination and the other in surprise.

The music changed, and the women took their places. She moved into an empty space near the window. It took her some time just watching to observe their movements, the repetition, and the cycles. But when she could mimic their gestures, as her body learned the moves, Alyssa gave herself back to the dance, back to the tempo, back to the beat. Her feet slid over the cold wooden floor, her arms moved in swift sharp movements. She watched Andrés lead, the dancers twirl, as the colors and twilight of sunset spilled through the stained glass window, bathing the room in blue. The music and dancers rose and fell like the whitecapped waves of the Aegean Sea. It was the most beautiful thing she'd ever seen.

It was only after the session, when the other dancers had left and the room was quiet, that the heady joy of dancing receded and the reality of her purpose for coming to the studio hit.

"The night of Lily's accident you had an argument."

Alyssa took a step away from the window. Andrés stood near the door, using the large space of the room as a wall between them, just as she'd used the dance class earlier.

"What about it?"

"Why were you arguing?"

He ran his long fingers through his hair and turned to look in the mirror. "I'd rather not talk about this."

Alyssa made sure to keep her hands by her sides as she took steps forward. She faced the mirror as well, making sure to maintain eye contact. "I'd rather not have blanks in my memory. What did you argue about?"

"Whatever it was, it's none of your business."

Although hurt by Andrés's frank answer, she continued to push. "Why are you avoiding my questions? She was running away and I followed her. Did you hurt her?"

"Yes, I mean, no. We were always hot-tempered." He shrugged. "There were many times we fought as siblings do, but we did not fight that night."

"If not you, then did she argue with Chad Worthington?" Her eyes narrowed as the name from her lips produced a visible start from Andrés.

He shook his head. "I will not discuss this, Alyssa."

"Then tell me why Worthington Enterprises, a multinational corporation, which was founded by the Worthington family and presided over by Chad Worthington at the time of Lily's accident, happened to fund my graduate fellowship to Oxford, and whose subsidiary happened to have given you this building and the land."

She paused, letting the information sink in to the silence of the room. "It is that same corporation whose former CEO and Chicago mayor was running for reelection at the time of the accident. Three days ago, Charles Worthington just happened to bid on a hundred-thousand-dollar painting of a dancer and have it delivered to my apartment. Connect the dots, Andrés, and they all lead back to that night and Chad Worthington.

What was his relationship with Lily? Was he driving the car that ran her down or was it his wife behind the wheel?"

"Leave now, Alyssa."

The lines of his face hardened and a sudden thought occurred to her. "Tell me, are you being blackmailed or bribed?"

Andrés turned away from her and stormed toward the back of the studio. "I said leave. This conversation is over."

"But my questions are not," she called out towards his back. "If you won't talk to me, maybe Chad Worthington or his wife will. I'm getting my life back and I won't stop until I uncover what happened that night. And I'll do whatever it takes with or without your help."

Chapter 18

"Where was she going at this time of day? And why the hell was she driving in the first place? Alyssa always takes the train." Nathan demanded answers as Bernard followed him into the hospital waiting room.

"Today she didn't take the train. Alyssa asked to leave a few hours early today. Said she got a call before leaving home this morning."

Something in Nathan's face made Bernard pause.

"Go on."

"She mentioned that the call was from an ex-detective who worked on Lily's case."

"She told you about it?"

"Sophie told me by accident."

Nathan picked up on the man's confusion. "What else?"

"Our assistant called the number in Alyssa's calendar to let them know that she wouldn't be there. She talked to the man's daughter and she told her that it was impossible for Alyssa to have had an appointment with her father."

Something cold and metal slithered down Nathan, and it took him a moment to recognize the sensation of fear. "Why?"

"The man died of a heart attack three years ago."

Everything hurt. Slowly Alyssa's senses returned to her . . . there was bright light behind her closed eyes, and the smell of disinfectant stung her nose. She could hear people talking in low voices somewhere close by, but it was difficult to tell who was speaking and what it was they were saying. She kept her eyes shut and focused on trying to manage the pounding in her head and to remember what had happened. The school bus . . . her pulse jumped at the panic of not being able to stop, the sight of the telephone pole.

"Alyssa."

She heard the soft voice along with a gentle squeezing of her right hand, opened her eyes slowly, and blinked at the beam of bright light that flared in her right eye.

"Just keep them open for a second more and I'll be finished, Ms. Knight."

"Where am I?" she whispered as soon as the doctor switched off the penlight.

"St. Luke's Hospital."

She tried to sit upright, only to come up against the barrier of a hand on her shoulder.

"Try to lie still."

"Listen to the doctor, Alyssa. Everything's going to be okay."

She turned her head toward Nathan and mustered a tired smile.

"Judge Hughes, your fiancée is not only smart but a very lucky woman."

Alyssa's brow creased in surprise. Her eyes sought and locked with Nathan's.

"Yes, indeed. The ambulance driver mentioned that if she hadn't steered into the barrier, she would have hit the back of a school bus, which could have ruptured the fuel tank and made it explode."

"The kids are all right?" Alyssa questioned.

"Everyone's fine, thanks to your quick thinking. Now you just relax. I just want to have them take you down for X-rays and a CAT scan just to make sure everything's working okay."

"Thank you for taking such good care of her." Nathan shook the doctor's hand.

"That's my job. I'll see you folks later."

As soon as the door closed, Alyssa cleared her throat. "I may have lost my memories once before but I'm sure I could never forget your marriage proposal."

"Look down at your hand."

"What?" Alyssa raised her left hand and stared at her ring finger to find a round solitaire diamond cradled in platinum.

"The doctor was suspicious at first, but I mentioned that I had to get the ring resized. Do you like it?"

"It's gorgeous. How on earth did you know my ring size?" Then she remembered that at the Hughes family barbecue, Sabrina's husband had inquired about the size of her ring finger. "Bernard's niece?"

"She is graduating from high school in two months but will be getting a trip to Paris from her uncle instead of a remembrance ring."

"Were you afraid I might not say yes?" she teased.

"I would have liked to propose after a wonderful meal at a nice French restaurant, but it was the only way they'd let me come in to see you." He tenderly ran a finger over her cheek. The need to touch her had gnawed at him like an addiction. To make sure that his eyes weren't deceiving him, that she was still alive. After being allowed into her room, the most wonderful thing in the world had been watching the rise and fall of her chest.

"So you didn't put the ring on while I was unconscious because you thought I would turn you down?"

"I'm going to plead the Fifth on that one." He grinned. "I'm not willing to take any chances where you're concerned. Now tell me, how are you feeling?" Nathan leaned in close over the bed and gently touched her cheek.

"Like I've been hit by a ton of bricks," she groaned, shifting her weight on the bed.

"Hey, didn't the doctor tell you not to move?"

"I'm fine, Nathan."

"If that were the truth, then you wouldn't be in a hospital bed, now, would you?"

"I hate it when you're right." She managed a weak smile.

"And I love it when you smile, sweetheart." He took her hand gently within his own. "I could have lost you."

"I wouldn't have made it that easy for you." She yawned.

"Tired?"

Looking around at the white walls and the sterile hospital room, she shivered. "I want to get out of here soon. Nathan, take me home."

"As soon as I can. I phoned your parents in New York."

Alyssa winced and then instantly regretted it. "Oh, no. Pop doesn't need to have any kind of stress. I wish you hadn't done that."

"Your parents have a right to know."

"Are they flying back?"

"They were ready to jump on the first flight to O'Hare but it's impossible. Most of the airports on the East Coast have been shut down due to a freak storm. But I have a feeling your uncle will be here soon."

Alyssa groaned, imagining that Uncle Ed would not only harangue the doctors and nurses but also make her stay at the hospital overnight, then under close watch at his house.

"Don't worry. I've got everything under control." Her thoughts read as easy as a Law 101 book. Nathan winked as Alyssa gave him a curious look. "I called in backup."

They both turned their heads as the door swung open. A young man in a white doctor's coat entered the room. "Ms. Knight, I'm Dr. Reed. I'll be taking you down for your scans."

Nathan stood but still did not release her hand. "How long will it take?"

"I'll have her back in less than an hour, sir."

"Hey." Alyssa squeezed his hand to get his attention. "I'll be fine, don't worry." An odd expression crossed his face and for a moment Alyssa thought she saw fear in his eyes.

"I'll be right here when you get back."

Nathan followed Alyssa's gurney as far as the elevator and when the physician pressed the up button, he pressed the down. Something wasn't right, hadn't been right since the night she'd had a nightmare about Lily's accident and he'd learned about her investigation. He was one for following his instincts and they led him back to his car. Nathan opened his briefcase and pulled out the leather-bound address book. Turning to the last page and the phone number that appeared without a name, he punched in the ten digits and waited for the ring.

Sara Hughes Knight didn't have to look left or right after exiting the hospital elevator; the deep commanding voice issuing orders was as familiar and easy to find as a light in the dark.

"Oh, Ed," she murmured, shaking her head disapprovingly. He was her best friend, her first and only lover, her heart and soul.

And he's your legally separated husband whom you will love for the rest of your natural born life, a small voice in the back of her mind whispered.

"My niece is somewhere on this floor and I'm going to find her."

"Sir, the only thing I can tell you is that we're running tests, but according to what's in her charts she'll be fine. If you'd like to take a seat in the waiting area her attending physician will be here soon and can give you an update as to Ms. Knight's condition."

"I didn't ask to see the doctor; I asked to see my girl."

"Oh, hush, Edward," Sara drawled once she stopped three feet away from him. Her heart fluttered slightly and her cheeks warmed from the sight of his black cap and its familiar white kangaroo.

For a moment, she let clandestine thoughts of satin sheets

and strawberries frolic in her imagination. Over a decade ago, she'd given him the black Kangol 504 as a birthday present. He'd called it lucky and she'd called it sexy. That cap had been the only thing he'd worn to bed that night. "I could hear you a mile away."

"Sara, love, what are you doing here?"

Before she could open her mouth, he swept her into his arms and moved them both to a more private alcove adjacent to the nurses' station. His eyes scrutinized her from head to toe.

"Are the girls okay? Why didn't you call me? Are you all right?"

The familiar feel of his arms made her want to weep or tell a lie just to stay as they were a little longer. Instead she pulled back but allowed him to keep possession of her hands.

"The girls are in school and I'm fine."

She watched as expressions filtered across his face, beginning with fear and moving rapidly to relief to settle upon puzzlement. How she still loved to gaze at the imperfect symmetry of his full chestnut-brown features. The artist in her had fallen in love with him because of them. It seemed that time with its lines and worries had only added more beauty to the man.

"I'm here for Nathan."

"That coldhearted pigheaded nephew of yours should have called me. Having to find out that Alyssa was in the hospital from my brother who's stuck hundreds of miles away is too much."

"No, he shouldn't have called you," she retorted softly. "You have no business here."

"She's my niece."

"She's Nathan's fiancée," Sara retorted.

He tore off his hat and then roughly pulled it back over his bald scalp. "Over my bullet-ridden body."

Sara put her hands on her generous hips. "What, we Hugheses aren't good enough for you? Didn't seem to be a problem when you rushed me down the aisle."

"Well, it apparently became a problem, because you left me quick enough."

"I'm not here to talk about the past," she asserted as her fingers gripped the leather strap of her purse like a lifeline. "Just trying to keep you from making a mess of things."

"You opened the door to the past and this time we're both going to step through it."

"This is neither the time nor the place."

"I think it is."

"You're being stubborn, Edward."

"Well, I guess you Hugheses don't have a monopoly on that trait. I'm part-time with the force, fully vested in my pension, got the house together, a nice IRA, and a nest egg. I'm tired of waiting for you to come to your senses, Sara."

She narrowed her eyes. "Come to my senses?"

He stood straight. "You want me to mind my business? Well, you're my business and you're coming home with me."

"I most certainly am not."

"I'm taking someone home with me. It's either you or my niece. You choose."

She chewed on her lips for a few breaths. "This doesn't mean a thing. I left you because I couldn't live with you, and that won't change."

Edward lowered his gaze to hide the gleam of triumph. "No, you moved to the Dominican Republic because of your crazy notion that I had to have kids. I could have lived my whole life without having crumb snatchers of my own as long as I had you. But you disappeared and then all I had left to keep me going was my job."

"You're wrong." Her voice shook with false denial. She'd purposely spent the past years in the company of others when she was around Edward. Just to avoid having conversations like the one they were having. Just to keep the feelings of affection at bay.

That man she'd married was as stubborn as a mule. She

knew that if he had his way, Alyssa wouldn't see the light of day or her nephew for a long time.

Only for Nathan would she do this. Even as a boy her nephew had never asked anything of her except love. Her niece and nephew were the only pieces of her older brother she had left. Family photographs and vacation movies could never take the place of blood and heritage. Lauren looked like her father, but Nathan had her older brother's heart. Her nephew's request in the matter of dealing with her husband seemed a small thing. If only she hadn't forgotten how his presence made her knees go weak.

"I could no longer stomach the idea that one night there would be a knock on the door and you wouldn't ever come home," she said, telling a partial truth.

"If I had really believed you would have come back to me if I quit the force, then I would have left the day I came home and found you gone."

"I couldn't handle being a cop's wife," Sara lied, making a mental note to heed the altar call the following Sunday and spend some extra time asking the Lord for forgiveness. She was strong enough to love with the knowledge that he risked his life to protect others. She'd meant every word of her marriage vows.

"You may have packed a bag and snuck out like some two-bit streetwalker on North and Sheffield Avenues, but you, Sara Knight, have never lied to me." Edward gave her a hard look. "Probably because you're the worst liar in the world. When we first met you told me you were a disaster in the kitchen. And even if I hadn't been a rookie on the force, I would have known you weren't telling the truth. Woman, I was there the afternoon that your red velvet cake started a fight in the church and Sister Anne got caught trying to sneak your pound cake out the back door."

She lifted her chin and sniffed. "I'm not going to stand here and be insulted."

He reached out and took her arm, holding her firmly yet gently in place. "I've got words to say to you. I've been saving them since I read that letter you left on top of the coffeemaker. I was raised to respect a person's decision and to respect a woman's mind. That and the fact that you never served divorce papers on me were the only reasons I haven't dragged you back home. I loved you before I put a ring on your finger, I was in love with you when you ran off, and I will love you when they put me in the grave. I didn't care about you not being able to have any children."

"You're lying." She choked. The tears wanted to come but she swallowed them back. "I heard you crying, Edward. I saw the tears in your eyes. I was awake when the doctor told you."

"I cried because I thought I might have lost you. I was scared that I would lose you. I'd never seen so much blood. I cried because the doctor told me how tore up inside you were and I hurt because it was my fault. You went through all that to have my baby."

"I wanted a child of my own." Her face hurt from the effort to hold back tears at the memory of the doctor's declaration that she would never be able to carry a child to term.

"I know you did, sweetheart." His voice was rough with emotion as he took her into his arms and squeezed.

"You don't know what that last miscarriage did to me. I felt like such a failure, and having to walk by the closed door of the empty room that you'd spent so much time and effort making into a nursery day by day killed a part of my soul."

"No, I won't ever know how you felt. I only know that I wanted to help, to talk, and you wouldn't. For a year, the space in the middle of our bed was as wide as the Mississippi and just as quiet. But I knew you were there on the other side and I could live with that. Then you left and tore out my heart."

"How you must have hated me," she whispered.

"No." He pulled her close. "I forgave you a long time ago and I waited for you to heal. But I'm not going to wait any longer. You're my wife and a mother; Callie and Tasha need a father, rooms of their own, and some grass."

He let her go and motioned toward the hovering nurses. "As I said before, I ain't leaving here alone. After the doctor comes out, you can either press the down button on the elevator or follow me down the hall as I search for Alyssa."

Sara had spent many a night awake in her new bed. Best on the market, the salesperson had bragged, yet she couldn't sleep. She wanted to sleep on the mattresses she'd left. The ones that were worn in just right. She'd come back to Chicago with two girls and gotten a new place, furniture, and life but all she wanted was the old.

Later when the physician had reassured them both of Alyssa's condition and Nathan had in no uncertain terms told Edward that he would be taking her back to his house to recuperate, Sara pressed the down button. She was going home.

"What are you doing?"

"Running a bath." Nathan watched as she glanced toward the doorway from her perch on the side of the marble tub.

"Damn it, Alyssa," he cursed. Anger born of fear made him pick her up and carry her back into the bedroom.

"Put me down," Alyssa ordered.

"Gladly." Nathan gently placed her in the middle of the bed and stopped her from rising. "You shouldn't be up."

"I'm not bedridden, Nathan, just bruised."

"I'll run you a bath, Alyssa." The expression on his face was impassive.

She opened her mouth to protest, but his next question stopped her cold.

"Is it so hard to let me care for you?"

Embarrassed by her own behavior, Alyssa shook her head, covering her face. "Yes," she admitted honestly. "I feel like an invalid."

"But what you are is a treasure." Nathan sat down beside her on the bed and reached out to gently take her into his arms. "Let me finish running your bath and then fix you a bite to eat, okay?"

She nodded as he placed a kiss on her brow. "Just stay here for a minute."

"Thank you, Nathan."

After Alyssa assured him for the fifth time that she had no intention of surviving a car accident only to fall asleep and drown in a bathtub, Nathan excused himself and went downstairs to the den. It had been one hell of a day and it wasn't over yet. He still had to call Damian.

He prepared to flip on the light when a voice broke the silence of the darkness. "Looks like your hunch paid off."

Nathan's head jerked up and his gaze locked with the man sitting comfortably in his leather armchair. Damian Béchard. Tall, athletic, and intelligent, the Canadian-born security expert had come to Chicago for an education and then disappeared into the U.S. military only to leave three years later due to family reasons. In helping Damian secure his rightful share of his father's estate, Nathan had gotten a crash course in the bedroom politics and infighting of one of Montréal's oldest families. "Where did you come from?"

"Back sliding door. You should get a better alarm. It's not wired to the system and a child could have picked the lock."

"Any news?"

"Sit down and have a drink first." He nodded toward the two glasses of clear liquid and a bottle of Nathan's vintage scotch on the coffee table.

Too wound up to sit, Nathan ran a hand over his head, rubbing his neck before taking a seat on the sofa and picking up the drink. The scotch was a devil on his tongue. Poured by the man he could call brother, it released a day's worth of tension in one sip. As he swallowed the strong liquor, enjoying the slow burn down his throat to his stomach, his attention returned to the present situation. Damian's presence in his home that evening confirmed what he'd suspected: Alyssa was in danger.

"Tell me."

"After I got your call, I sent a man down to the police impound. He took the brake pumps and lines to the lab. According to the preliminary report, your woman was meant to die today."

"Why didn't the police find anything? They've seemed pretty convinced that it was an accident."

"Probably busy solving homicides. My people found microscopic tears in the line. The police didn't know where and how to look. The job was done by a professional who knew the standard operating procedures."

"You know what's next?"

Damian nodded. "I'll assign one of my best men to watch her."

"Not good enough." Nathan shook his head. "You already told me the accident was done by a professional, and if I'm right, someone very powerful is involved with this."

"What are you saying, Nate?"

"I want her protected by someone who won't hesitate to pull the trigger. I also want you to find evidence against the man trying to kill her."

"Just so that we don't have any conflicts of interest, who do you suspect is behind the hit?"

"Chad Worthington."

A raised eyebrow was the first show of emotion Nathan had seen Damian display that evening. "Former Chicago mayor's son, upstanding corporate leader, and heir to the Worthington millions? She should be more careful of the enemies she picks."

Nathan brushed the comment aside with an irritated flick of his wrist. "Alyssa is determined to find the person responsible for the hit-and-run death of her best friend eight years ago. Worthington is on the short list of suspects."

"Men like him try to keep their hands clean." Damian stood up and Nathan followed suit.

"One more thing. Alyssa isn't to know about any of this."

Damian shrugged and adjusted the collar of his leather coat, then pulled something out of his billfold. "Whatever you say. Take this."

Nathan eyed the unusual business card. No address, no name, only a phone number.

"Be sure to call this number in the morning. Tell him I gave it to you and he'll eliminate your security problems."

With that Nathan saw his friend upstairs and out the sliding back door and went into the kitchen. Mentally, he made a note to call the number the next morning.

Chapter 19

Alyssa woke to the sound of singing. *Gospel,* she thought, her brow wrinkling as the fog of sleep refused to dissipate from her mind. She inhaled and the scent of Nathan's cologne brought with it some idea of where she was, but only when she opened her eyes and saw stray beams of sunlight through the heavy curtains did she realize that she had no idea about how much time had passed since . . . She moved to sit up, only to gasp as pain flared through her muscles. Then she remembered the accident, the hospital, the shadow of waking in Nathan's arms as he carried her up the stairs, and taking a bath.

"Sleeping Beauty has risen." Alyssa turned her head toward the masculine voice. She noticed Nathan sitting in the bedroom's only chair, back straight, arms resting on the side.

"Good morning." Her voice was husky.

"Good afternoon." He smiled and leaned forward to brush his fingers across her cheek.

Alyssa welcomed his touch and turned her unbruised cheek into his hand. His presence, the sound of his voice made everything more real. "Is it really afternoon?"

"Oh, yes."

"How long have you been watching me sleep?"

"Not long."

Alyssa glanced over to the side of the bed and noticed that the covers remained unwrinkled.

"Nathan, please tell me that you didn't spend the night in that chair."

"All right."

"All right what?"

"I won't tell you."

"Why didn't you sleep in the bed, or better yet, another bedroom?"

"You flinched when I touched you last night, Alyssa. I can't sleep in the same bed with you without holding you, and the thought of my touch making you hurt is more painful than sleeping in this chair."

"You look tired." She pushed herself up, gritting her teeth to keep in the groan of pain. It was only the brush of cool air that made her aware of her own lack of clothing. Surprised, Alyssa reached down and grabbed the sheet and pulled it over her lace-covered breasts. He not only sounded tired, but she could see the shadows under his eyes.

"Here, take these." Two white pills lay in the palm of his hand.

She shook her head. She knew painkillers when she saw them. She remembered them. The doctor had promised that the codeine tablets would make all the pain go away, but when she'd woken from her drugged sleep Lily was still dead. "I don't like taking pills."

"Doctor's orders." He took a seat on the side of the bed, careful not to touch her. He'd slept in the chair and woken in the predawn hours. Something in him had reached out to turn on the bedside light and she hadn't woken. When he'd slid back the sheet to see the bruises marring her skin, acid had filled his gut. Only by chance had her face managed to escape harm; her arms had taken the direct impact of the airbag. Even now, his hands shook. He was unsure that he could handle loving Alyssa, handle the intensity of his own emotions, namely the fear that she could leave him.

"Nathan, I won't tell the doctor if you won't."

"You're acting like a child."

Damn if he wasn't right. She had broken a rule by spending the night in his bed, in his house, something that she promised herself she wouldn't do so early in the relationship. Yet she couldn't rustle up any other feeling than regret that she hadn't spent the night doing other things besides sleeping.

"Open your mouth and take this pain medication."

She shook her head, glaring. He might treat her like a child but she was a woman in possession of all her facilities. As a dancer she'd fallen and gotten up, danced until her feet bled from blisters and her muscles ached with exhaustion. The pain from the bruises would pass. "I don't need them."

"The doctor says you do and in this case I believe him."

"I have to go to the bathroom." She looked right and left. She needed to get up and away. It wasn't exactly a lie, she had to use the restroom. She hadn't gone in forever.

She moved to swing her legs off the bed but found them blocked by Nathan's hand.

"You will leave this bed after you take the pills."

"You are not my father or my keeper, Nathan."

"The ring on your finger says something different, Alyssa."

"I can always take this off." She moved to remove the ring, but his hand locked on her wrist. Nathan had never touched her in anger before. It caught her off guard, and it wasn't until her lungs began to burn that she unfroze.

She found her voice but it was small and hollow. "Let go of me."

"Don't," he warned in a quiet voice. "That ring belongs on your finger, like you belong in my bed and my life. I will take care of you always."

They stayed like that, for how long she couldn't remember. The issue went far beyond the mere taking of pain medication. Nathan had taken her heart and she had given it reluctantly, but now he would have her newly rediscovered independence as well.

"I can deal with the pain, Nathan. What I cannot tolerate is being forced to do something against my will."

He released her wrist and to prove his point, he reached out and barely touched her arm and she flinched away in pain. "You may be able to take it, but I can't, Alyssa. I love you, angel. And I can't see you hurting, not after knowing that you could have died yesterday. For my sake, take the pills."

Anger fled her eyes and Alyssa went quiet as reality set in. Nathan was right; she could have been permanently injured, or worse, killed. It was her turn to reach out and touch Nathan on his cheek. He had spent the night in a chair, held her, cared for her, and she had fought him over such a little thing. It made her feel small and mean, ungrateful. And if there was something that she was not, it was ungrateful.

She leaned forward and placed a gentle kiss on his lips. "I love you. I just don't know what's gotten into me."

"Nothing for the moment. You need to eat, but first—" He nodded toward the codeine.

"Nathan Hughes, you could give Fidel Castro a run for his money should you ever decide to get into the dictator business." She held out her open hand and screwed up her face in an expression of defenselessness. He ignored it all and placed the medication into her empty palm.

His lips curved into a full grin. "And here, I will provide water for my people. Am I not generous?"

"You're too kind," she quipped. Without breaking eye contact, Alyssa put the pills in her mouth and then, cradling the glass in both hands, brought it up to her lips to drink, only to realize how thirsty she'd been. Even finishing the entire glass didn't manage to cleanse her tongue of the bitter aftertaste of the medication.

"When I woke up, I thought I heard a woman singing, or was it my imagination?"

"That was my housekeeper, Mrs. Earls. She will see to your needs while I'm in court."

"Really, Nathan, I don't need a babysitter."

"I know. She's not here to babysit. Just to look after you. It wasn't my idea, she insisted."

She gave him a suspicious look. "I haven't even met her yet."

"But I've told her a lot about you." He stood up. "She has a granddaughter about your age."

"I wonder about you sometimes, Nathan Hughes."

"Wonder all you want, angel, but lunch will be ready in about thirty minutes."

"I can't go downstairs in my underwear."

He gave her a hungry look and her body tightened with the thought of events that had occurred when he had given her that look in the past. She closed her eyes and took a few breaths, then got out of bed, carefully wrapping the light sheet around her like a robe.

She suspected with the pain she felt that getting hit by a bus must be a lot easier than hitting the airbag in a car. From her shoulders down to her hips she ached from where the seat belt had bitten into her skin. "I need to borrow some clothes."

"Already taken care of." Nathan smoothed his hands over her hair. "I took the liberty of stopping by your place on the way home and picking up some clothes."

She had to stare at him and blink like an owl. Before Alyssa had even opened her mouth to reprimand him, he winked at her.

"You're welcome." Nathan grinned. "You need help getting dressed?"

"I'll be just fine, thank you." She started for the dressing room. She heard his quiet chuckle and gave in to the urge to slam the door shut behind but forwent the temptation to lean up against it. When she looked to see over half of her clothes and a wide selection of her shoes, she shook her head; she'd had more than enough help for one day.

Alyssa finally ventured downstairs dressed in twill pants and a three-quarter-sleeved blouse. After she'd combed her hair and washed her face, she'd looked in the mirror and blanched at the sight of her own skin. The natural light made the purpled bruises all the more ugly.

Alyssa stood in the kitchen doorway and enjoyed the sight along with the murmur of the aquarium's water filter. Copper cookware hung neatly on the far wall as Nathan moved to pull open the door on the gas oven. Before her first dinner in Nathan's home, she had opened the cabinets and kitchen drawers for a peek. Just as she'd expected, every spoon, fork, and champagne flute looked ready for a color advertisement in a gourmet magazine.

She tiptoed across the tile floor, snuck up behind Nathan, then covered his eyes with her hands.

"Guess who?" she whispered in his ear.

"Mrs. E., I don't think your husband will appreciate your getting so close, but if it's okay with you . . ."

"Wretched man." She laughed.

"You must be feeling better?"

She smiled and took his outstretched hands while biting back a sudden yawn. "I think the medication has kicked in. The pain is gone but so is my energy."

"But not your appetite, right? Because Mrs. E whipped up a roasted turkey, garlic mashed potatoes, and broccoli."

Alyssa's stomach took that moment to growl and she smothered a laugh. "I think you've got your answer." She peered at the myriad dishes. "Can I help?"

"Yes." He leaned down, pressed a slanted kiss upon her lips. "You can go have a seat at the table."

"Where did your housekeeper go?"

"She'll be back later to prepare dinner."

"I can cook, Nathan."

"I know, but you'll be busy."

"Doing what?"

"Resting." He directed her toward the dining table, pulled out a chair, and guided her into it.

"I have to work, Nathan, and make calls. There's the insurance company."

"Already taken care of. I had my assistant fax over the police report to the insurance carrier this morning."

"How did you know my insurance company?"

"Your father and I had a long talk yesterday. I may be overly optimistic but he's coming around to the idea of having a son-in-law."

Her breath caught in her lungs at the excited look on Nathan's face. The scolding she'd planned to unleash upon him at his high-handed handling of her affairs died at the back of her throat. "I have to talk to my insurance agent," she said stubbornly.

"What you have to do is eat," he admonished. "You didn't wake up when I brought you dinner last night, Alyssa."

She looked down at the loaded plate and imagined her overfull stomach. "I can't eat all this."

"But you'll try? Wouldn't want to disappoint Mrs. E."

"Why is that?"

He wiggled his eyebrows and Alyssa giggled. "She'll sit you down and describe in great detail the story of Moses, the Hebrews, and the starving children in Africa."

Alyssa picked up her fork and sampled the mashed potatoes. "This may not be so hard after all."

"Good. Because you know I'm easy." He grinned.

Alyssa let loose a soft snort. "Easy as a Monday morning after a tropical vacation." Her lips trembled with suppressed laughter.

Ignoring the comment, Nathan raised his fork. "I picked up some books that you had on your bedside table."

"Glad you approve of my reading. But back to more important matters, I really do need to call the detective back."

"No, you don't."

Her fork paused halfway between her lips and the plate, then she lowered it. "Why?"

"Bernard had Carol call the agency after he learned about your accident."

"I'll have to remember to thank her tomorrow."

"I'm sure she'd like to hear from you. Do you need the phone number?"

"I don't need it since I will be thanking her in person."

"You're not leaving this house for at least a week, Alyssa."

She opened her mouth to protest but Nathan was faster and placed his forkful of garlic mashed potatoes between her lips.

"Chew and swallow," he ordered. "Doctor's orders. Bernard should be coming over tomorrow with a project for you."

"Then I'll call and reschedule my appointment with the detective for next week."

"How about we discuss this stuff after lunch? We don't want all this good food to get cold."

"You're right." She took another bite of the roasted turkey.

Nathan gave her a devastating grin that she felt down to her toes. "You're right," he said, mimicking her voice, then wiped a bit of juice from the corner of his mouth. "Now I love the sound of that. So much so that I'd like to hear it again."

What he wanted and what he got were two different things. Nathan could only laugh as the broccoli floret hit him square in the face.

Later after eating, they settled on the couch with the low trembling of the piano in the background.

"Were you listening to this song the first time you called me?"

"No. I was playing the piano."

"You still play?"

"Whenever I need to exorcise my demons."

"And you needed to think that night?"

"Oh, yes. I'd had dinner with this beautiful woman and I could not for the life of me get her out of my mind."

"So I'm a demon, huh?"

"No." He pulled her legs into his lap and began to massage her feet. "You're my angel."

"Hmm," Alyssa groaned and closed her eyes at the sensation of his hands on her feet. "That feels wonderful. If you keep doing this I might have to—"

"What?" He let go of her feet and bent forward to pick up a small jar from the coffee table.

She opened her eyes. "I may have to marry you."

He paused from opening the lid and smiled. "Oh, you're going to marry me anyway. That ring is a promise."

"Which you put on my finger while I was unconscious."

"Nevertheless." He scooped out something brown and pasty. "It's binding and I would hate to drag you into court for breach of promise."

Alyssa inhaled sharply as he pulled the drawstring on her twill pants. She aimed a glance at the glass jar in his hand. "What is that and what are you doing?"

"A present from Liz."

"Liz?"

"My judicial assistant."

"Nathan, does everyone in the world know I've been in a car accident?"

"I couldn't get in touch with my mother and stepfather. Weather down in the Bahamas is playing havoc with the international lines."

"Good Lord, what is that?" She wrinkled her nose at the scent. Old and new combined, her grandmother's attic drenched with a heavy hand of peppermint.

"She said it was an old family recipe guaranteed to get rid of your bruises." He rubbed it in his hands to warm it up a little. "Now lie still."

Although feeling lethargic from the lunch and the pain medication, Alyssa managed a convincing scowl. "So bossy."

"No more than you, angel," he said, depressingly smug. She'd bet that he was enjoying this. She was putty in his hands and they both knew it.

"So instead of you kissing my bruises and making them feel better you're going to put that stuff on me?" she joked. She could have died in that car accident, yet she had not. Lily's death had robbed her of the feeling of immortality that came with youth, but she would let nothing take her sense of humor or her faith.

"Wait until you're better, I'll give you all the kisses you'll ever need," he vowed, pulling back the strap of her lace panties. He stopped when he heard her draw in a shallow breath the second his fingers came into contact with her skin. "Does it hurt?"

"Not the kind of pain you're thinking about."

He felt himself swell beneath the weight of her legs, wanting. It humbled him, the love he felt for her rocked him to the core of his being. He was a lawyer, a judge, a man of self-control and logic. The practice of restraint, an ability he prided himself on, had all but disappeared. The ability to control the most basic responses weakened, like the beliefs of the sailors who set out to find the end of the world only to discover no edge.

"I'll be done in a minute," he murmured.

Alyssa hoped it would be more like a second. He had such a command over her body that she found it impossible not to respond to his touch. Even his scent aroused her and made her forget about the soreness of her muscles, the rawness of her skin. She wondered if it would always be so even when she was gray-headed.

She closed her eyes and the image of his face lingered, but it was his eyes that calmed the surge of longing that heated her blood and pooled in her center. Although she could feel the press of his arousal underneath her thighs, his eyes were still brown and gentle, soothing like a first cup of tea in the silence of morning. She had so many things to do, but her body would have none of it, and with a smile on her lips she drifted onto the shores of sleep.

Just as her first morning in Nathan's bed, Alyssa again awoke to the sound of singing. Opening her eyes, she began to stretch, to test how much her injuries had healed. The soreness was less, but not by much. She winced, feeling her muscles contract.

After she'd finished her morning ablutions, she happily noted that the shadows under her eyes had lessened. Only as soon as she'd gotten dressed, Alyssa learned how to breathe all over again. Not the normal inhale and exhale. She learned to suck in deep gulps of air and swallow. Each step she took down the stairway hurt. Hurt so much that she would gladly have accepted the pain medication from her lover, but Nathan wasn't home and the pills sat alongside a glass of water by the left side of the bed.

"Well, good afternoon. How are you feeling?"

Alyssa looked up from her rapt study of the staircase banister. The annoyance of having someone watch her disappeared with the thought of not climbing the stairs. "I'm good, ma'am."

"Well, you don't look it. And don't call me ma'am, just call me what Nathan does."

"All right. Mrs. E."

"Honey-chile, you look like death warmed over in a microwave, and I hate those things. Always tell my daughter she shouldn't use the thing 'cause you don't know what it's doing to that food. Speaking of food, why don't you come in here so I can fix you something to eat?"

Alyssa smiled and loosened her death grip on the banister. "Thank you."

"Don't thank me yet, Nathan called about five minutes ago and told me to make sure you took your medicine. Did you?"

"No, not yet." She lowered herself into one of the chairs in the kitchen.

"Should have known." She shook her head. "Does it taste bad? Is that why you don't want to take it?"

"I just don't like taking pills."

Alyssa watched Mrs. E bustle around in the kitchen putting together a sandwich and a glass of milk. Nathan's housekeeper had short curly silver-gray hair, a wide face to frame deep-set eyes. Dressed in a saronglike purple and gold skirt and a black blouse, she could have gone straight from the house into a dinner club and hit the dance floor. "I hated cod liver oil as a little girl and I still do, but I have to be thankful my mother cared enough to put up with my mess and make me take it." She paused to put the plate of food on the table. "Now you start eating and don't stop until you're through. I'll go get your pills."

As she looked down at the oversized turkey sandwich, a smile curved Alyssa's lips. She felt like a kid again. And it was good that she didn't see the housekeeper as she paused in the doorway. For the woman's sympathy-filled gaze at the bruises of her arms would have taken the joy of the moment away.

Chapter 20

"I need some help with this." Nathan grinned after putting another box on the floor.

"Where did all these boxes come from?" Alyssa asked.

"The back of my car."

She looked toward the open front door to see her boss carrying two large shopping bags.

"Bernard, you drive a Porsche."

"True, but as of Tuesday evening, yours truly also drives an SUV. Figured it was safer and I need more space."

"For who?"

"For Sophie and Curtis. I just broke ground on a new house, got a lot more acreage this time. I figure I can put in a basketball hoop over the driveway, a swimming pool, space for her to garden."

"You've got it all planned out, huh? She agree to this?"

"She doesn't know yet. I've got Curtis softening her up and then when the time is right . . ."

"Hey, Bernard," came Nathan's booming voice. "Can you grab this box? I need some help out here."

"Nathan." She reached out and touched his arm, forestalling another exit. "What is all this stuff?"

"Remember that project I mentioned the other day?"

She nodded slowly. "Vaguely."

"This is it."

She read the labels on the boxes: Columbia, REI, L.L. Bean, The North Face, Gore, etc. . . . The list of companies read like an outdoor enthusiast's fantasy shopping spree. "Why is the mother lode of camping equipment in your living room, Nathan?"

Bernard responded instead. "That's because my ace program director can't come to the office, so the work will come to her."

"Where did you get all this stuff?"

Her boss put his hand on a box. "Ran into an old friend in the entertainment industry on the golf course last week and talked to him about the camping trip. He got excited and now he wants a camera crew to come along and film the trip. Put together a virtual reality show. Urban kids in the wilderness."

"You're kidding."

"No, and all this equipment is courtesy for the free publicity. Now all you have to do is pick the camping gear the kids will use."

Alyssa's frown deepened. Camping she knew how to do, but in all her experiences in the woods and underneath a tent, it was always someone else's job to bring the supplies; all she had to do was carry and set it up. "Not that I don't like the chance to pretend it's Christmas and open all these boxes, but wouldn't an expert be best?"

Nathan came up beside her and gingerly placed his arm around her. "Who needs an expert? It'll be just you and me tomorrow and I can't think of a better way to spend a Sunday with my woman."

"Well, I can." Bernard grinned.

"I'm sure you could because you don't have a woman."

Bernard spread his hands. "I'm just biding my time. You know how stubborn women can be."

"Oh, yeah. This little one over here is a perfect example."

"So what's the secret?"

Alyssa narrowed her eyes at Bernard, but her boss deliberately avoided eye contact.

Nathan boldly replied, "First you get her in the car, take her to the woods, feed her all her favorite foods—"

"Okay, boys," Alyssa interrupted with a silly smile on her

face. "I think the pizza's getting cold." It was wonderful to be around when Nathan let go and relaxed. She loved the way his dimple stayed put, not just visited, but moved into his face because his mouth curved into a full grin, revealing white teeth.

Sleeping in a man's house constitutes a step toward marriage, she mused, looking at the ring on her finger. She'd known him half her life, but something niggled in the back of her mind. Did she know him well enough? Putting those thoughts aside, she let herself keep falling more in love.

First thing Nathan did that Saturday morning was ease out of bed quietly so as not to wake Alyssa. He bent over the bed and moved the pillow so that her arms curved around it. She'd been restless last night and he had woken to the sound of her harsh breathing and small moans. He had only to put his arm around her and she settled down, but he couldn't close his eyes. Instead, he'd spent half the night staring at the ceiling thinking. Not about the upcoming conformation hearing, the political fund-raiser, or Senator John Thorpe's push for a wedding. No, he thought of the faceless man who would take from him the one woman he'd waited his life for.

Nathan picked up the cordless phone in the kitchen and dialed Damian's number. At that early hour on a Saturday morning his friend picked up on the first ring.

"Yeah."

"Any news?"

"None of it good. The man's a ghost, Nate."

"What?"

"If the man who tried to kill her is the same man whose image I managed to pick up a still photo from off the video camera at your woman's condominium, then she's in some serious danger.

"He has exes, Nate. He's ex-military, ex-DEA, and ex-Colombian cartel. Everything on file is strictly confidential and none of the cases against him have gone to trial."

"How does this tie in to Worthington? How did he get this man?"

"Money makes all things possible."

"Can you do anything? Call him off? Scare him?" Nathan grasped at straws.

"By reputation, he works alone and under contract. The only person who can shut this thing down is the person who took it out."

"Damn the man. What the hell am I supposed to do, Damian?"

"Keep her close and I'll see what I can do about your woman's new friend."

A click ended the conversation, but nothing would stop the anxiety in his mind. He looked toward the placidly swimming fish, the boxes littering his living room, and then up toward the ceiling and wondered if justice was worth any cost. Wondered how much would he have to pay.

"Is it getting hot out here or is it just me?" Alyssa murmured in Nathan's ears. Her bruises had finally faded enough and the pain had gotten to the point that she no longer shied away from his touch, could curl her body alongside his and think more about what was underneath his clothes than what was hiding underneath her own. She'd been so tired after unpacking all the equipment and setting up that they collapsed on the first comfortable stop: the hammock.

"It's getting a little warm." Nathan lifted himself up and supported himself on his elbow so he could stare down at her face, still flushed with excitement. "Thinking about going inside?" He traced the outline of her brow with his finger.

"Among other things."

"Sure you're up for that?"

"A woman has needs, Nathan. This woman has needs."

"Well, if you're in a hurry we can test out those high-tech foam sleep mats."

At the mention of the mats, they both turned their heads to look at what had taken two hours of confusion to build. The perfect campsite sat in the middle of Nathan's back-yard—the blue convertible four-season tent complete with color-coordinated ground cloth.

"It looks good, doesn't it, angel?" Nathan grinned.

"Uh-huh, now that it's finished. I'm still amazed that the mass of fabric and aluminum poles looks exactly like the picture on the box."

"The problem comes later when we have to put it back in the bag."

"Do we have to? I think that this makes a wonderful addition to your house."

"I'll have to keep that in mind for our son. We could all have little getaways in the backyard." Nathan's gaze traveled to her stomach and he imagined Alyssa swollen with his child.

In the space of a breath, he realized that he had the power to make fantasy a reality; he could get her pregnant and bind her to him all the more firmly while hastening their marriage. He dismissed the idea with an internal shrug. The scales of his conscience were already weighed down where Alyssa was concerned; he would not add another. A child would be conceived only when they both were ready.

"Or daughter," Alyssa automatically corrected.

"As much as I would love to have a daughter with your beauty and my temperament, I don't think my heart could take it."

"And why is that?"

Nathan put a hand to his chin and shook his head. "The day my daughter brought a boy home would be the last day she saw sunlight until her thirtieth birthday."

"And our son?"

"As long as he keeps his mind on getting an education, we can move him out at eighteen."

"Nathan Hughes, for a judge you are such a hypocrite."

"No, I'm honest. No man wants his little girl to grow up and leave. I can't imagine how hard it was on your father when you went off to school."

Alyssa shifted her head on his shoulder, remembering the day Pop had taken her to the airport for her flight to London. It was as though the sky had changed colors when she saw her father cry. "It was hard, but he managed."

"Speaking of managing, we haven't finished here yet, have we?"

"No." Alyssa looked at the unpacked boxes. "We still need to look at the cooking equipment, try out the stove, put together the water purification kit and the lantern. I think maybe we should just call it quits and leave everything there." She finished the sentence with a yawn.

"Not possible, it's taking up prime real estate."

"It's only grass."

"Call it a male thing. All a man needs on weekends when he can't play golf is a lawn mower and grass."

"Really?" She trailed a finger from the tip of his chin down to the end of the V in his polo shirt. "That all?"

"Not by a long shot."

"That's good because I could use a shower."

"Mind if I join you?" Nathan sat up, careful not to tip the hammock.

"It's your house; you don't need to ask my permission."

The smile dimmed from his eyes and he took her hand and placed a kiss on her knuckles. "Our house, Alyssa. Every possession I own is yours to do with as you please."

She saw the playfulness leave his face and would have it back. Alyssa batted her eyes and waved her hand as though she were holding a fan. Move over, Scarlett O'Hara, Alyssa Knight was coming through. "Oh, Nathan," she drawled with a butter-couldn't-melt-in-her-mouth southern accent. "I love you, but you most certainly have"—she sniffed delicately—"a most ungentlemanly smell."

"As do you, little lady." He laughed. "And it's not the scent of roses. Now let's go have that shower." He scooped her up carefully and carried her inside the house.

When her feet next touched the ground it was to the cool shock of tile. She looked around, observing the master bath in natural light, noticing the green of the walls that blended into blue minimosaic tiles, admiring the Japanese style with its theme of glass, chrome, and porcelain. It was a perfect space for two. Biscuit-white his-and-her pedestal vanities, tucked-away cabinets, candles, overhead nooks.

She watched as he slid back a small door to the cabinet and pressed a button. Immediately the sounds of the piano filled the bathroom.

"Nice, I would never have thought to have a stereo in the bathroom."

"One of the many fringe benefits of having an interior designer in the family. But you haven't seen anything yet."

"Oh?"

He reached behind her and slid open the opaque shower door. Alyssa turned and peered inside. Nathan turned the knob and a fine spray of water poured from not one but two showerheads.

"Impressive." She stepped onto a thick cotton bath mat.

"I aim to please." He patted her on her rear.

Nathan made short work of removing his clothes, but Alyssa took longer. This was a moment of firsts. The first time she'd ever shared a shower, the first time she'd stood naked with a man in the daylight. She stepped into the shower behind him and the hot water poured over her front. "This feels wonderful."

"Glad you like it." He leaned over and kissed her neck. Nathan picked up the bath sponge and began to run it lightly over her back and then her front. It was only a few moments until he turned her around, leaned down, and lost himself in her lustrous eyes. The kiss began as a sweep of his lips across hers, a hide-and-seek game played with tongues, a mingling of moans, a meeting of lips.

They tested the hot water heater to its full capacity and made puddles on the floor, and turned the mirror white with steam. But while the sun sank in the horizon, she rose to his possession and for a time they had each other and that was all that mattered.

"Alyssa Knight, how could you get engaged without talking to your mama first?"

Alyssa pulled the phone away from her ear and exhaled. She had spent the night in Nathan's loving arms, only to spend the morning squirming under the onslaught of her mother's vigorous scolding. Placing the receiver back to her ear, she spoke in a slow voice as though speaking to a small child. "It was a surprise, Mother. I had no idea Nathan would propose."

Her eyes automatically glanced at the ring on her finger. In the month that she had been seeing Nathan, she had yet to wake or sleep without thinking of him, loving him, caring for him.

"And how in the world did you get into a car accident? You just got home, just bought the car."

"I couldn't help it that someone ran me off the road."

"At least you could have waited until your father and I were home."

"Nathan is taking excellent care of me."

"He better. I talked to his mother yesterday night. Do you think I need to call the church and talk to Reverend Carter tomorrow? I can only imagine how slow they are about getting things together, and we need to plan this."

Alyssa leaned her elbow on the table and rubbed her head. Her mother switched topics faster than a politician. "We're planning on a long engagement. Speaking of weddings, how are Alan and Cassandra? Are you enjoying New York?"

Ten minutes ticked by as she listened through the cordless phone that was tucked between her ear and shoulder. Every now and then she chimed in just to let her mother know that the line had yet to be disconnected. Her eyes followed the random swimming patterns of the tropical fish in the aquarium.

"That's nice," Alyssa commented.

"Have you been listening to a word I've been saying?"

"Every last one of them. I'll stop by the house tomorrow to water the plants."

"Are you sure you're okay?"

"Just a few bruises and a scrape or two. The doctor recommended that I take it easy for a couple of days. So when are you coming back?"

"Well, that depends on your father."

Her mother's slow response tied a figure-eight knot in her stomach. "Is Pop all right? Is he having a relapse?"

"None of that. He's fine. Just calm down. In fact, I can hear him downstairs playing video games with Alan. He thought that since we're here on the East Coast already, it might be good to go visit my relatives down South."

"That sounds like a good idea." Alyssa smiled, releasing her tension. Like a woman on death row, she'd been granted a reprieve.

"I've got Nathan, his family, Aunt Sara, and Uncle Edward checking up on me, Mama. I'll be fine."

"Are you sure?"

"Very. Just book the ticket and give my love to everyone for me."

Alyssa hung up the phone and wandered aimlessly from room to room until she stopped in the den. She needed music. When Mrs. E had left the house to go grocery shopping, she'd taken the comforting sound of her humming as well.

She perused Nathan's wide variety of compact discs. The collection spanned languages, time periods, and genres. After picking through Luther Vandross, Curtis Mayfield, and Etta James, she finally settled on Miles Davis's *Sketches of Spain*. She slipped the disc into the carousel and, reading over the back cover, skipped to one of her longtime favorite classical songs, "Concierto De Aranjuez." It ws a composition she and Lily had danced to many times as ballet students.

Alyssa put down the controller, then closed her eyes as the strumming of the guitar filled the room. Slowly, her body began to sway and her feet moved over the carpet. The song was halfway to the end when the strength of an image of a black car made her stop dancing.

No. She shook her head and reached out blindly, grabbing hold of the side of the couch. Alyssa whimpered as a flash of blinding white pain hammered her skull. The fragment of a memory was filled with snow, the high pitch of tires squealing, the sight of hands and rectangular headlights. Black. No, dark blue.

She closed her eyes and held on to the image, studied it, committed it to her memory. Over and over again she replayed the scene, so much so that when she closed her eyes the after-image remained. Carefully, Alyssa walked into the kitchen, picked up the phone again, and took another step forward to finding Lily's killer.

"Thank you again, Uncle Edward." Unconcerned with the other occupants in the room, she hugged her uncle tight and burrowed into his chest like a child. His presence reassured her, but her uncle's having brought a sketch artist with him was a sign that he believed her. No matter the incredible amount of time that had passed since Lily's accident, he believed Alyssa's vision was indeed a memory of the car that had run her best friend down.

"You just quit thanking me and take care of yourself. I'll let you know something as soon as I can, and in the meantime you take it easy."

"I will."

"Promise?" His gray-streaked eyebrows rode upward.

"Promise." She nodded.

"Now that's my girl."

"You won't tell Aunt Sara about any of this, will you?"

"I don't keep stuff from her if she asks."

"Then you'll tell her."

"Yep."

"Well then, I'll have to cross my fingers and hope she doesn't."

Alyssa turned to the young man standing with his pad and pencil. "Thank you."

"No problem, ma'am. Anything I can do to help."

She detected the faint New York accent and offered him a wide smile. "Do you think that you'll be able to match it?"

"I'm not a car expert but it's an import, and if I'm not too far off the mark, I think it's a Jaguar. The guys down at the DMV will be able to identify it."

Nathan's gaze had rarely left Alyssa as he stood back next to Edward. His eyes narrowed as she reached out and shook the young sketch artist's hand. He hadn't missed the man's look of interest. He couldn't blame him, for even when she was dressed in jeans and a T-shirt with not a trace of makeup on her features, his lady was a beauty to behold.

"You look after my niece."

"No worries, Mr. Knight."

They saw him to the door and Alyssa took the opportunity to lean back into Nathan as he held her.

"I could be getting my memories back." Her voice should have been excited but instead it was tired. She may have just taken one step closer to proving her suspicion that Chad Worthington was the person responsible for Lily's death.

He rested his chin on the top of her head. "It's been a long day. How about I grab up a bottle of wine while you light some candles and we head upstairs for a nice, relaxing soak in the bathtub?"

"Oh, Nathan, I'm sorry I didn't even ask about how your day at work went."

"You can make it up by scrubbing my back." He hugged her close.

"I can do more than that," she said in a purr and tapped him on the cheek.

It had been a while since Alyssa had entered into the halls of Chicago's famed Field Museum of Natural History. That morning she returned and she was not alone. Glancing over her shoulder, she watched the "it's hip to look bored" teens jockey for the best place to view Sue, the fossilized sixty-seven-million-year-old tyrannosaurus.

In a few minutes, she was sure they would want to go to the second-floor balcony just to get a better look at the giant skull and the creature's razor-sharp teeth. Alyssa suppressed a small shudder; she'd inherited her mother's intense dislike of insects, rodents, or lizards, no matter how dead or well preserved they were.

It was good to get out of the house and better to be around people. She liked Nathan's house. She liked the woven rugs, the large windows, the silk-covered cushions, and the multi-colored, decorative objects that were perfectly arranged in each room.

What she didn't like was a week of Nathan treating her like an orchid whose petals would drop at the slightest touch, and her family's constant phone calls had come close to driving her up the wall.

"Thinking of the devil," she muttered as her phone began to vibrate in her purse. She pulled it out and walked away from the sound of children's laughter, the murmuring of voices, and the noise of hundreds of kid-sized feet filling the room.

"Uncle Edward?"

"Can you talk?"

"Not really," she replied in a low voice, well aware of the disapproving glances coming her way from a group of camera-touting tourists.

"That's all right then, just listen. Heard back from my

buddy at the Department of Motor Vehicles. Cost me a few beers because he had to do some powerful digging. Putting that aside, a car matching the make, color, and year that you described was registered in ex-Mayor Worthington's name, not his son's."

"Thanks, Uncle Ed." Alyssa held the phone between her shoulder and her ear as she wrote down the information.

"That's not all," her uncle continued. "Chad Worthington reported it stolen the day after Lily's death and it's listed as never being recovered."

"Damn." Alyssa bit her lip after letting the curse slip out. "Why is it that for every step forward I take, I have to take three back? Without the car, I can't tie Worthington to the accident."

"I know I can't change your mind about trying to find out who killed your friend, but be careful. I got a surprise visit from the president of the police fraternity the other day. Seems yours and Nathan's digging into this case has made the people high up uncomfortable."

The hairs on the back of her neck stood up at his words. Alyssa looked up and scanned the area, only to have her heart jump at the sight of the red-haired security guard from Bernard's cabin on the upstairs balcony. He was wearing a billed cap, yet she recognized his face, the precise mustache.

Uncle Ed's voice pulled her attention back to the cell phone. "Alyssa, you be careful."

"I will," she promised and clicked off the phone. When she looked back up, the man had been replaced with a rather studious-looking African-American male. Shaking off her sense of unease, she rejoined the group as they moved to another exhibition.

"You okay?"

Alyssa turned to find Sophie at her side. "I'm all right. Why do you ask?"

"You seem a little shaky. Are you sure you're over the accident?"

"Positive." She linked arms with Sophie after casting a

glance over her shoulder. "I'm not too fond of reptiles and I think big Sue back there was giving me the evil eye," Alyssa quipped.

"She's probably hungry, says here in the brochure that the dinosaur weighed about seven tons when she was alive."

"How's Curtis liking this?" Alyssa turned her eyes to see the youngest member of the group, who had taken that exact moment to snap a picture of some of the girls as they posed in front of another woolly mammoth display.

"He's in heaven. Basking in the attention from the older girls and getting to hang out with the boys. I'm really glad you invited us."

"It wasn't my idea. You should thank Bernard."

"Should have known."

"Speaking of Bernard, he's going to be at the center all day today and I'm sure he'd love it if you and Curtis dropped by."

"Alyssa, I know what you're trying to do, and don't think I don't appreciate the gesture, but you need to stop. Not only am I not ready yet, I'm not sure when or if I'll ever be."

They stood side by side, neither taking her eyes off the kids. Alyssa silently apologized to her boss before making her next statement. "He loves you."

"I know."

Her head swung in Sophie's direction. The serene expression of her friend's face prompted Alyssa to add, "I mean the man has been and is in love with you."

Sophie nodded. "I know. Bernard came by the house the night of your car accident. Seeing how close you came to losing your life shook him up."

"What did you tell him?

"That I wasn't ready to get involved."

"How did he take it?"

"Like a man."

"Meaning?"

"He's dead set on ignoring the obvious and changing my mind to suit his liking. He's already gotten to Curtis."

"How?"

"Took him up to the cabin last weekend for some man-to-man time."

"Sounds innocent enough."

The comment earned her a nasty look.

"And now Bernard's got Curtis designing his own room in the new house."

"What's he planning on doing with his old one?"

"Already sold it for twice the price he paid for it. Told me that he's building a bigger house to get the tax write-off. I don't believe him though. I just think he's trying to work on my last nerve."

Alyssa chuckled. "That's what they do best. Nathan has his moments too."

"No kidding, I eat lunch with his assistant." She sighed. "Now let's get this troupe together and get over to that Eternal Egypt exhibit. I'm itching to see what the real pharaohs of Egypt look liked."

"You've been studying history?"

"No, I've been reading one of my coworkers' romance novels." Sophie fanned herself. "If the statues look half as good as the man on the cover, I'll be a happy woman."

Chapter 21

Alyssa removed the bobby pins from her hair and it fell around her shoulders with a slight curl on the tapered ends. Having had the ends trimmed plus adding additional red-gold highlights, her tresses looked fantastic. It had been a treat to leave work on time and take a cab to the upscale African-American salon.

For the past week Nathan had insisted on taking her to and from work. True to his word, he arranged to have an identical yellow Jeep Wrangler ordered. She smiled while running a brush through her hair. Dan, her car salesman, had so appreciated her business that he'd delivered a courtesy vehicle to Nathan's home the same evening.

He still didn't want her to drive and she had acquiesced for the moment, but needed to face her fear and get back in the saddle, or in this case behind the wheel. Today, however, she'd driven to work, then to the beauty salon.

Walking through the doors, she was bathed in the smell of vanilla, soothed by the soft sounds of jazz that poured through recessed speakers, and stunned by the beauty of women of color. Professional photographs of women with numerous hairstyles, designer gowns, and dazzling jewelry were arranged along the walls.

She'd sipped fruit juice while under the dryer, and read one of the latest magazines while indulging in the luxury of a spa manicure and pedicure. Yet her best moment was sitting in the shampoo chair, letting someone else handle her thick tresses, feeling someone else's fingertips massaging her wet scalp, listening to the other clientele's drama instead of thinking of her own.

Alyssa pulled her hair so that it hung straight down her back and her neck looked golden brown and bare save for her favorite silver necklace with opal pendant. Unzipping her cosmetics case, she dotted on a sheer foundation and blended it as needed, brushed a blush on her cheeks, then a shimmery eye shadow and taupe lip color with a gloss hue that finished off the evening look.

She stood up and moved back to admire her own handiwork, but stopped upon catching sight of Nathan in the mirror.

"Um-um-um." He'd gotten into the shower right after she'd gotten out of the whirlpool bath. The arousal caused by the mere scent of her that lingered in the space had prompted his shower temperature to be lowered by more than a few degrees. Yet all his efforts were in vain.

Entranced, Nathan stopped in the doorway, drinking in the sight of the fluid silk sheath dress with a high collar that left her shoulders bare, the perfection of her skin like a ray of sunlight.

He walked into the guest bathroom and wrapped his arms around Alyssa's waist. Her three-inch heels made her taller, but Nathan still exceeded her height.

"Hello there." She smiled at him in the mirror.

"I'd wondered where you were hiding." He nuzzled her neck while his attention focused on their reflections in the mirror.

"Sometimes two people in the same place can be a little hectic. Besides, I didn't want a perfectly unused bathroom to go to waste."

"Waste not, want not," he said huskily in her ear, while his hands moved from the curve of her hips and carefully pulled up her dress to stop at his destination. He watched her eyes darken as his fingertips caressed the baby-soft skin between the old-fashioned silk stockings and garter.

"I know what I want," she said shakily.

"And what's that?"

"For us to make this a very early night."

"Sweetheart, we will eat, greet, and leave."

"Good." She turned around and placed her hands on the cotton of the shirt in the triangle formed by the jacket. She reached up and made a small, inconsequential adjustment to his tie. Just watching Nathan cross the room had moved the heat of her heart to the center of her thighs. Up close with the musky scent of his cologne, the man sent a shiver down her spine. She would never tire of being with him, looking at his high cheekbones and wide-spread nostrils that shadowed perfectly firm lips.

"Ready to go?" he asked.

"I just need to dab on a little perfume."

"You don't need it."

"But I'd like to wear it."

"Let me."

"All right."

Nathan took the glass bottle from her hand and lifted her hair with appreciating slowness. He loved the feel of her hair in his fingers, the silk threads when they touched his skin. "I like what you've done."

"Fiona convinced me to do something different."

"I like all that you've done, angel." His gaze fixed on the golden brown curve of her neck and the curve of her breasts, and he touched the heart-shaped opal pendant. It filled his heart to see her wearing his gift and his ring. "I am truly a blessed man to have you in my life, to have you as my future wife."

"Just remember those words when I'm fussing at you for no other reason than that it's my time of the month and you're the closest target."

"I will." He laughed low in his chest and brushed her hair to the side to spray the perfume on the juncture of her smooth shoulders and slender neck.

"You're proficient at this," Alyssa murmured, shivering at

the cool spritz of perfume on her bath-warmed skin. He saw the spark of jealousy and it amused him.

"I lived over half of my life in a house with women. You learn all the basics and then improve."

He took her left wrist and gently pressed the spray, then placed the bottle on the table. He took her other arm and rubbed her wrists together.

"The way you look right now . . ." He marveled again at the way in which the soft material skimmed her curves and stopped just above her knees and revealed acres of leg.

She leaned up on her tiptoes and brushed her cheek alongside his and whispered, "Make this a short evening, Your Honor, and we can make the night all the more enjoyable."

"Wear your seat belt tonight," he growled. "Because I think I may be getting my first speeding ticket."

Much later, after she kissed another cheek, commiserated with the governor's wife over the deteriorating educational system, delicately shook an unknown hand, and smiled a practiced smile at another round of congratulations on her recent engagement and Nathan's assured confirmation to the bench, if someone offered an opportunity to kick off her shoes and crawl into a soft bed, Alyssa would have sold her soul for it.

"What a great networking event, don't you think?"

"Yes, it is." Alyssa took a sip of her soda and studied everything about the woman, from the razor-cut bob, dusty brown skin, sloping eyes, dainty nose, and petite frame. As she moved to place an appetizer into her expertly painted lips, the subtle yet expensive diamond tennis bracelet caught the light and twinkled like a thousand stars.

"I saw you arrive with Nathan Hughes. Are you friends?"

Alyssa's eyes narrowed, but seeing only curiously in the woman's body language, she relaxed and smiled. "We're engaged."

"You are very fortunate. He's a wonderful man."

"I count my blessings every day and he has accounted for many." She stopped. "How do you know Nathan?"

"We met through a mutual friend," she replied.

"I'm sure he'd love to see you."

Alyssa watched the elegant woman's smile, which didn't match her eyes: sadness or regret lay in their depths, and Alyssa wondered what she had missed.

"I've got to get home. Please tell him hello and congratulations for me."

"I'm sorry I didn't get your name."

"Gillian Mathis."

Alyssa watched her until she disappeared in a sea of black. *Gillian.* Her brow wrinkled in concentration. Where had she heard that name before? Shrugging her shoulders, she raised a hand to lift her hair off of her neck; the temperature in the atrium had risen with the additional arrivals. Looking around, she moved a little farther to the outer rim of the gathering.

Not for the first time since she'd agreed to marry Nathan did the voice in the back of her mind whisper misgivings about her choice. There was no question that she loved him. A love that she wanted to hold, to cherish, to adore, but the political fund-raiser was too reminiscent of the corporate events Harrison had insisted she accompany him to. And that memory made her uncomfortable.

She pivoted on her black sling shoes and from her spot under a palm tree watched as Nathan charmed the socks off of a state representative from Indiana. Only knowing how much her presence at the event meant to him kept her from walking out onto the pier and spending the rest of the evening in solitude.

The beautiful Crystal Gardens was a one-acre glass atrium filled with palm trees, flowers, and plants. Dancing fountains and seating areas provided a perfect backdrop for the political fund-raiser. Finding a quiet place near the window, Alyssa peered out of the window at the twinkle of the Ferris wheel's light off the water.

Taking a sip of her sparkling water, she observed Nathan.

His manners were excellent as he focused his complete attention on the people around him. He knew that his interest in their lives, agendas, opinions would win their approval and pull their support like moths to a flame. She knew Nathan had a lot of work to do. He had a lot of people pulling for him, making calls, writing letters, showing their support, and she was there to show hers. He had arranged for the housekeeper to come every day, and Alyssa had come home from work to find wonderful meals in the oven, only to sit at the kitchen table alone.

Although she had yet to leave his house, they had barely seen one another the past week. He left before she woke and arrived long after she went to bed. His insistence that she remain until the doctor cleared her was a mere technicality that would be taken care of tomorrow when she went for a follow-up visit.

"You must be very proud of him."

Alyssa smothered a sigh as she turned to face a new well-wisher, then forced herself to brighten her expression. The voice's owner was a tall man with silver-peppered black hair, olive-tinted skin, and an aura of power. Even under the soft glow of the tree lights, he had eyes the color of winter's skies and hard, even features that spoke of confidence. She smiled politely. "Yes, I am."

"Alyssa Knight." He extended his hand. "I've followed your brother's career from the time be hit that grand slam at the college baseball finals to the day he got drafted to the Astros and then when he went to New York. I must say that there's more than a passing resemblance between the two of you."

She shook his hand and noticed that he held it long enough to make her feel uncomfortably aware of his presence in her personal space. "I'm sorry, but if we've met I don't recall your name, and if we haven't, then you have me at a severe disadvantage by not giving it to me."

He took a swig of his drink and then placed it down on a passing waiter's tray. "Senator John Thorpe."

"Senator Thorpe." Alyssa shook his proffered hand, surprised that she hadn't recognized him before. Out of the corner of her eye she saw a young red-haired woman with an earpiece. The large group of high-profile elected officials necessitated an even larger contingent of suit-clad Secret Service agents. "It's a pleasure to meet you."

"Likewise, and please call me John." His smile when he gave it was big and looking unabashedly into her eyes. "Behind every powerful man there will always be a smart and successful woman; it's about time that I met Nathan's."

"Nathan told me that it was because of you the president nominated him for the job."

"Yes, he was one of my top students at law school. He is an exceptional judge and both the president and I agree that, given experience and the proper political guidance, he will be a strong candidate for the U.S. District Court of Appeals on—"

Alyssa felt a prickle of forewarning across her skin. She didn't like politicians as a rule, but this was something more.

"I'm glad you feel that way." She cut him off accidentally.

"My support, as helpful as it might be, isn't as important as yours."

"Why do you say that?"

"This is only the beginning, Alyssa. Thurgood Marshall and Clarence Thomas may have paved the way, but Nathan still has a difficult path to follow to the Supreme Court."

She barely managed to keep from sloshing the contents of her barely sipped glass of sparkling water onto the carpet. A wave of disbelief left her feeling weak. Nathan hadn't said a word.

"Are you all right?"

"I'm fine, just a little nervous."

"Don't be." His grin was charming. So much so she wondered if he practiced it in the mirror after brushing his pearly white teeth. "The press likes a good love story and politics, a fresh face. How about we go rescue Nathan from my fellow elected official over there?"

Alyssa placed a hand on his tendered arm and thought of a

fairy tale she'd seen as a child. She couldn't remember the story, only that it had been acted out in the form of a puppet show. She imagined the wooden dolls moving with the help of hidden masters as the senator escorted her through the crush toward Nathan. With every step she took, an ever-growing suspicion dogged her steps. And when she stood next to Nathan, with his arm comfortably around her waist, she wondered, if she looked upward, would it be his hand gripping her invisible strings?

"Nathan, I think I've found something that belongs to you."

He turned to find Alyssa with her hand on John's arm. He moved to stand by her side and kissed her cheek. "I missed you."

Nathan watched the senator smile down into Alyssa's up-turned face and fought the urge to pull her away.

"If I wasn't married to the best woman in the world, I'd be tempted to keep her. My best wishes for the both of you."

"Thank you for returning her to me."

After the Senator Thorpe's departure, Nathan led Alyssa to a less crowded corner of the room. "Honey, you look tired. Do you want to leave now?"

"Can you?"

Taken aback by the strange undertone in her voice, he watched her closely. "What is it?"

She shifted her gaze toward the secretary of state as he took the stage to give his closing speech. "I would have thought that you'd want to stay and put in a good show. This is, after all, your opportunity to shine."

He took her face within his hands and turned it firmly toward his own. There was a trap in her words and for the life of him he couldn't figure it out. "This is one of many fund-raisers and nothing compares or takes priority over you."

"You say that now, but will you say it when the time comes for you to take on the role of a Supreme Court justice?"

Nathan's hands dropped to his sides. "You're wrong on this, Alyssa."

"Am I? Are you telling me that you don't want the job?"

Her lips curved into a caricature of a smile. Nathan silently cursed himself for not anticipating John telling Alyssa of his plans.

"Alyssa, my career ambitions have nothing to do with us."

"I disagree." Her expression shifted from impassive to hurt. "You tell me that I am your partner, your confidante, your future wife, and yet you concealed this from me."

"It's only speculation, Alyssa."

"No. Not with you, and I'm struggling with the why. Give me an honest reason, Nathan."

"Because I love you."

She stared at him and all emotion drained from her voice. "I asked for a reason, not an emotion."

Nathan closed his eyes and then opened them again to draw in a deep breath. He would give her more than a reason; he would give her the truth. His mind made up, he answered with firm resignation, "Because I needed you to marry me."

At that moment, everyone stood to give a rousing applause for the party's success. Yet for Nathan the applause seemed to mock his personal defeat. He watched as Alyssa turned away and raised her hands as well. He turned and joined in, but his heart and mind lay elsewhere. In the past hour he had secured most, if not all, of the votes he needed to be confirmed to the federal bench. But his efforts would be in vain if he couldn't convince the beautiful woman at his side that she had his heart.

"I won't be here tomorrow night."

Nathan opened his eyes in the darkness of his bedroom. He'd taken five steps forward and now it seemed that she would send him back. He had confessed everything during the drive back to his house. Withholding nothing, he told her of his intentions to marry in order to gain a family image before his upcoming Senate confirmation hearing.

He had hoped by Alyssa's silence that she had accepted or

was at least going to give him the benefit of the doubt. Nathan closed his eyes again and took a deep breath. He'd taken her into his arms and loved her with such passion and care that he'd hoped to wipe the slate clean of his earlier confession. Yet she still planned to leave him. "Talk to me, Alyssa."

"I need to spend a night or two alone."

"Is this because of my wanting to be on the Supreme Court?"

"No," Alyssa whispered, glad that she wasn't facing him, relieved that the night hid her face. "This is much deeper than that. I don't trust that the man who has swept me off my feet is the same man who just told me he planned to marry a woman he didn't love in order to improve his career standing."

"Angel, you can't think that I would want you for my wife for any other reason than that you own my heart."

"Really? You say that with such conviction that a part of me can't help but believe you." She closed her eyes to trap the tears from falling onto the pillow.

"I am not Harrison."

"If you were I wouldn't even consider coming back here." Alyssa turned on the lamplight, then sat up while holding the sheet to cover her nakedness. "I love you, Nathan, and if I sincerely believed that you would choose ambition over me, I'd have given you back this ring, your keys, and ripped holes in your boxer shorts. Nathan, ambition can be healthy and good, but as with everything, too much can blind you. You are a noble and fair man that I love more and more each day, but I can't overlook that you kept something important from me not once, but twice."

"You're not well enough to be alone," Nathan said, pushing up to lean against the headboard as her declaration echoed inside his head. Not only that, somewhere out there was a man trying to kill her.

"I'm fine and we both know it. I need to go."

"You love me, yet instead of staying to work out our first disagreement, you plan to leave?"

"This is more than a *disagreement* and it's something that we can't fix in the bedroom talking." She turned her body toward him so she could see his face in the shadow of the incandescent light. "I'm spoiled rotten by my family and I'm used to getting everything I've ever wanted."

"Are you giving me an excuse or a reason?" The flash of anger in his eyes belied the ice in his voice.

She ignored his sarcastic comment. During the lull after making love, she'd searched her heart for the whys of her own behavior. "I'm also a Knight. In my family we give and take, we fight and love and live with everything we've got. The guts, the glory, the pride. I need to be number one. Like Alan I want to have it all. I want all of you. Not just the good, but the bad. I want your hopes, fears, dreams, and nightmares. I want to be your number one and have access to a part of that inner life you keep under lock and key. I have to know that when push comes to shove you'll be committed and honest; that no matter what, you'll fight for me and with me."

"Shouldn't that work both ways?"

She nodded. "I was ready to be the wife of a federal judge, but I'm not ready to share my life with a man who can't share all of his. It should have been you who told me about your Supreme Court ambitions."

"I would have told you."

"When?"

"After the wedding."

"For what reason?"

"To keep you from doing exactly what you plan to do now: leave."

She shook her head. "I'm not running away or hiding. Just taking some time, that's all."

"I thought it was the man who was supposed to pull away." He stood up, wrapped his arms around her, and pulled her tight into his chest. "I don't want to you leave," he repeated. "But I won't apologize for loving you and wanting you as my wife. I have and will always have our best interests in mind."

For one second he contemplated telling her about Damian's

surveillance, but stopped. Knowing at that moment he was making the wrong move, but ignoring his gut feelings, he remained silent. There was no doubt she would fight it and he couldn't afford to take the risk, not when she was on the verge of leaving him.

And I don't want to go, Alyssa mentally responded. She laid her head on his bare shoulder. Of all the things she would sacrifice for love, emotional security or commitment would not be one of them. She had to trust that through the good, through the bad, no matter what, he would be there for her and their future children and she could be the partner he needed.

"You want time." Nathan tightened his arms around her in an embrace that was almost painful. He couldn't deny what she'd said and he couldn't lie and tell her that he would have changed his actions if he could do everything all over again.

"I'll give you forty-eight hours. After that I will spend my nights in your bed or you in mine. From the moment you lay in my bed, Alyssa, you made a commitment. We are in a relationship and we will be married. When the next two days have passed there will be no time-outs, pulling back, or pleas for space. We will fight, but never go to bed angry."

He took her face with his hands, looking down into golden eyes that glistened like sunlight on brown water. "Are we agreed?"

Her chin rose. "You haven't left me with much of a choice, have you?"

"No, I won't let you run, walk, skip, hop, or stroll out of my life, Alyssa."

She aimed one last searching look in his direction before nodding. "I'll come here."

"Good." He kissed her. "Now that we've got that out of the way, how about you join me for a shower?"

"I'd like to shower alone, thank you."

"Suit yourself."

She watched him stand up and walk toward the bathroom,

naked as a jaybird. She sighed and lay back down on the bed. Only forty-eight hours to decide whether to follow her heart or her mind. Shaking her head on the pillow, she closed her eyes and sighed. *I am such a fool, but I will make him wait.*

Chapter 22

"Don't scream. I'm here to protect you."

Alyssa struggled, clearly intent on disobeying as a gloved hand clamped down over her mouth. Refusing to let panic swamp her, she managed to elbow her attacker twice in the ribs before he dragged her into the stairwell and positioned her facing the door.

"Just stay still and watch," he whispered into her ear. She ignored him and instead attempted to stab her heel into his foot. In the silence of the stairwell she could hear his breathing and feel the moisture on her throat. Her heart pounded in her ears as terror grew with every beat.

As seconds seemed to slow to minutes she waited until a man dressed all in black and carrying a toolbox emerged from her apartment door. Her brows knitted together. She hadn't requested anything to be done to the apartment and had not been informed of any necessary maintenance work.

He moved to stand in front of Alyssa and her throat went dry as she struggled to keep panic at bay. The man who stared back at her could have jumped off of a most-wanted list on the post office wall. Thick eyebrows on a heavy brow, an unshaven jaw, and lips pressed into an unforgiving line. "I will move my hand away, but it is imperative that you remain quiet. Nod one time if you understand."

Careful to keep her eyes locked with his, she nodded slowly and was rewarded with a loosening of his arm around her stomach and the removal of his hand from her mouth.

"I'm going to leave you for five minutes. Promise me you won't leave until I come back."

With his hand away from her mouth, she whispered, "All right."

Alyssa turned to demand what was going on, but the man who'd called himself her protector had slipped silently down the stairs.

Sometime later, the emergency exit door opened and she followed the stranger into the hallway. At once she wrinkled her nose at the overwhelming smell of gas. The heady scent made her stomach heave but the surprise that the source of the smell was coming from her apartment floored her.

"There was a wire on the door and a backup in the light switch."

She looked at him, confused. "What?"

A bright beam appeared to illuminate the light switch by her door. "If you'd opened the door, the spark produced by that"—she followed his gaze upward to see a small black box taped over her door frame—"or the rigged light switch probably would have taken out maybe two or three floors."

"I need to sit down," Alyssa stated as her knees began to tremble at the reality of what could have happened to her.

The man shook his head. "No time. Stay here while I gather some clothes. Don't touch the light. He's most likely watching the place from a safe distance."

She narrowed her eyes and watched as he slipped into the darkness in the direction of her bedroom. He avoided the sofa, the painting, and the boxes of books she'd yet to unpack. It took her a moment to realize that he'd been in her apartment before. The thought sent another chill racing down her spine.

Five minutes later he came back and, taking her hand, led her down five flights of stairs only to pause at the emergency back door. She watched as he took a pair of wire cutters out of his pocket and cut the alarm.

But he paused before opening the door. "Where did you park?"

Her brain froze for a moment as she thought of her Jeep and then remembered the dealer's car. "Three blocks down on the right."

"Give me the keys."

She fished them out of her purse and put them into his hand. "We are going to walk slow and steady. Just pretend we are a loving couple out for a stroll. I want your arm around my waist and your face in my shoulder at all times. Don't look straight, up, down, just walk. Do you understand?"

She swallowed, hoping to moisten her fear-dried throat. "Yes."

She glimpsed a set of perfect white teeth as he smiled. "Let's go."

She allowed him to lead her out of the apartment building, into the cool evening air, down the empty sidewalk, and into the passenger side of the car. After they were well away, Alyssa continued to bite the inside of her lip to keep her teeth from chattering. A myriad of questions pressed her mind from all sides. The loudest voice wondered, who was trying to kill her and why?

"Yesterday. I saw you yesterday at the supermarket." Alyssa's eyes opened and focused on the coffee table. He hadn't said a single word during the drive from her apartment to Nathan's house, but each and every second she'd been afraid. She shook her head as her glance caught on the full glass of dirty brown liquid on the table.

"Drink it all." His tone had an air of natural authority.

She ignored his order and asked the only question that was tearing around in her mind. "First tell me who you are."

"The man whose sole purpose is to keep you safe."

"Safe." Alyssa tasted the word on her tongue as she stared at the stranger's profile.

Her rescuer moved back from the window, allowing the heavy drape to fall back into place. She couldn't help but notice that his booted feet moved silently across the room. He could have been a dancer, part of her mused.

As he came to a stop on the opposite side of the coffee table, Alyssa looked upward and into honey-brown eyes locked with obsidian, and the chill that crept across her skin had nothing to do with the temperature of Nathan's living room. She'd seen similar eyes before, only then she'd had the safety of thick glass between her and a reptile with sharp fangs and constricting muscles. For a split second she didn't know who frightened her more: an unknown assassin or her rescuer.

Had she been standing, his height alone would have been intimidating. Yet, added to the way he watched her, this made Alyssa want to run from the room and take her chances with the faceless killer rather than the silent savior. He was dressed in all black with a short-sleeve cotton shirt that only seemed to highlight his muscular arms and powerful shoulders. A lone shard of silver at his temple could be found amongst the thick, coal-colored, wavy hair. Angular features, thick eyebrows, and a crescent-shaped scar underneath his prominent cheekbones made her aware that he was good looking.

Alyssa started to repeat her question but before she could blink, he'd moved to hold the glass in front of her lips.

"Drink it." This time it was not a request; she could hear the barely leashed impatience in the order. The tone as well as the brief glimpse she'd seen of the gun on his left side had her reaching a shaking right hand out to take the glass from his grasp.

"What is your name?" she managed to gasp after the fiery liquid burned a rolling path down her throat.

"Damian."

"What are you?"

That question was greeting by a tiny response as his lip

curled upward slightly. "African, Canadian, Sioux, and French."

"Are you a police officer?"

"No."

"FBI?"

"No."

"Bodyguard?"

"I am none of those things, Alyssa."

Seeing that she was not going to get an answer, she decided it was time to try another question. "How long?"

He raised a dark eyebrow.

"How long have you been watching me?"

"Since the first murder attempt."

Alyssa took a deep breath in her lungs as he moved away. Something about the man was unnerving. The hint of leashed violence seemed to permeate the air.

"What are you taking about?"

"The car wreck wasn't an accident. You were meant to die. Someone tampered with the brake cable and tried to run you off the road."

The room tilted and she brought an unsteady hand to her brow, as the temperature in the room seemed to have gone from cold to an inferno. She'd had the suspicion that her brakes hadn't just given out, but to hear the truth . . .

"Nathan—" she started.

"Hired me while you were still in your hospital bed."

"He didn't tell me." She shook her head in disbelief. "Why would he think that someone was trying to kill me?"

"The names connected to the investigation, the painting, out-of-town career opportunities, and Chad Worthington's involvement. Nathan wasn't sure, but the pattern called for him to suspect that someone wanted to get you out of the picture permanently. Your car accident was all the proof he needed."

"Why didn't he tell me?"

"He didn't want to frighten you unnecessarily and I agreed with him."

Alyssa dropped her hand as everything began to feel heavy. She struggled to breathe as her heart thudded in her chest. Yet it was more than the shock of Nathan's actions that caused the sensation.

"I feel woozy." Her speech was slurred.

Alyssa's alcohol tolerance wasn't all that high, but it wasn't low enough that a glass of brandy would have such a potent effect. Her gaze fell on the empty tumbler.

"You put something in my drink." Her long eyelashes fluttered upward to reveal accusing eyes. She stiffened as she looked at Damian standing across from her. The man's dark eyes traveled up the length of her and settled on her face.

Her hands came down on the sofa and struggled to straighten as a wave of lassitude threatened to drown her in its wake. She stood up slowly but stopped as the room began to sway. When her eyes drifted shut, then snapped open. Damian stood less than a foot away from her, or was he? She saw three of him. Alyssa tried to move, but instead her legs wouldn't hold her, and her hand shot out and clamped onto the back of the sofa.

"You have beautiful eyes, Alyssa." Damian reached out and tucked a strand of hair behind her ear, then his fingers traced the length of her jaw.

"Do I?" She stared into his eyes, mesmerized as much by their darkness as by the resonance of his voice.

"Pure gold, yet with a luster found in precious metal ingots. I had wondered these past few days."

"Go . . ." Her voice trailed off. "Away."

"Love is not a zero-sum game, Alyssa. There is no win or lose. Nathan is a good man, not perfect, and he needs you now. Let that be enough."

Alyssa inhaled and the subtle ginger scent of his aftershave went to her head as she struggled to speak; her voice was less than a whisper. As her heavy lids closed, the sight that followed her into oblivion was the serene expression on Damian's face.

* * *

Nathan pushed open the door of his house and turned toward the right. Catching sight of Damian standing next to the window, he skidded to a halt. "Where is she?"

"Upstairs asleep."

"Don't go anywhere," Nathan ordered, tossing his jacket on the sofa before spinning on his heel. Rushing back to the hallway, he took the stairs two at a time. It wasn't until he'd entered his bedroom and caught sight of the fully clothed woman on his bed that Nathan allowed the air out of his chest.

In the space of twenty-four hours, he'd missed her more than he'd ever imagined, more than he'd thought possible. The emptiness of his bed, the emptiness of his house, the silence made her absence all the more intolerable. Even the prospect of never holding her, never kissing her, never making love to her paled alongside the realization of the possibility that he might lose her not to death but because he'd acted like a fool.

He kneeled down on the edge of the bed and gently unfastened her sandals, then sat down beside her and pulled her as close to him as possible. She was sleeping deeply, thick lashes soft against her cheeks, one hand loosely wrapped around a pillow and the other trailing over the edge of the bed. His gaze moved from her sleeping face over her slender figure.

"Alyssa," he whispered. "You're safe and you're home." He tucked her hair behind her small rounded ears. He wanted to trace his hands all over her body, to touch her, to ground himself in her, to make sure that she was real and unharmed. She murmured and buried herself against his chest, eyelids fluttering, but did not wake. He couldn't mask the feeling of disappointment when her eyes didn't open to meet his.

"I gave her something to make her sleep." An all-too-familiar voice came from the doorway.

Nathan rose from the bed and covered her with the blanket before following Damian out the bedroom. He made sure to close the door firmly behind him.

"What happened?" Nathan asked after they'd entered the den. Pulling off his tie, he went behind the wet bar and proceeded to pull down two glasses and an unopened bottle of Jack Daniel's.

"Someone rigged her apartment to blow. Very clean, very professional. Would have looked like her stove had a gas leak, and the trigger point could have been anything. Would have taken at least three or four floors in the blast, wiping out any evidence."

"My God." Nathan poured a shot of whisky and tossed it back without thinking.

"The stakes are getting higher and she may not be so lucky next time."

"Next time?" Nathan repeated as something heavy slammed into his chest. It took him a moment to realize that it was mortality. Not his own but that of the woman he loved, the one woman he would hold above all others and protect at the cost of his own life.

"Cause and effect. Action and reaction. She's gotten too close to being able to pin the hit-and-run on him. Up until now he's tried to make it look accidental. Next time he probably won't."

Fear was a physical thing and it clawed the insides of Nathan's stomach. "Get her out of here, Damian. Take her up to Canada and stash her there until this blows over."

Damian shook his head and took the drink from Nathan's hand. "Maybe her leaving after the accident worked once before, but as long as she's alive she's a threat to the person who committed the crime."

"Let's not pussyfoot around. Worthington is behind this. I think it's time we brought in the police."

Damian shook his head. "You're smarter than that, Nate. Think with your head and don't act in fear. Not only is there not enough evidence, but as far as I can tell the man's kept his hands clean."

Nathan rubbed his head vigorously. "What do I do?"

"You wait for them to make a mistake. I've got a man shadowing Worthington and the hit man. All we need to do is link the hit man to Worthington and we've got leverage to get him to back off."

"How long will that take, Damian? I don't think I can handle another phone call."

"Five days."

His gaze sharpened. "Alyssa's appointment at the district attorney's office."

"Yeah." Damian's gaze was steady. "It's also the day of your confirmation hearing."

"I can't leave her."

"Yes, you can. Listen to me, Nate, because I've been there, I've seen stuff like this go down before. He will come after Alyssa whether you're in Chicago or in Washington."

"Do you know what you're asking?" Nathan asked after spending three minutes staring down into the bottom of his empty glass.

"The same thing you asked of me before meeting with my family's lawyers and regaining my full inheritance. I'm asking you to trust me."

"She's my life, Damian," Nathan confessed shakily to the man who had been his roommate in college, his line brother when he'd pledged, and his first legal client. "Promise me that she won't come to any harm."

They locked eyes and it was Nathan who was the first to look away to stare down at the tumbler in his hand.

"I promise you that I will take any means necessary to keep her safe."

When Nathan next looked up, he was alone.

Chapter 23

Alyssa rolled to her right, expecting to encounter the edge of the bed, and hit a big, warm object. The next thing she noticed was that the only clothing she had on was her undergarments. Her eyes opened slowly as the memories of the apartment, Damian, and the drugged drink raced through her mind. Their eyes locked and she tensed; she was alive because of Nathan, but yet again he had failed to trust her, failed to tell her the complete truth.

"I was worried about you." Nathan spoke in a whisper, reaching out to her through the distance his manipulations had created between them.

"Why—"

His fingers came up to cover her lips. "You're alive and you're safe and you're home."

"But—"

"No," he whispered, shaking his head. "I won't lose you, Alyssa. Either to ambition or death." His fingers moved to caress her jaw as his lips soon followed suit.

"I should leave you." A large yawn took that moment to split her face, making her ears pop and the threat laughable.

Nathan wrapped his arms all the more tightly around her. "I've hidden your clothes and you can't have them back until I'm forgiven."

"Fine, you're forgiven." She pulled back. "Now let me go and give me my clothes."

"I haven't apologized yet."

"Well, hurry."

"Alyssa. . . ."

"What?" She shook her hair out of her face. "Were you expecting me to be so grateful that I would forget that you held out on me again?

"Ouch!" She tried to pull away again and only managed to hurt her toes while kicking him in the shins. "Don't you have to go to work today? Some corporation that you need to make a little richer?"

"It's Saturday."

Nathan kissed her on her bare shoulder, thoroughly enjoying her struggles. "See what happens when you try to leave me?"

"Yes, someone tries to kill me. If this is your way of skipping over the 'until death do us part' thing, I don't like it at all," she bit out.

Laughter rumbled in his chest. "I'm glad you still kept your sense of humor."

"If I didn't, I would be either crying hysterically or yelling at you. Nathan, how could you have that man following me and not have told me?"

"I didn't want to frighten you." He lowered his gaze and trailed his fingers over her shoulder.

"Congratulations," she said sarcastically. "You've succeeded brilliantly, Your Honor. I'm one exit past terrified."

"Baby, I told you I would do anything to make you happy, and anything to keep you from harm. Damian is inclusive in that."

"You could have told me."

He put his leg on top of her thigh, settling her against his hardness. "I believed that you would resist having a bodyguard, so I opted for a shadow instead."

"Who exactly is Damian?"

"A friend." He dipped his head and began to nibble on the curve of her neck. His fingers slid down the curve of her back, then lower until his hand settled on the swell of her hip.

"A friend?" she repeated. Doubt didn't just drip from her

voice; it flowed like an open tap. "A gun-carrying, lock-picking, and absolutely terrifying friend?"

He lightly stroked her skin, running his thumb ever closer to the valley of her thighs.

Alyssa worked hard to ignore the strings of desire that seemed to be pulling tight against her skin. Nathan's hardness pressed close to her stomach, and the musky scent of him wreaked havoc on her senses.

"I have never liked guns, Nathan. I don't want to be around people with guns. Uncle Edward was the only exception and Aunt Sara never approved of his having a pistol in the house."

"I'm sorry, but I need you safe and he is the only person to do it. I trust him with more than my life. I trusted him with the most precious thing in my life and he brought you back home early."

"I had twenty-four more hours." She recalled their agreement.

"Sooner is better than later. Until we can put Worthington and his lackey behind bars, I want you to remain here. I'll talk to Bernard and get Damian to pick up your laptop from your apartment. You can work from the office downstairs."

"No, thank you."

"This house is more secure than your condo, Alyssa."

"Really? Well, your pal Damian didn't seem to have trouble getting past the alarm last night," she pointed out.

"He wouldn't. Damian designed the security system."

"Go figure. Is there anything else you left out?"

He sidestepped the question. "I'll go ahead and call Bernard in the morning."

"No, Nathan." She touched his arm. "I know how much you want to protect me and I love you for it, but I will not cower in this house like some helpless victim."

"It will only be until we can put a stop to these attempts on your life."

"One hour is too long. Chad Worthington won't keep me from finding justice."

"He's already taken a year off of my life," he murmured while toying while the lacy strap of her bra. "How about we find a compromise?"

"I'm listening."

"Damian continues to go wherever you go and you spend your evenings and nights here."

"Where's the compromise in that?"

He moved over and kissed the soft hollow of her collarbone. "It's either that or I cancel my trip to D.C., Damian watches you during the day while I'm in court, I pick you up after work, and I move into your place."

"You would give up the opportunity of becoming a federal judge and risk losing the chance at a seat on the Supreme Court?"

"I love you, Alyssa." He watched her face for signs that she understood the depths of his commitment to her. Not seeing the response he'd hoped for, Nathan got out of bed and put on his boxer shorts. Reaching into his armoire, he pulled out a college shirt.

"Catch."

"What's this for?" she asked, puzzled, with not just a little disappointment at his abrupt action.

"Put it on and come with me."

Alyssa sat up and tugged on the oversized T-shirt. He led her downstairs into the basement, into his study.

Nathan opened the door to his inner life. She had been in the room before, yet with him standing beside her it became more than pictures of family, law books, books on philosophy, and a library of other books and the smell of leather. She followed him over to the shelves filled with model trains of all different colors, shapes, and sizes that represented different ages.

"My father's dream was to see the entire United States by train. He did whatever was necessary to get on a train and get out of Mississippi. He managed to get all the way up and down the East Coast, from top to bottom, before changing directions and trying for the West, but he didn't accomplish his goals."

"Because of the accident?"

He was silent for a long moment, then continued, his voice low, confessional. "No, he discovered a better dream." Nathan wrapped his arms around Alyssa from behind and turned her toward his favorite photograph. He knew every small silver fleck of the black and white photograph, could describe the day it was taken, from the smell of the air, to the shrill whistle of the train. "Her name was Rosemarie Wilkens.

"Dad could have crossed the continent on that train over there." Nathan pointed to the glass case. "But he chose to take the sum of his wages to a small jewelry shop that catered to colored people and he bought a ring. The ring I put on your finger."

Alyssa stood quietly, her back to his chest with his arms still wrapped around her waist as he returned his solemn gaze to her face. "Spell it out for me, Nathan. I need to hear the words. I need to trust that you are committed to this because of love, not duty."

Inhaling the sweet scent of Alyssa's skin, he caressed her stomach. "At this moment I know what matters. I love you. When I am on my deathbed surrounded by loved ones, I want to be remembered first as a good father and your loving husband. If I am granted the privilege of seeing my life before I see God, then I want most of that time spent watching you in my arms. I swear to you that like my father chose my mother, I shall place no other before you. My father knew what mattered and like him I'd rather have a lifetime with you than a few decades on the Supreme Court."

Alyssa's eyes misted at the sincerity of his sentiment and emotion. She turned around and placed her cheek next to his, feeling the roughness of his shadow, the trembling of his jaw. She had lived by the creed that actions spoke louder than words, but as she looked up into his eyes and straight into his heart, she rediscovered her faith in things unseen and futures undreamt. "I believe you, but there can be no more secrets or skeletons in the closet. If we're going to be in this for the long haul, I need you to be straight with me always."

"Well, there is one . . ." His dark eyes twinkled. "I knew I would marry you from the moment you stole my tuna sushi. Are you mad at me?"

"Mad? Yes. I'm madly in love with you, Nathan Hughes."

Lowering his face, he touched his lips to hers. "That makes two of us."

For Nathan, the week sped by in the blink of an eye. Every moment that he was not called upon to answer questions, preside over cases, or sign his name to another document giving rights to some bureaucrat to peer into the crevices of his life, he spent it with Alyssa.

Walking through the doorway of his home had never been so peaceful. The threat of Chad Worthington hung over their heads, but by some unspoken agreement they never spoke of it. And he took each minute, each hour, from the moment he called out his greeting in the entranceway until he whispered his good nights to her in his arms, to show Alyssa he loved her. He loved seeing her in his shirt, seeing her legs intertwined with his, having her singing in the shower, the way her body sang as they made love, the way she marked him with her teeth when she climaxed, pulling him even deeper into her body.

Every morning he woke to the soft warmth of Alyssa's skin touching his own, the rhythm of her heartbeat, the beautiful privilege of seeing her honey-brown eyes, and her lips curving in in a sleepy smile. This last morning proved to be no exception.

He watched as her long, slender eyelashes fluttered upward to reveal sleepy pupils. "Good morning."

"You overslept, little one."

Her smile stretched as she flattened her palm against his chest. "No, I didn't. I took today off."

"You didn't have to."

"I know, but I want to see you to the airport."

"My flight isn't until this afternoon." He moved in for a kiss only to freeze in surprise as she drew back.

"Oh, no, you don't. I have morning breath, remember?"

"Alyssa. You know I wasn't serious."

"And how do I know—" She broke off as he pulled her to him. "That?"

"Because I love you." He crushed her lips to his and rested his thickening sex against her stomach. Nathan heard her moan and ignored it.

"Do you believe that?" He looked into her eyes.

"Well . . ." Her voice trailed as she gave him a coy glance before lowering her eyes.

"Yes or no?" He didn't wait for her answer; instead he moved lower on the bed, caught her foot, and brought one toe into his mouth. In his desire to give her pleasure that would make up for time they would spend apart, he took his time and licked every inch of her skin while making his way up her body. With his fingers and tongue he staked his claim to every part of her heart, body, and soul.

Alyssa couldn't catch her breath. Just when she thought her body would shatter, he'd begin again. And she took it all with reckless abandon while offering moans of pleasure intermixed with cries of joy.

Pulling away from her, Nathan reached over to the bedside table and placed the contents of the silver-foil packet on his sex. Soon he would see her standing by his side pregnant with their child, but not yet.

She reached for him, but he avoided her touch and took her hands within his own. Every muscle in his body strained to bury himself in her softness, to fulfill the promise of their joining, but he forced himself to slow down, and he buried his face in her neck, smelling her scent, his tongue leaving hot trails up her neck's graceful line as he managed to whisper in her ear, "Yes or no, little one?"

And she turned her face and he leaned down to kiss the tears from her eyes as she panted.

"Yes," she moaned, gripping the sheets. He thrust himself into her slick, tight heat, and she cried out. His hands on her hips, he pushed into her, harder and harder, relishing the way her breasts moved with his thrusts, the dark nipples swollen by the results of his touch.

Her climax came so suddenly she didn't have time to get ready for it. It slammed into her and made her breathless as it rocketed through her. He growled his fulfillment. She prepared herself for the finish as she thought he would stop, grow soft within her, and she would be left with that pleasant throbbing but somehow empty feeling she had when it was all over. But Nathan did not stop, he pulled her up and positioned her in his lap.

"I will always cherish you," he whispered, his breath caressing in her ear.

He slowed down then, cradling her hips gently. And as he began to move her again, this time it was sweet, and he held her close and made love to her with even, tender strokes and then stopped. He caught her face in his hands, his eyes tightly closed as he kissed her, his kisses strong, and when her second orgasm came it was with him, feeling the powerful shudder of his body as they clung to each other and a second, unexpected bliss rolled over her in heady waves.

Mine, Nathan thought, then buried his face in her neck, groaning, the taut muscles of his shoulders and back trembling beneath her hands. He didn't know if he would be able to leave her that afternoon.

"I wish I could be there to support you," she said again.

Alyssa alighted from the backseat of the Mercedes after Damian parked the car next to the departure terminal. The sun beamed down on the both of them and Alyssa peeked up at Nathan from underneath her sunglasses.

They'd only had time for a shared quick shower before the phone rang, signaling an end to their morning tryst. With him dressed in a three-piece suit and a tie he'd asked her to pick out, Alyssa eyed him with more desire than she'd eyed the banana-nut muffin she'd grabbed as they ran out the front door.

Nathan leaned down and placed a lingering kiss on her lips. "Funny, I was thinking the same thing, but you don't have to be by my side for me to know you're there for me."

Nathan let go of the handle to his luggage and pulled her close. "I want you here and safe. Lauren and her future mother-in-law will be taking the train down together to show some support. Does that make you feel better?"

"Yes." She took off her glasses and slid them into her hair before stepping through the automatic sliding doors. She blinked twice, waiting for her eyes to adjust.

"Good." A woman's voice came over the loudspeaker. Alyssa nestled in his arms while people walked past, accompanied by the sounds of rolling wheels. Goose bumps rose on her skin as a gust of hypercool air swept over them. Although the morning sunlight streamed into the terminal through expansive glazed windows, the temperature inside was one degree above freezing.

"You need to catch your flight," she pointed out, yet didn't move from the cradle of his arms.

His lips curved into a grin. "One more kiss before I go?"

Reaching upward, she used her hands to guide his face down to press her lips upon his. She kept her eyes locked with his, letting the love show, and while her tongue stroked his, her fingers rubbed the stiff strands of his hair.

"Promise me you'll be careful and listen to Damian," he whispered against her mouth.

Alyssa crossed her fingers while he squeezed her tight. "I promise." She looked over his shoulder and straight into Damian's penetrating gaze. Meeting his stare with one of her own, she turned back to Nathan, kissed him hard on the lips, then playfully pushed him away. "Go knock 'em dead and give my love to Lauren."

After seeing Nathan go through security, Alyssa adjusted her sunglasses and exited the terminal to see Damian leaning against the Mercedes. She nodded politely as he opened the passenger-side door. Even after they had gotten on the road she remained silent.

"Alyssa?"

"Yes, Mr. Béchard?" She didn't take her gaze off the passing scenery as they drove toward the city.

"Call me Damian."

"Damian," she said through gritted teeth, determined to be civil even if the effort killed her.

"Look into the side mirror."

She opened her mouth, then shut it quickly before snapping out a question.

His attention never wavered from negotiating the highway traffic. "Do you notice anything familiar about the charcoal-gray SUV two cars behind us on the right?"

"No, should I?"

"It has been parked two houses from Nathan's for the last two days. The man behind the steering wheel goes by many names except his real one. Ryan Buhl was once a member of the U.S. Special Forces, dishonorably discharged, and then he turned mercenary in Latin America. He is a killer with a reputation for success and he happens to be the same man who attempted to run you off the road, tampered with your brakes, and rigged your apartment to explode. Mr. Buhl has attempted to kill you twice. I believe that he will make another try."

He paused at her indrawn breath.

"I tell you this not to frighten you, but to make you aware of the seriousness of this situation. Our only options are to catch him with evidence or kill him; to do that I need to stop him before he gets to you. Alyssa, you may not like my presence, but it is absolutely necessary that when the time comes you will follow my orders without question. Are we agreed?"

She locked her hands together and squeezed. His comments upset her but it was still Damian's presence that sent the contents of her breakfast on a merry-go-round in her stomach. Something in the way he moved, the way he watched everything, let her know that he wasn't someone she wanted to cross. *No,* the voice in the back of her head screamed in warning. He intimidated the hell out of her but she'd be damned if she would let him see it. "So I get to be bait?"

"That's one way you could see it. Are we agreed?"

She looked into the side mirror as he switched lanes, and sure enough the charcoal SUV followed them off the freeway. Alyssa thought back to the first time they'd met and the subsequent drugging of her drink. "Yes, as long as you don't touch my glass or my plate."

Two nights later and less than a thousand miles away from Chicago, Nathan adjusted his tie and took in a deep breath before knocking on the door of the Ambassador Hotel's suite 573. He had not seen his sister in person for over a year. Growing up they had been best friends. They both had their established careers now and lived their separate lives; he would never be able to see her as anything but his little sister.

"Nate!"

He held out his arms and the familiar warmth of her cheek alongside his dissipated his earlier fears.

"Come on in."

"How are you, little bit?" As a lawyer he'd learned never to ask a question when he already knew the answer. And he knew the answer from one look at Lauren. Although just shy of thirty, she glowed with the vitality and luster of a girl half her age. He noticed the sparkle in her eyes, and the tenor of her voice hummed with excitement.

"You look good," he commented, taking off his raincoat and looking around the space.

"Thanks to a quick sit-down in the hotel's sauna." A mischievous smile played on her face. "I thought I'd get rid of some tension before dinner. The wife is an avid art collector and the husband is a minimalist. I have no idea how it is those two got together."

An interior designer at a prestigious firm, Lauren decorated and renovated many kinds of living abodes, but her true passion lay with brownstones. It was more than fitting that she would fall in love with Nicholas Randolph while turning his Brooklyn brownstone into a home.

Lauren patted Nathan's arm. "Enough talk about work. What's the plan for dinner?"

"I've got reservations for eight o'clock."

Lauren stood next to the television hutch. "Nathan?"

"Yes?"

She tilted her head to the side and smiled at him like a little girl. "Would it be okay if we ordered room service and ate here?"

Startled, he looked at her. Just looked. His little sister was beautiful but her resemblance to their father made her all the more wonderfully precious to him. "Little bit, we can eat anywhere you want."

"It's just that I haven't seen you in a while and I'd like to spend as much time as I can with you."

After they had consumed three-quarters of a loaded pizza and numerous breadsticks, Nathan wiped his grease-covered hands on the napkin and leaned back in the deep-seated chair.

"Now how did the two of you meet again? Mom gave me this crazy story that you were going to take a long vacation and get married."

"Well . . ." She leaned back in her chair. "The scheme isn't so crazy. I planned on going around the world and finding a husband. Alan put Nick up to hiring me to do some renovations on his brownstone. I fell in love with the house, its owner, and a stray cat we found in the backyard."

Nathan let out a loud laugh, which trailed off into a chuckle. "You sure know how to make life exciting."

Lauren finished nibbling a pizza crust, then aimed a twinkling eye his way. "According to family gossip, you're the new hero. You and Alyssa reunited Aunt Sara and Uncle Edward, got Sabrina to give up her weekly pilgrimages to Marshall Field's shoe department, in favor of volunteering, and hopefully you will soon be the parents of a kitten."

"Whoa." He almost choked on his soda. "Back up. Dog, maybe, but no cats."

"Brooklyn's pregnant."

"Brooklyn." He searched his memory. "Is that the stray cat you adopted?"

"Nick and I adopted her. Actually, we found her in his backyard and we both thought she was a he."

His brow creased. "How did— Never mind."

"Nick accidentally let her out a few weeks ago. She didn't come back for three nights, and when she did come home . . ."

Nathan's mouth curled upward. "Did you find the father?"

"Maybe another stray, but I'm hoping it's the Persian across the street. The kittens will be adorable."

"Sorry, little sister. I'd do anything for you, but sacrificing my fish isn't one of them."

"No worries." She laughed and the light sound warmed his heart. "Brooklyn only likes canned food and tuna. Her kittens will be the same."

Knowing that he would do anything to make his baby sister happy, Nathan decided to change topics before she managed to change his mind. "You're going to be getting married. I feel as though I'm going to lose what I've only just found."

"You can't lose me like you lost Barbie's Ken doll, Nathan. No, you're getting the brother you've always wanted and the family gets another lawyer. You'll always be my big brother."

"I only met Nick Randolph one time. Tell me about him."

"He's a lot like our father, I imagine. He'll do anything for family, loves me beyond measure, and he accepts me unconditionally."

He looked down at her hand as it curled around the can of cola. The circlet of diamonds on her ring finger twinkled in the overhead light. "Guess it's a little late to act like the overprotective big brother."

She put down her beverage, stood, walked around behind him, bent down, and hugged him close. Lauren kissed him on the cheek and rested her head atop his own. Nathan's heart caught at the familiar gesture.

"It's never too late."

Chapter 24

The final straw came, not with the ringing of the phone, Damian's constant presence, the breaking of glass, or a thump in the middle of the night. No, Alyssa got fed up when she spilled her morning tea at the sound of the refrigerator clicking on.

"No more," she muttered while cleaning up the spill. Fear had made her sleep restless and her favorite foods tasteless. She was no longer going to hide out waiting for the other shoe to drop, counting the hours until she met with the district attorney to give her testimony. No, she wasn't going to wake up dead and buried or floating in a lake.

Damn it, I'm a Knight and we don't run and hide. We stay and fight. She wasn't going to sit and wait as Worthington's hired killer came after her. No, she would get to him first.

Alyssa stood up, moved to stand next to the aquarium, and took a moment to gaze at the tranquil fish. A plan began to form in her mind. First, she needed to get away from Damian. Everywhere she went he followed; the man didn't seem to eat or sleep. Picking up the cordless phone, she pressed the soft rubber button. It was time to see the man behind it all.

"Good night, sweetheart."

"Night, Uncle Edward," Alyssa repeated, stepping out of the bear hug with a smile on her face. It made her feel like a kid again. Some part of her expected her aunt and uncle to tuck her into the bed as they did when she was seven years old.

"If you need anything, you just give a shout, okay? We're right down the hall."

Her overnight visit to her aunt and uncle's house, although unexpected, had been welcome. No questions and no deceptive answers to give. Only Damian had pressed her to know why she would leave the security of Nathan's town house. As if wanting to be with family wasn't enough, she missed Nathan. Longed for him to come home and quietly slip into bed next to her. She missed falling asleep in a semi-fetal position with his arm around her stomach—protecting her from nightmares.

After taking a shower, Alyssa opened the door to the guest bedroom to hear her cell phone ringing. She crossed the hardwood floors and managed to dig it out of her purse on the fifth and last ring before it switched over to the answering service.

"Hello." Her voice was still husky from the steamy shower.

"Alyssa?"

"Nathan?" She repeated his name in the same tone, making it sound as though she were unsure it was him on the other line.

"I got your message. You plan to spend the rest of the week with Aunt Sara and Uncle Edward?"

"Damian wouldn't let me go back to my condo and I don't like staying in that big house without you."

"As long as you're safe."

"This neighborhood is filled with grandmothers who don't sleep, police officers, and dogs. I'm sure no hit man in the world is that foolish, so stop worrying."

In the silence, Alyssa heard the rustling of papers.

"Were you sleeping?" Nathan asked.

"No." She placed her bag on the floor, then sat at the bottom of the double bed. "I just got out of the shower and put on my pajamas."

"So what are you wearing?" His voice lowered, sending goose bumps down her skin.

Alyssa lay down atop the bedcovers, enjoying the feel of the cool air on her heated skin. A smile curved her mouth. "You first."

"Boxers."

"Aunt Sara's orange muumuu," she lied, looking down at the yellow two-piece pajama set.

"The one with pockets?"

"Uh-uh."

His voice lowered. "Sexy. Model it for me the night I get home."

"Not even if you paid me." Alyssa laughed softly. "By the way, when are you coming home?"

"Miss me?"

"No, just tired of Damian. I'd rather have you."

"Only two more days."

"How are things?"

"Haven't had any problems. In fact they seem to be treating me with kid gloves. And I spent last night eating Italian with a beautiful woman."

"That's nice."

A smile blossomed on Alyssa face. "I left her hotel room at three o'clock in the morning."

"Aren't you two a pair of night owls? Did heartburn from the pizza wake you up this morning?"

"My mother?"

"No," she chuckled. "Technology, big boy. Your sister sent me an e-mail to say hello and asked if Alan was as possessive of his little sister as you were."

"I love you."

"I know." She paused. "Nathan?"

"Hmm . . ."

"I'm not wearing a muumuu."

"I know. Aunt Sara doesn't have any."

"Smarty-pants."

"I'm waiting, Alyssa."

"I love you, too."

"Go to bed, angel. I'll be dreaming of you."

Alyssa clicked off the cell phone and placed it back in her purse. Climbing into bed and pulling the light coverlet over her shoulders, she stared into the darkness. Tomorrow was the day; she just hoped she could pull it off.

Alyssa Knight was blushing. It wasn't an unusual occurrence, except that she'd begun blushing fifteen minutes ago and the shade of her cheeks had yet to change. The memory of the lie she'd told her aunt Sara when she borrowed both the nurse's uniform and her aunt's car that Thursday morning wouldn't stop the replay loop in her mind. Pulling up to a stoplight, she brushed her hands over the plain white cotton outfit. She doubted that Nathan had ever had any kind of fantasy about playing doctor and nurse, but the idea was intriguing.

She slowed the car as she drew near her destination. The large brick houses, manicured lawns, and pristine streets with elegant lamps lining the sidewalks. Alyssa pulled up to the front of the Worthingtons' iron gates, rolled down her window, and pressed the intercom button while looking into the small video camera lens.

"Yes?"

"I'm here to do a surprise check of Mr. Worthington's attending nurse."

Alyssa held her breath until the gates began to open. "Park your car on the west side near the garage and use the servants' entrance."

Too relieved to be angry, Alyssa smiled. "Thank you. Please don't alert the attending nurse of my arrival."

"Certainly."

After parking the car, she grabbed the clipboard. She'd succeeded in getting in, but could she get by? All she needed was to be seen by the maid that had served her tea during her previous visit, and it would be all over. Lady Luck was with her. The cook opened the door.

"Just follow me."

They went through the large, immaculate restaurant-sized kitchen, up the back stairs, and down a long corridor.

The nurse was sitting in a chair reading when Alyssa opened the door and entered.

"Good afternoon."

The older woman closed her book and stood up quickly. "Who are you?"

"Alyssa Knight."

She turned her head sharply at the sound of a strong voice from the other side of the room, locking eyes with the man sitting in a wheelchair in front of the window.

"I've been waiting for you."

"Sir, your son—" the nurse began.

He waved a hand, cutting off the woman's tirade. "Ms. Shaw, you may go."

"But—" She took an aggressive step toward Alyssa.

"You may leave and let Jorgen know that I have a guest and would like to have refreshments sent up."

When the door had firmly closed behind the nurse, Alyssa spoke. "I apologize for the deception, Mr. Worthington, but I felt that this meeting would never take place if I relied upon your son."

"I agree with you wholeheartedly. Please indulge an old man and take a seat near me."

After settling in the chair he indicated, Alyssa studied his face. He had neither the looks nor the presence of the politicians she'd dealt with in the past, although he would inspire confidence with his steady gaze and voice. There was something surprising in one who had spent eight years as a mayor.

"What is it that you wish to talk about?"

"I need you to stop covering up for your son and tell me what you know about the night of Lily Santiago's death."

He didn't bat an eye but she caught the quiver in his chin. "What makes you think I know anything, and even if I did why would I talk to you?"

"For whatever reason possessed you to purchase a painting for a hundred thousand dollars and have it delivered to my apartment. Because it was at your order that Oxford University gave me a fellowship, for the reason that your Jaguar was reported stolen one day after the hit-and-run. I believe your son killed Lily in a fit of jealous rage and now he's hired someone to kill me."

"That is a very slanderous accusation, young lady."

"I was there that night, Mr. Worthington. I saw the car. I saw your car. The same blue Jaguar that you reported stolen the day after Lily's death."

"But did you see the driver?" he parried.

"I'm not sure." Alyssa searched the older man's face, hoping that her scrutiny would shake something loose and give her some idea as to how he fit into Lily's death, how much he knew about his son's actions.

Mr. Worthington's blue eyes widened. "You don't remember it all yet, do you?"

He turned away from her and toward the door as a tall man walked inside caring a tray. She recognized him from the charity auction. She watched the odd sight of the large man handling the silver serving tray and placing the two glasses filled with brown liquid and topped with a lemon wedges on the table.

"Jorgen, Ms. Knight has come to pay me a visit."

He took his glass and smiled. "Please have some tea."

"Thank you." She placed the glass to her mouth and pretended to sip. The lesson of never taking candy from a stranger had been reinforced when she'd drunk Damian's doctored glass of brandy.

"What do you have to do with all this? It revolves around you and your son. I can't prove it yet, but I know that it was his car that hit Lily. I'm certain he's the one behind the attempts on my life. But what I don't understand is, why did you send me the painting? What happened that night? You were there, weren't you?"

"Ms. Knight, I am truly sorry but I can't answer your questions. I can promise you that all will be revealed to you in due time."

Alyssa stood up but maintained eye contact. "Tell that to the district attorney, Mr. Worthington. Because I'm going to tell him everything."

"I'm afraid I can't allow you do that, yet. I need more time to put things in place."

Unnerved by the sudden fierce gleam in the older man's eyes, Alyssa swung around but was not fast enough. Before she could move, a strong arm clamped around her and something nauseous was placed over her mouth and nose. The world swam and she sank into blackness.

"What happened to Alyssa?" Nathan jumped into the car with Damian. Any luggage he had was still in his hotel room in D.C. He'd gone straight to the airport and jumped on the first plane out to Chicago after receiving Damian's phone call. It had to have been the longest flight of his life.

"Gone. I've got a lead, but that's all. They fished Worthington's hired killer out of the lake two hours ago. Someone made it look like a boating accident."

"Damn it." Nathan barely stopped himself from punching the dashboard. "Why weren't you following her more closely?"

"Alyssa gave me the slip, she wasn't kidnapped. Save your anger for your future bride."

He took a shaky breath. "You're right, my apologies."

"If it'll make you feel better I'm beating myself up over this as well. She borrowed her aunt Sara's car and drove right past me. It wasn't until after she was due for work that I knocked on the door and found out she'd left." Damian's fingers cut into the wheel as he accelerated onto the expressway. "I must be losing my skills."

Nathan wanted to punch something to relieve his tension

and worry, but instead he shook his head. This was Alyssa's doing. Damian was not to blame. "No, my friend. We both failed to remember the golden rule: never underestimate a woman."

Chapter 25

Alyssa woke with a dry mouth, headache, and upset stomach. Barely five minutes had passed from sleep to wakefulness before nausea sent her stumbling through the door in search of a bathroom to hang her head over the toilet as dry heaves racked her body. She flushed the toilet, rinsed out her mouth, and looked in the mirror. Her face was ashen and her eyes seemed to engulf her face.

Looking around the bathroom, she could see that the place had been prepared for visitors. A brush, comb, toothbrush, and toothpaste along with other assorted toiletries lay displayed on the marble top. She shivered after looking over into the shower and seeing a set of her favorite French shower gel, shampoo, and bath oil.

Alyssa made her way back to the bedroom and pulled back the heavy curtains. The sight of the windows made her stomach lurch. They were barred from the inside. Between the dark metal bars were micromini blinds. To the outside it would look as though there was nothing amiss. Not that it mattered; all she could see through the cracks were trees and bushes.

Someone had tried to kill her twice, Damian had drugged her, and now she'd let herself be kidnapped and locked in a cottage.

She shook her head and winced at the residual headache. She almost giggled in disbelief. In an effort to remain calm, she explored her custom-fit prison and tried opening every door. The first led to a closet with ten changes of clothing approximately her size.

Rubbing her arms, she went through every item in the cottage. The galley-sized kitchen was stocked with plates, cutlery, pots, and pans. It also contained a basic selection of appliances and included a microwave. The small cupboard was filled with canned goods and pasta; the refrigerator and freezer contained a number of fresh vegetables, fruits, meats, and frozen dinners.

The living area lacked a television or radio. There were no phones, no way for her to communicate with the outside world. *The place won't be getting a four-star rating,* Alyssa thought, trying to cheer herself up. She bent over and looked up the chimney, actually contemplating crawling up, but it would be impossible for her to make it up the small space.

Giving up, she went back and crawled into bed as the pounding in her head grew louder.

Two days passed before the man of her dreams became the voice of her reality. "Alyssa, it's time to go."

"Nathan?" She opened her eyes and reached for him. The flashlight dropped unheeded on the bed as he wrapped his arms around her and all the emotions Alyssa had kept in check through the whole ordeal came spilling over into tears.

"Am I glad to see you!" She sniffed.

"Sweetheart, are you okay?"

"No, I'm angry. Worthington's pet guard put something over my face and I woke up here feeling sicker than a dog."

"Chloroform." Damian's voice intruded on their reunion. "No time for happy reunions, we need to leave." Alyssa turned to see the bodyguard's shadowy figure in the doorway.

"Not before I find out why." She rushed to put her shoes on. "Worthington said he needed more time. That he would 'protect the both of us.' Why would he want to keep me safe if he hired someone to kill me?"

"If Nathan is discovered here, it will turn into a case of trespassing and his career could be ruined."

"It was kidnapping," Alyssa snapped.

"Sara Knight mentioned that you borrowed her nurse's uniform the day you disappeared, Alyssa," Damian stated. "My guess is that you gained entrance to the estate under false pretenses."

She opened her mouth to protest but stopped when Damian gestured for silence, then looked upward and his fingers tapped the device in his ear.

"We've got company: two cars. Chad Worthington is in one."

He paused. "Second driver identified as Andrés Santiago."

"We need to warn him, Nathan. He could be in danger," Alyssa said.

"I doubt it," Damian responded dryly. "Nate, let's move. My man can only keep the gate open for five minutes before the malfunction alarm trips."

Alyssa didn't get the chance to ask the question. Nathan grabbed her hand and pulled her out of the room and out of the cottage behind Damian. She let him lead her as far as the edge of the garden and the driveway, then came to a dead stop behind the manicured bushes. They were close enough to hear two people standing underneath the floodlights.

"Alyssa," Nathan whispered urgently.

She stared straight, unseeing, at the sight of Chad Worthington, then her breath caught upon seeing Andrés step out of his vehicle. Their voices carried across the driveway.

"Why are you here?"

"To stop you before another innocent woman is killed."

"I need to speak with my father," Chad said dismissively. "This can wait until later."

Andrés called to the man's departing back, "No, it can't. Is it your turn now, Chad? Your father left my sister bleeding in my hands! Will you leave Alyssa there as well? She's missing and I want to know what you've done to her."

"How dare you have the audacity to come to my family's home and accuse me of anything? This is your fault, Santiago. You should have taken the money I offered you and stayed the hell away from my mother." Chad's voice was filled with such venom that Alyssa shuddered.

"We loved one another." Andrés didn't raise his voice. "Susan meant more to me than your precious money."

"She was a married woman, who had a family, who had responsibilities."

"None of those things you mentioned made her happy. I did that."

"It was not your right and no matter what the doctors said, I will never stop believing that my mother is dead because of you."

Andrés took a step forward. "Blame me if you will but leave Alyssa Knight out of this."

"You don't know what you're talking about."

"Oh, yes, I do. Better than anyone in this city, I have always known how ruthless you could be when your father or family reputation was at risk. Alyssa Knight didn't just have a car accident, you arranged it."

"She wouldn't leave well enough alone and I won't let her blacken my family's good name."

"Alyssa is doing what I couldn't. She just wants to find justice for my sister."

"Don't try that holier-than-thou act with me, Santiago." He turned around. "You were not ready to admit to your family that their son had had an affair with a married woman."

"My cowardice has haunted me ever since," Andrés said. He didn't need his sins paraded before him. "I have prayed, I have confessed and been forgiven, yet still I dream of that night. I still hear my sister's screams. This madness will end because I plan to go to the police."

Chad Worthington could have been made of stone. During the entire heated conversation he had not moved; nothing of life showed except for his eyes. "You swore to my mother that you would remain silent."

"Yes, I did. It was a promise I never should have made. And I won't keep it at the cost of a friend's life."

"Your parents will disown you and you could go to prison for covering up a crime."

"Then so be it," Andrés replied. "I will not let you hurt an innocent woman."

A sickening burn rose up in Alyssa's throat. She lifted her tongue to the roof of her mouth to hold it back, but instead of losing the contents of her stomach, a barrage of memories tightened like a band around her chest.

She felt as though she were watching a movie on fast-forward; the events leading up to and after Lily's death played in her mind. Shaken, she closed and opened her eyes. Tears began to stream, one after another, as shudders racked her body. Alyssa made no effort to suppress the fury of emotions, which began with grief and heated to anger.

She stood up and Nathan's hand fell from her shoulder. "She pushed me out of harm's way."

Andrés turned toward her and there was surprise underneath the shock. "Alyssa, I—"

She curled inward away from him and held out a hand as though to avoid a blow. "Don't say a word. Don't you dare say you're sorry! Don't think it. Don't even feel it. I remember what happened that night, Andrés. I remember it all now. We overheard the two of you arguing. Chad Worthington came backstage to offer you money to break off the affair. Lily dropped her bag and ran. You followed her outside." Alyssa shivered, remembering the wet snow falling on the street. "I ran out to stand between you. The headlights kept coming brighter and she pushed us."

"Yes, Ms. Knight. She pushed you both out of the way."

All of their heads turned at the unexpected voice.

"Father, what are you doing? You should be inside." Chad Worthington rushed to his father's side, then stopped and stared coldly at the blond bodyguard. "You're fired. Pack your belongings and get off this property within the hour."

"Stay where you are, Jorgen. I own this estate, I hired you, and I will fire you. I am not dead yet, Chad," the old man said coldly. "Kindly wait until that day to take my place."

"What about your health?"

"It's failing, son," Worthington Sr. said. "I will die, Chad, but I won't go to my grave with this stain sitting on my soul. I won't let you destroy what little piece of your mother you have in you. I promised that woman I would never let anything happen to you."

He turned away from his son and locked eyes with Alyssa. "The police and the attorneys are making their way to the estate. Jorgen, if you would be so kind as to open the front gates. Ms. Knight, how I envied you. How ironic that a man who had a brilliant memory and a good life wanted to forget. I have lived the past few years with my health as well as my faculties deserting me. But I could never erase the memories of that night. The look on the young woman's face, the sounds."

"You ran her down and left her for dead," Alyssa spat.

The son answered, "He was upset."

"I was full of gin and hate, Chad. I came to the performance furious that your mother could be so weak. How could she jeopardize my election, the reputation of our family, and our marriage to have an affair with a dancer? A Hispanic boy still wet behind his ears—"

"She loved me," Andrés said, cutting him off.

The old man nodded slowly, as though the weight of the years had come crashing down upon his shoulders. "My shock turned to anger and then denial. I knew that you had changed my wife, seduced her." He paused for several moments, struggling for breath. "I thought that if you were gone, things would go back to the way they were."

Chad bent over the ex-mayor's chair. "Father, you promised never to talk about this to anyone."

"I've promised many things, but I will not have you committing murder or going to prison for me. I need my grand-children taken care of far more than I need a good reputation. You've kept me from facing my own mistakes for too long, Chadwick. The sins of the father shall not be visited upon the son."

Several moments passed before Nathan stepped forward. "I'm not a criminal judge, but your son has tampered with evidence, conspired to commit murder, and covered up a crime. I won't let him get away with this."

"You don't have a choice. The contract on Ms. Knight's life has been irrevocably canceled. I've confessed to the crimes you have mentioned and provided evidence of my sole accountability.

"Ms. Knight, Judge Hughes, Mr. Santiago, I must apologize, but you have to leave. I am sure the press will descend upon us as well and I'm sure that the future Chicago northern district federal judge doesn't need the negative publicity of trespassing and libel charges to darken his upcoming confirmation ceremony."

Nathan took Alyssa's arm and gently led her away. The vacant expression on her face scared him almost as much as when he'd gotten the phone call informing him that Alyssa had been admitted to the hospital.

When she stumbled, he picked her up and carried her to the waiting automobile. As Damian pulled away from the edge, she turned and looked out the back window as the flashing blue lights of the arriving police cars chased them away.

"How could he? How could I?" Alyssa's breath came out in uneven gasps and tears welled in her eyes and dripped down her cheeks. Of all the things she'd imagined, none could have prepared her for the devastating truth. It made her wish she'd never remembered the accident. Even the pure feelings of gratitude she had knowing of Lily's sacrifice couldn't wipe away the stain of Andrés's betrayal.

"Baby, please don't cry." Despite the seat belt biting into his chest, Nathan reached and pulled her toward him.

Angela Weaver

"All along he'd known who killed Lily." Alyssa rocked back and forth, uncaring of Damian's eyes in the rearview mirror. Looking into Nathan's face and seeing the understanding reflected in his eyes, she broke down. At first a single tear fell and then the storm came. She tried to breathe and all that came forth was a gasp. Shudders racked her body as her lungs struggled to pull in the dry, cool air.

Nathan held her all the way to his house, never saying a word. He carried her to the bedroom and laid her on the bed, undressing her like a child, and wiping her face with a warm cloth. He took off his shoes, pulled Alyssa into his arms.

"I don't understand."

"Love and hate can do powerful things to a man, angel," he whispered, pressing his lips to her brow.

"What happens now?" Alyssa pulled back enough to look Nathan in the eyes. "Will he get away with what he's done?"

"Right now all I care about is our future. I promised to protect you and I failed. I should have been here."

"No. You were where you were meant to be. God had His plans tonight, Nathan."

"I'm not sure the Lord would endorse your foolish actions, Alyssa. I didn't know if I was going to kiss you or strangle you when Damian told me you'd snuck off."

"I'm glad you chose the first."

"I'm glad I got to you in time."

"He promised not to hurt me."

"Alyssa, the man Chad Worthington hired to kill you was fished out of the lake this morning. That man's promises mean nothing to me and I will personally do everything I can to see that the both of them pay for their crimes."

Her eyes widened as another thought crossed her mind. Alyssa shook her head. "Wait, you told me that the hearing would take all week. You could have forfeited your confirmation by leaving early—"

"Shh." He pulled her into his arms and grounded himself

in her scent, in the way she fit in his arms like a part of him. "Just say you still love me. Nothing else matters."

Alyssa closed her eyes; his hands stroked her back and her heart sped up.

"Say it," Nathan said again. "I need to hear the words." The touch of his lips on the nape of her neck made her dizzy and she clutched at his shoulders, afraid she would lose her balance. His breath was warm across her mouth, and yet he held back, only letting his lips brush across hers in butterfly kisses.

"I won't let you go until you say the words."

His hands roamed over her body and for a moment Alyssa had the perverse thought of saying nothing so that he would have to hold her forever. "I love you."

"Then nothing else matters."

Just then the phone rang.

"You should get that," she advised. Late night phone calls were always the most important.

"No, I haven't checked my messages. That was fairly quick. Thank you for calling." Nathan hung up the phone and returned his attention to his future bride.

"Well? Did you get the job?"

"Yes, baby, I did it."

Her eyes widened and the smile that graced her face took his breath away. Alyssa kissed him on the cheek and settled against his shoulder. "I knew you would."

"Really?" He grinned and eased them both down onto the bed.

"Never had a doubt." She yawned. "I knew you would come for me too."

"Just remember that before you get any crazy ideas about leaving me," he whispered in her ear. "Because I will never let you go."

Epilogue

A passing of four seasons

While Alyssa stood in the doorway to Nathan's judicial chambers, her lips curled into a smile that went unseen because the object of her affection continued to look down at the documents on his desk. She would never tire of looking at her husband of only twelve months. And if the past year of weddings, her brother's team playing in the World Series, Aunt Sara and Uncle Edward's renewing their vows in Jamaica, and his new job hadn't given Nathan strands of silver in his jet-black hair, then she could look forward to many decades married to a devastatingly handsome, dark-headed man.

They had spent Thanksgiving with her family, Christmas with his, and New Year's attending a blowout party hosted by the matriarchs of both families. With so many blessings in her life, Alyssa didn't know what to do, and the best of them all, she'd announced at Christmas. She'd beat out all her sisters-in-law. She and Nathan were having a baby.

For the first time she'd managed to bring her mother to tears of joys, not frustration. With Lauren and Nick's Christmas gift of a kitten, they had expanded their pet family as well. The tortoiseshell cat's diesel-engine-like purr had managed to capture her heart and twist Nathan around its paw just like a string of yarn. Now when she asked him to go to the grocery store for potato chips and ice cream, her husband brought home bags of kitty treats and cans of gourmet cat food, too.

She glanced down at the watch on her wrist. She intended to spend as much time with her husband as possible before their lives turned into a succession of diaper changes, bottle warming, and midnight feedings. "I'm sorry to have kept you waiting," Alyssa drawled, adding a heapful of southern sweetness to her tone. "But I do believe I have an appointment with Judge Hughes."

Nathan looked up from his desk and then nodded at the attorneys present in his office. "Gentlemen, if you'll excuse me, our meeting is over."

After the door had closed, leaving them alone in his chambers, Nathan gently put his arms around Alyssa and inhaled deeply. He loved his job but would walk away in a second just to hold her in his arms. "How'd it go?"

"I put them on the plane myself," she replied. Her mom and pop would spend the next month down in South Carolina. If their schedule and her pregnancy permitted, she and Nathan would join them soon. The thought of planting seeds alongside her mother and watching them grow brought the threat of tears to her eyes, which she blamed on crazy hormones.

"Not that."

"Everything's fine and . . ." She reached up to tug at the point where the zipper of his robe intersected with the white of his collar. The magic of his scent and the strength of his presence had never ceased to ignite her desire. "The doctor said we could . . ."

"Yes?"

Her lips curved into the seductive smile he loved so much. "Well, before I go any further I was hoping you would clear up a little mystery for me."

"And what's that?" Nathan grinned, pulling her into his arms. As each day went by, things just kept getting better. Her smile kept making his day brighter and the love she brought into his life took away any and all of the frustrations of his job. He knew that the past few months with long hours and the media attention generated by the criminal trial against Charles and Chad Worthington hadn't been easy. Through it all she had been strong and when the time came for her to cry he'd been there for her as well as her family.

This evening they would celebrate their one-year anniversary dining with friends. And tonight he would give her the diamond bracelet, which had been burning a hole in his pocket since he'd picked it out one month past. She'd given him a world of happiness and soon she would give him a child.

He put his hands on her round belly and looked into her twinkling eyes.

"Your Honor." Alyssa smiled wickedly. "What exactly do judges really wear under those robes?"

Dear Readers,

As Alyssa and Nathan flourish under the spotlight that comes with having Marva Knight's first grandchild, my wish is that by the time you've reached this page you've enjoyed their story of intrigue and laughter as much as I've had fun writing it.

Many thanks for your e-mails, your words of encouragement, and support.

Take care,

Angela Weaver

angela@angelaweaver.com
http://www.angelaweaver.com

ABOUT THE AUTHOR

A Southern girl by way of Chattanooga, Tennessee, Angela Weaver has lived in Philadelphia, Atlanta, Washington, D.C., New York, and Japan. She is the author of *By Design* and currently at work on her next goal, that being her next novel.